How to Win Her Heart on the Nth Try

Ichine Kamijo

YEN ON

NEW YORK

How to Win Her Heart on the Nth Try

Ichine Kamijo
Illustration by Yu Shiroya

Translation by Judy Jordan
Cover art by Yu Shiroya
Original cover, table of contents, and frontispiece designed by Mai Maeda + Bay Bridge Studio

nKAIME NO KOI NO MUSUBIKATA
©Ichine Kamijo 2022
First published in Japan in 2022 by KADOKAWA CORPORATION, Tokyo.
English translation rights arranged with KADOKAWA CORPORATION, Tokyo,
through TUTTLE-MORI AGENCY, INC., Tokyo.

English translation © 2023 by Yen Press, LLC

Yen On
150 West 30th Street, 19th Floor
New York, NY 10001

Visit us at yenpress.com
facebook.com/yenpress
twitter.com/yenpress
yenpress.tumblr.com
instagram.com/yenpress

First Yen On Edition: May 2023
Edited by Yen On Editorial: Emma McClain
Designed by Yen Press Design: Andy Swist

Yen On is an imprint of Yen Press, LLC.
The Yen On name and logo are trademarks of Yen Press, LLC.

Library of Congress Cataloging-in-Publication Data
Names: Kamijo, Ichine, author. | Shiroya, Yu, illustrator. | Jordan, Judy, translator.
Title: How to win her heart on the nth try / Ichine Kamijo ; illustration by Yu Shiroya ; translated by Judy Jordan.
Other titles: N kaime no koi no musubikata. English
Description: First Yen On edition. | New York, NY : Yen On, 2023.
Identifiers: LCCN 2022057317 | ISBN 9781975362416 (hardcover)
Subjects: CYAC: Love—Fiction. | LCGFT: Romance fiction. | Light novels.
Classification: LCC PZ7.1.K2158 Ho 2023 | DDC [Fic]—dc23
LC record available at https://lccn.loc.gov/2022057317

ISBNs: 978-1-9753-6241-6 (hardcover)
       978-1-9753-6242-3 (ebook)

10 9 8 7 6 5 4 3 2 1

LSC-C

Printed in the United States of America

Contents

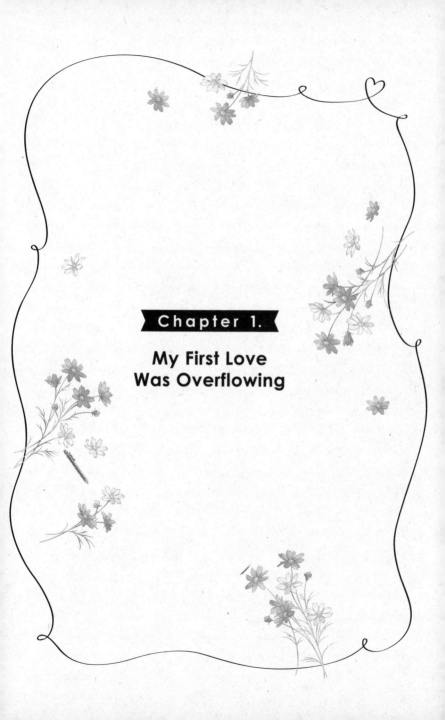

Chapter 1.

My First Love Was Overflowing

First Try

I hate birthdays. You're supposed to have gained a year's worth of experience, but I always feel like I've lost something in equal measure.

Ever since I was little, I've always had one dream or another. When I was five, I wanted to become a princess and live in a castle made of sweets. When I was eight, I wanted to become a singer and appear on TV wearing cute outfits. When I was twelve, I wanted to become a pastry chef and bake cakes that would make the whole world happy. Those dreams were so dear to me, I wanted to squeeze them tight in my arms. They practically glittered.

When I was fifteen, I wanted to live my own "Cinderella" story by marrying the president of a big company. When I was eighteen, I wanted to become a civil servant with a stable income. When I was twenty, I wanted to become an office worker at a halfway decent company and quit when I got married. When I was twenty-two, I wanted to get a job with whatever company would have me. Now that I'm twenty-seven, I've totally forgotten those dreams overflowing with hope from when I was young. Now the bar has lowered considerably, and I'm desperate to achieve even an average level of happiness.

If I try to remember when, exactly, I became like this, an empty feeling overtakes me. Everything I've learned as an adult is important and yet ridiculous. Like the fact that it's shameful to rely on others if you haven't struggled to make it on your own. Or that there are some people you must never argue with, even if what they're saying is completely wrong. Or that sometimes, no matter *how hard you work, you won't be rewarded for it. The older I get, the more I take these "important and yet ridiculous" things for granted. And whenever I'm reminded of that, I get fed up with myself. If you ask me, that's more than enough reason to hate birthdays.*

"Ms. Yoroizuka, may I speak with you for a moment?"

Nagi Yoroizuka stopped typing.

"Yes?"

She glanced in the direction of the voice. Her coworker Ai Saotome was looking at her hesitantly.

"I've finished the revised design specifications for Yummy Foods," she said. "The document is in the shared folder."

"You're done already? I swear, you're almost *too* fast!" Nagi answered.

"Oh, no, not at all," Saotome replied bashfully.

Two years younger than Nagi, with a sweet face, a polished style, and a voice like cotton candy, Saotome was the embodiment of "femininity." She was so ridiculously attractive that after she was hired, Nagi heard guys who weren't even in their department were getting weak in the knees over her. It wasn't just her appearance, either—her personality was cute, too. And to top it all off, she carried out her work with admirable efficiency. Nagi felt constantly grateful to have such an amazing team member.

"Please look it over when you can," Saotome said with a polite nod. Nagi thanked her before turning back to her computer.

Nagi had joined the software development company Sync.System straight out of university five years earlier. The company had two development divisions, and the one Nagi belonged to was called System Development Division One. Her department mostly built systems for small and midsize companies in a range of industries, from medical and food to apparel and e-commerce. Simply put, they did a little of everything. When she was first hired, she didn't know a system or a software program from a sandwich. But at this point, she was an engineer on the cutting edge of her industry. She'd never dreamed, back in her days as a humanities major, that she'd end up doing anything like this, but life was unpredictable.

"...Right, back to work."

Nagi took a gulp of coffee from her tumbler and brought her focus back to the monitor in front of her, where she'd pulled up the system design specifications for Yummy Foods. The food-processing company was launching an e-commerce project, and Sync.System was developing the website. As a project manager, Nagi spent most of her time meeting with clients, managing schedules, and designing systems. They'd been working on the current project for about three months and were supposed to hand it over the week after next, which meant it was crunch time.

Just then, a notification popped up on Nagi's screen. She had a message on the internal chat system from Takumi Saiga, a younger coworker who had just been hired that year. Saiga was in charge of programming for the Yummy Foods project, but according to his message, he was taking a little more time than planned. Nagi stood up and walked over to Saiga's desk, which was located diagonally behind hers.

"Saiga...?"

"...Yes?"

Saiga, who'd seemingly been in a staring contest with his computer screen, turned around. With his lightly permed, bleached-brown hair and baggy suit he didn't yet seem used to wearing, he still looked like a university student. Nagi was a little put off, however, by the frown on his face which clashed with his otherwise youthful aura, and the grumpy mood he was making no effort to hide.

"Um...it sounds like you're running a little behind schedule. Is everything all right?" she asked.

"Oh, yeah... Sorry about that," Saiga replied. "Something is tripping me up. The part that issues members-only discount coupons should stay on the screen when you scroll, but it seems to disappear under certain conditions."

"Ah, gotcha. That part could be tough."

Saiga had been a STEM major, and Nagi had heard he'd taken programming courses. But book knowledge only counted for so much in the real world, and he seemed to agonize over that gap. He tended to work at about half the speed of more senior programmers.

"I still don't know what's causing the problem. Would you mind if I stayed late tonight?" he asked.

"No worries, I'll do that part. Why don't you handle the newsletter? That should be easier. Sorry for sticking you with such a tough job."

Nagi was grateful for Saiga's willingness to tackle the issue, but she wanted to avoid overburdening him when he still had so much to learn. It would be better for her to stay a little late so that he could leave on time.

"...Okay, if you think that's best," Saiga answered. For some reason, his tone seemed a little short. He turned back to his computer and began pounding the keys in a suspiciously violent manner.

"K-keep up the good work...," Nagi mumbled to his hostile-looking back before retreating to her desk, inwardly troubled.

The truth was, she had failed to build a positive relationship with Saiga, and he seemed to have a low opinion of her, though Nagi had no clue why. She thought she'd treated him normally, but before she knew it, the guy hated her. System Development Division One was broken into smaller teams, and the one Nagi led had only three members: herself, Saotome, and Saiga. As team leader, Nagi genuinely wanted to get along with him. She bought him little snacks and attempted to chat with him, but Saiga's attitude remained unchanged. Conversation might have been easier if they were closer in age, but Nagi was five years older than him.

And her birthday was coming up, which would only widen the gap even more. Oh well. She made up her mind to stop thinking in circles. Yet no sooner had she cleared away these mental distractions and gotten back to work than she heard someone calling her name.

"Hey, Yoroizuka."

Immediately, any optimism she'd had vanished. It was Kojima, head of the sales team. He was gesturing to Nagi from his desk, which was some distance from the development team's area. Nagi stood up immediately and hurried over to him.

"What's going on with Yummy Foods?" he asked right out of the gate, leaning back in his chair with his arms crossed. He was in charge of marketing on the project.

"I posted a status update in the regular thread."

"Did you? I haven't opened it."

Don't talk to me until you have, Nagi thought, but she was used to this. She stood by silently as he read the thread.

"Aha...so you're on schedule," Kojima muttered, still looking at his monitor.

"Yes. We're managing to keep up."

She added emphasis to the words *managing to*. Problems were a fact of life in system development, and Yummy Foods was no exception. But they'd worked through the issues methodically and were finally nearing the end. If they continued at their current pace, they should safely make their deadline.

"You can't work a little faster?" Kojima asked.

Nagi gaped at him.

"Are you seriously asking me to move up the deadline?"

It wasn't unusual for clients to request an earlier date, but this late in the game? Accelerating the schedule any more would be impossible. As Nagi panicked, Kojima shook his head.

"You don't get it, do you? You need to keep internal costs in mind."

It wasn't that she didn't understand Kojima's point. The faster they finished one project, the sooner they could take on the next, which meant more profit for the company. But the truth was, while individual skill did impact speed, building a system took a certain amount of time no matter who did it. System development required testing, after all. If you slacked on testing, you ended up with a system full of bugs. The quantity of bugs was directly proportional to the quantity of customer complaints, which would ultimately drag down the company's reputation. For that reason, Nagi and her team had to run tests on dozens, sometimes even hundreds, of patterns to hone the system's quality. Everyone knew that, which was why no one else in Sales would ever say something like this to the development team. In fact, in an industry so plagued with problems, finishing a system on schedule was cause for celebration.

"I realize that's important. But at this stage, I don't think I can move up the schedule very much. I'll do what I can, but…"

There were plenty of things she wanted to say, but she did her utmost to sound humble. Kojima clicked his tongue anyway.

"People like you who get hired through connections always mouth off," he spat. Nagi could feel her cheek twitching. "Listen, Yoroizuka. You may think you're hot shit because you're the president's niece, but you won't get any special treatment from me."

The founder and current president of Sync.System, Ryou Yoroizuka, was Nagi's father's younger brother. When Nagi was a university student, hiring was at a virtual standstill. She applied for dozens of positions and didn't get a single offer, so her uncle gave her a job. Kojima was right—she *had* been hired through connections. Nagi was painfully aware of the fact, and at first, she'd been desperate to gain her coworkers' acceptance. She studied programming every night after work and eventually earned a certification. At one point, she was only sleeping three or four hours a night and became so run-down, those around her constantly remarked that she looked like a ghost. She wasn't sure if it was thanks to her hard work or simply the passage of time, but now most of her colleagues treated her as a regular employee. Still, she guessed Kojima wasn't the only one who still resented her. Deep down, it frustrated her, but there was nothing she could do about it. They had no way of knowing all the time she'd put in, let alone any obligation to find out.

"Of course not," she replied. "I'm still inexperienced, and I welcome any guidance you have to offer."

She bowed her head deeply, which led to an obvious softening of the crease between Kojima's eyebrows.

"That's the attitude," he said with satisfaction. "That's the smart way to see it. Respect your elders."

Sometimes Nagi wasn't sure what skill she'd learned most thoroughly since entering the working world. Was it how to program, how to draw up winning proposals, or how to talk to people—or was it how to tell herself that someone completely wrong was actually right?

◆

It was after ten by the time Nagi got back to the apartment where she lived alone. As she was unlocking the door, her cell phone rang. The caller ID read Nae Yoroizuka. Her mother. Nagi kicked off her pumps, let them lie where they fell, and answered as she trudged into the living room.

"Hi, Nagi, done with work?" came a familiar, easygoing voice from the other end.

"Yeah, just got home."

"Late again, eh? Such a hard worker."

Nae lived about twenty minutes away by train. She was raised in the lap of luxury, as they say, and had a gentle disposition. Personality aside, she was much shorter than Nagi, who was close to 170 centimeters tall, and had quite different features. Most people were surprised to learn they were mother and daughter.

"Thanks. What's up?"

Nagi collapsed onto the sofa. The soft cushions gently embraced her exhausted body.

"Saturday after next is your birthday, right?"

Nagi glanced at the wall calendar. Her stomach sank as her eyes landed on the box labeled SEPTEMBER 17, but to keep her mother from catching on, she asked, "Is something going on then?"

"Are you free that night? I thought I'd make reservations at the usual restaurant."

Nagi didn't need to check her datebook to know she had zero plans that day. It was a little sad, but even if someone had invited her out for her birthday, she would have turned them down. The Yoroizuka family went to the same restaurant every year on Nagi's birthday. Her only worry was that the day before, September 16, was the deadline for the Yummy Foods project. But at their current pace, everything should be fine.

"Yeah, I'm free," she told her mother.

"Oh good!" Nae answered. *"We're going to have such a nice time. I invited Ryou, but he said he had plans he couldn't get out of. It's too bad."*

She was talking about Ryou Yoroizuka, Nagi's uncle and the president of Sync.System. He always joined them on her birthday if he could, but leading a company was unfortunately a busy job.

"Anyway, I was thinking of inviting Keigo this year. What do you think?"

"Did you say Keigo?"

Nagi hadn't been expecting to hear that name. Keigo Yuuki was her childhood best friend. They were the same age, and their families had lived across from each other, so they'd grown up like brother and sister. Not only did they go to the same school all the way through high school, but they had even attended the same nearby national university. And that wasn't all—after graduating, Nagi signed on with Sync.System while Keigo got a similar job at a different system development company. It was like they were glued to one another for life. For a while, they hadn't seen much of each other, but then, strangely enough, Keigo had transferred to Nagi's company. Although they were in different departments, the degree of coincidence was a little scary.

"I don't mind, but... He probably won't come, will he?"

The two families still spent New Year's Eve at one or the other's house, but Nagi was skeptical that Keigo would sacrifice a precious Saturday night to celebrate his childhood friend's birthday.

"The more the merrier, I say," replied her mother. *"Also, last time I saw Keigo, he mentioned that he wanted to come."*

"He did? I suppose it wouldn't hurt to ask, then."

"Great, I'll get in touch. Call you soon. Good night."

"Good night."

Nagi ended the call, changed into loungewear, and heated the stir-fry and rice she'd picked up for half off at the local supermarket. When it was ready, she set it on a low table with a can of beer and the seaweed salad she'd bought in a feeble attempt at staying healthy. Lately, her evening routine was to wash down some premade food with beer as she watched her favorite gangster show on her phone. When she wasn't too tired, she cooked at home, but recently, work had been so busy she never even took out a frying pan. Nae would probably scold her if she knew, but for Nagi, quality of life was less important than securing a scrap of free time.

The first can of beer was empty before she knew it, so she grabbed a lemon Chu-Hi. As she popped the tab, a little tipsy, her phone dinged. She paused her show to check the incoming message. It was from a friend who was getting married next month. She was thanking Nagi for the congratulatory coffee maker she'd given her the other day. Probably because fall was wedding season, Nagi had ceremonies to attend two weeks in a row next month in October. Nagi liked weddings. When she looked at the bride and groom, she felt included in their happiness. The prospect of attending two back-to-back didn't dampen her excitement in the least, and as for the money customarily given to newlyweds, she considered it a happy expenditure. The only part she didn't like was the lonely feeling she got as she went home by herself after the ceremony. The lovelier the wedding, the more strongly she felt it.

Thirty was right around the corner. Sometimes she worried about still being single. Even if she met someone tomorrow, it would probably take at least a year for marriage to come up. After that, if she didn't plan the wedding, hold the ceremony, and have a baby right away, she'd be thirty before she knew it. All her friends with children said it was better to give birth in your twenties when you still had lots of energy, like they were trying to scare her or something. Part of her figured that even if her friends were right, she could just start working out at the gym and everything would be fine, but she knew that wasn't really the point. To start with, she was too busy at work to even feel like going to the gym. At any rate, thinking about it wouldn't get her anywhere. For now, all she could do was make a strong effort during the bouquet tosses at next month's weddings.

As she was sending a quickly typed response to her friend, another notification dinged. It was from Nao Kousaka. Kousaka was three years younger than her, and she'd started corresponding with him after a friend who was worried about her being single introduced them. They'd still never met, but as far as she could tell from his profile picture, he looked like a nice guy with a cute face. He took things slow, but they'd been messaging each other every day for three months now. Nagi felt like it was high time for at least a dinner date, but she couldn't bring herself to ask him, and since he showed no sign of making a move himself, their relationship was at a standstill. As she was carefully composing her reply, her phone started buzzing. The caller ID said Keigo. The hulking form of her old friend flashed across her mind.

"Hello?"

"Happy twenty-eighth!"

She couldn't help grinning.

"Shut up. It's not my birthday yet," she said, pretending to be mad.

"Pardon me," Keigo teased.

Keigo's birthday was in spring, making him slightly younger than her, and over the past few years, it had become a standing joke for him to tease her about it.

"Your mom just called me. I'm going to your party."

"What? Really?"

She found it extremely surprising he would make time for her on his day off.

"I'm in shock. Are you going to foot the bill, too? Handsome men are the best."

"You should say that more often!"

He matched her tone and played right along as easy as breathing. He'd always been smart, and even if they weren't friends, she'd have said he had a nice enough face, but women drawn in by his looks tended to be put off by his stupid jokes. Nagi, however, liked the fact that he didn't try to hide who he was.

"Seriously, you're very sweet, a real stand-up guy. Though it's a little sad you have nothing better to do on a Saturday... Oh, sorry. That one just slipped out."

"What a pity. I just lost my desire to pay for your dinner."

"Hey, wait! I was kidding!"

Keigo burst out laughing.

"I know. And I mean it—don't bring your purse."

"Are you sure?"

"Of course. This is a special occasion."

"Yay! Thanks, I can't wait! I'll get you back on your birthday, so you better be ready!"

"Don't worry, I won't expect too much. Anyway, I'd better go."

"Okay, 'night."

Nagi hung up and lay on the floor with her arms and legs

stretched out, still excited. The Yummy Foods project was going fairly well, and Keigo was treating her to dinner on her birthday. And while things with Kousaka were moving slowly, they were developing a good connection. Maybe by her birthday, they'd be closer.

Life is good, Nagi thought as she gazed at the wall calendar. *I won't pursue overblown dreams like living in a castle of sweets anymore. I'm satisfied with a few jelly beans scattered on the road in front of me. That's enough to make me happy.*

Second Try

It happened early the next day.

"Yoroizuka. Can I speak with you?"

It was just after eleven when Kojima approached Nagi with that line. Instead of his usual tyrannical tone, he sounded formal, which struck her as odd. She followed him into the meeting space, where they sat down across from each other. After a pause, Kojima began speaking.

"We received a call from Yummy Foods just now."

Nagi could tell from Kojima's solemn demeanor and serious expression that this was not going to be a happy conversation. She nodded and said, "I see," but she had a bad feeling in the pit of her stomach.

"It's about the e-commerce site you're developing for them. They want to add a number of functions. I've written them down here."

Nagi took the paper Kojima was holding out and looked it over.

"There's…a lot here," she said glumly. It wasn't at all unusual for a client to request additions midproject. If the changes were minor, her company often accommodated them without extra charges. But what Yummy Foods was currently asking for could not be called "minor" by any stretch of the imagination. If Nagi's company accepted the request, the deadline would inevitably have to be pushed back. Plus, if Nagi was right, the price tag would have to be increased significantly. She wondered if they would agree to pay without a fuss.

"Can you tell the client that if we implement these changes, we need to extend the deadline by about two weeks? I'll get right to work on a quote for the additional work."

"I want you to do the work within the existing budget and timeline."

Nagi's mind froze at Kojima's unexpected reply.

"...What?"

"They begged me. Said their budget was tight. I said yes, so now it's up to you."

Nagi felt dizzy. How many times had this happened? Kojima would give in to whatever the client wanted, saying he had to show the company's best face, and then Nagi and the other systems engineers and programmers would be forced into an insane schedule. No matter how often she tried to explain to him that their programmers would die from overwork at this rate, he wouldn't listen.

"Please hear me out. We can be flexible within reason, but this is just too much work. And with no change to the schedule...it's impossible."

The same guy who had spouted off to her about "internal costs" thought it was okay to make idiotic promises to the client like this? It was obvious that if they did this much work for free, they would be way in the red. And on top of that, they were supposed to meet the original deadline? Did he think Nagi and her coworkers were a band of super hackers or something?

"I need you to do this. Help me save face here," he said.

Not much of a face to save, Nagi thought as she stared, dumbfounded, at his insincere expression. Catching herself, she gathered her thoughts. Saotome and Saiga would be pulled into this mess along with her. No matter what, she had to be the breakwater protecting them.

"Saotome already has a full plate working on another project, and Saiga was just hired, so I can't subject him to excessive overtime. Please, let's just talk to the client one more time about the deadline. If you'd like, I can speak with them directly."

"Not possible. Whatever it takes, I need you to use Saotome and Saiga to get this project done. Your job is to finish it, even if it means working overtime or sleeping less."

Everything about what he had just said was so offensive, she wasn't even sure which words pushed her over the edge. She could handle him belittling her. But now he had gone and denigrated the junior team members she valued so much. She had done him the favor of keeping her temper this long, but now her patience snapped like a twig.

"I beg your pardon."

Respect your elders? To hell with that!

"If you're saying my job is to build systems even if it means working overtime or sleeping less, then isn't your job in the sales department to keep client expectations reasonable? Any pushover can swallow whatever outrageous requests the client serves up!"

After she finished this tirade, a painful silence descended upon the meeting space.

Had she said too much?

When she came to her senses, Kojima's demonic face was hovering in front of her.

"Is that how you talk to your seniors, you ingrate?!" he screamed, pounding the table. "Who do you think gets you work?! I'm the one who pays your meal ticket! If it weren't for me, idiots like you wouldn't have a job!"

Nagi wanted to scream at the top of her lungs, "That's bullshit!" For one, another member of the sales team had secured the Yummy Foods contract. Kojima had only ended up in charge of the project because the person who got the job was too busy, and Kojima wasn't. Otherwise, he'd still be sitting at his desk twiddling his thumbs and doing who knows what—definitely not bringing in jobs. That's what she would have shouted if she were alone anyway.

" … "

But that was out of the question. *Calm down!* she desperately

told herself. It was obvious that if she answered back, she would
only get into a pointless argument. She swallowed the rage
surging inside her and muttered in a low voice, "I understand. I
will speak with the department head about increasing the fee. As
for the deadline…I'll see what I can do."

She most definitely did not think she could make the deadline,
but there was nothing else to say. Probably because she was so
furious, her dizziness had evolved into a headache. As she grimaced at the stabbing pain, Kojima turned back arrogantly and
said, "Anyway, you don't need to worry." Apparently, her concession had assuaged his anger with surprising ease. "I'm going to
help with the programming," he added.

"What?"

Nagi had heard that Kojima worked as a programmer before
he was transferred to Sales. But that was long before Nagi was
hired, which meant he likely hadn't done any programming for
over ten years. And if her memory was correct, he'd been reas-
signed because he was so horrible at his previous job.

"Can't wait to get back to it after all these years. You can rest
assured with the project in my hands. I was one of the better programmers we had," he said confidently. But Nagi couldn't shake
the anxiety rising in her chest.

◆

After that, life became hell. Kojima claimed to be helping, but
they were still shorthanded on programmers. This forced Nagi
to work on the additional requests while also serving as systems
engineer. Naturally, the worst happened: They soon fell behind
schedule, and Kojima got angry about the poor progress and
forced Saotome and Saiga to work overtime. Nagi apologized profusely to them, but Saotome said she was happy to take on the
extra load for Yoroizuka's sake. For his part, all Saiga said was
"Is that so? Fine." Nagi was convinced her relationship with him

was now beyond repair, but for better or worse, she was soon so swamped with work she didn't have time to worry about it.

Every day, Nagi, Saotome, and Saiga worked until the middle of the night. Meanwhile, the all-important Kojima traipsed home at the regular time, making Nagi sick with worry over whether he was actually completing his part of the project. But since every time she asked how things were coming, he brushed her off by saying "Who do you think I am?" Nagi quickly gave up and only assigned him the minimum work possible. The three of them (Kojima excluded) fought through exhaustion and sleepiness, and by the deadline, their goal was somehow in sight.

"Saiga, do you think you'll be able to finish the master data…?" Nagi asked.

"Yes… As far as I can tell from my review, I haven't missed anything…"

"Thank you…"

In a corner of the hushed floor, Nagi, Saotome, and Saiga were busy working on the final adjustments. It was ten at night. Maybe because it was Friday and everyone was out on the town, the office was abandoned. Nagi had only cut it this close once or twice since starting her job, but thanks to Saotome and Saiga, it looked like they were going to deliver the project by midnight. As soon as they turned it in, Nagi was planning to go have a drink, which she hadn't done in weeks. Heck, she was going to buy an expensive wine and drink it all in one day. That was her sole wish as her hands flew almost automatically over her keyboard.

Suddenly, she heard an ominous cry.

"…What?! I can't believe this!"

It was Saotome, who had been conducting a final check.

"Ms. Yoroizuka! The common processing code I wrote, I noticed it was behaving strangely, so I checked it, and it's been replaced by some weird new code…"

"Huh? What do you mean?!"

"I looked at the log, and for some reason, several days ago Mr. Kojima seems to have gone in and rewritten everything…"

"No way… Can I see?"

As Nagi took the mouse from Saotome and began checking the code, she felt herself grow faint. She had no idea why he'd done it, but it looked like Kojima had changed Saotome's processing code without permission. Worst of all, he'd somehow zeroed in on the places with the greatest impact on the entire system. Systems are extremely delicate, and if even one of tens of thousands of pieces of code is wrong, totally unforeseen bugs can pop up. Given that code is written by humans, however, errors are inevitable. That's why so many tests have to be performed—to kill the bugs. Even with limited time, Nagi's team had frantically tested their work to ensure its quality. But thanks to Kojima's "help," they now had to rewrite this section. Then, as an added bonus, they had to retest it.

"We're not going to make the deadline, are we…?" Saotome said. Her face was pale, and she looked on the verge of tears. Nagi guessed she had more or less the same expression herself.

"…Let me call the client."

Even though their deadline was that same day, the company wasn't officially launching the site until Sunday. Nagi figured they might still be able to finish by then. She hurriedly called the client's system contact, explained what was happening, and received an extension until midnight on Saturday. But while she was relieved to have escaped total disaster by the skin of her teeth, they were by no means in the clear. They had to complete the project in the next twenty-four hours no matter what. If they focused on fixing the messed-up code by midday Saturday and then started testing, they should just barely make the new deadline. There was no time for sleep. They were going to have to blast through on pure grit.

Having made up her mind, Nagi looked up to find Saotome and Saiga peering at her worriedly. They looked completely wrung out, with dark circles under their eyes. It was obvious that thanks to days and days of overtime, their exhaustion was at its peak. There was no way she could force another all-nighter on them.

"I'll take care of the rest. You two go home. Thank you both so much for working this late," she said as cheerfully as possible. Saotome gaped at her.

"What?! We can't do that! I'll help you!"

"Don't worry about it. I wouldn't feel right making you come in on the weekend. If I work on it tonight and tomorrow, I'll be able to finish."

"But you'll never make it on your own! I want to stay! Please let me!"

Saotome looked so adorably plaintive, Nagi wished she could give her a big hug.

"Really, it's fine. I'd feel even worse if I asked you to stay."

"But…!"

As Saotome refused to give in, Saiga, who had been silent until now, spoke up.

"Ms. Saotome, Ms. Yoroizuka is trying to be considerate. We should do what she's asking."

"Yes, exactly!" Nagi said. "Go home and rest. Please."

For a moment, Saotome looked conflicted, but at last she grudgingly nodded. Nagi saw them off—Saotome endlessly apologizing and Saiga looking ready to die from exhaustion—then turned back to her computer. Where on earth should she begin? Wait—before even starting, she had to tell Nae she'd have to skip the birthday party on Saturday night. She gloomily picked up her phone and dialed her mother's number.

"*Hello?*" Nae said in her usual laid-back way.

Nagi told her she was drowning in work and would have to miss the party.

"*I understand,*" Nae answered soothingly. "*We'll reschedule. We can go when things have calmed down for you.*"

"I'm so sorry… You went to all the trouble of making reservations."

"It's no big deal. But is everything all right at work? Does Ryou know how busy you are?"

Nagi's heart jumped at the mention of her uncle's name. Employees were supposed to submit a special form if they wanted to work on the weekend, and she'd have to fill in the reason. That would put the culprit, Kojima, in an awkward position, which was why she had planned to skip the form and not tell anyone she was working on Saturday.

"No… He doesn't know about it. Would you mind keeping it between us?"

"If you think that's best…but please don't overdo it, okay? I'll let Keigo know you can't come."

Dammit. Keigo had offered to treat her to dinner, and now she was standing him up.

"Thanks. Will you tell him sorry for me?"

Filled with regret, Nagi hung up and flopped listlessly onto her desk. Why was this happening to her? If it weren't for Kojima, the project would have been turned in by now, and she'd be at home drinking a glass of wine and getting excited about her birthday party. Unable to gather the will to sit up, she simply lay like that until she heard a soft buzzing. She glanced at her phone and saw it was a call from Keigo. Given the timing, it was probably about tomorrow.

"…Hi," she said dully.

"Hey there. Nae told me you can't come tomorrow," he said, sounding worried.

"Oh…yeah. I'm so sorry. You said you'd come, and now I can't go. I feel awful."

"Don't worry about that!" he answered casually. *"Work problems?"*

"Yeah, basically. A senior coworker did some programming, and it's pretty buggy."

"You're kidding. When's it due?"

"In twenty-four hours."

"Shit…"

He seemed to immediately grasp the hopelessness of the situation. That alone was enough to make her feel somewhat better.

"Where's this senior coworker?"

"At home, I guess."

As usual, Kojima had gone home exactly on time that evening. Nagi smiled wryly as she remembered him leaving.

"He seriously just left?"

"I don't even think he knows we're in this situation."

"That's outrageous," Keigo said in a low voice.

His reaction was natural, but since she was dealing with Kojima, Nagi had already moved past anger into resignation. If he'd been the type of boss to step in and help in a situation like this, the whole thing would probably never have happened.

"…Should I come down to the office?" Keigo asked hesitantly, breaking into Nagi's daze.

"Ha-ha… At this point, I'd be happy just to have a warm body sitting next to me cheering me on…"

"That's not what I mean. I'm asking if you want me to help you with the job."

Keigo's uncharacteristically serious tone caught her off guard.

"What? I'm sorry, I thought you were joking…"

"Would I joke at a time like this? Anyway, just tell me where the specifications and environmental information are. I can figure out the rest from the log."

"Hey… Hold on a second!" she said in a panic when she realized what he was saying. He was forging ahead with his plan at a rapid clip. "It's really fine! Besides, if you try to help me…!"

"I know what you're thinking. If anyone finds out, we'll both be in big trouble. I'll make sure not to leave any evidence I helped you."

At those appealing words, Nagi couldn't help swallowing her

protests. Even though they worked at the same company, it was taboo to do work in a different department without permission from the higher-ups. But Nagi had heard how good Keigo was at his job. She couldn't imagine anything more reassuring than having his help.

She imagined the worst-case scenario if she didn't finish the job in twenty-four hours. It wouldn't be so bad if she was the only one who got punished, but there was no question everyone on the project team would be impacted. Saotome, who had worked so frantically and without complaint to support her. Saiga, the new hire she'd pushed so hard and who had nevertheless managed to get the work done. The Yummy Foods employees who had poured their blood and sweat into the project. Even the division head and company president, who would probably have to take responsibility for her actions. She shivered as she reflected once again on the gravity of the situation.

After almost six years as a systems engineer, she had a fair amount of experience. But that didn't mean she was extraordinarily smart or gifted. There was no way she had what it took to overcome a situation this tough. She'd only made it this far by pushing herself not to complain in front of her junior staff or make them uneasy.

"Listen, Nagi. It's okay to lean on me sometimes."

Keigo's voice was like a balm on her frayed nerves. The truth was, she was overwhelmingly afraid. She hated the situation she was in. It was absurd that after working so hard, she had to take responsibility for Kojima's actions. She wanted to tear it all up and run away. She wanted someone to rescue her. She wanted to be unconditionally comforted. Without that, she didn't feel the tiniest bit of motivation to go on.

"...No, it's fine," she said, despite her feelings. She didn't want to cause Keigo any more trouble.

"It's not fine," he said, sounding fed up.

She was grateful for the sentiment, but when she thought about the consequences of being found out, she knew she couldn't let him help her.

"I know I said it was a bad situation, but if I work hard, I think I can finish by the deadline. I'm sorry for making a big deal out of it," she said, trying very hard to sound positive.

"That doesn't change the fact that if you're working on it alone, you won't be able to make dinner tomorrow, does it?"

"No…"

"And you always go out to dinner with Nae on your birthday, don't you?"

He was right. It was their ritual. September 17 was a "special day," and she and Nae had promised each other that they'd go to a restaurant to celebrate every year.

"That's true, but this year it can't be helped."

"I think it can. Listen, Nagi. I hate to see you neglecting these things—"

"I told you it's fine!" she snapped.

Keigo fell silent.

"No matter how hard I work, I won't be able to make it…so would you drop it already?"

She knew she sounded childish. She probably should have tried to smooth it over, but she was too exhausted.

"Nagi," Keigo said, quietly breaking the brief silence. *"You wouldn't tell me to drop it if we were talking about the anniversary of your father's death, would you?"*

His voice was sympathetic, but she still couldn't speak, because she knew he saw right through her. He was right. She didn't want him to drop it. Of course she didn't.

"Listen, I'll help you. Let's get this thing done one problem at a time. It's going to be fine."

Those were the words she was hungry for, but they never reached her ears. Maybe she'd given up on listening altogether. She knew that if she let herself register even a fraction of his kindness, she would sink to the ground, unable to move. She must not lean on him. She didn't want to cause anyone any trouble. She had to do this herself, no matter what.

"…Thank you. But I really am going to be fine," she managed to say at last. "I'd better get back to work. Thanks for calling."

"Hey, Nagi…"

"Talk to you later!"

She escaped by hanging up. Her phone started buzzing again right away, but she ignored the call and shoved her phone to the bottom of her bag. There were several more calls before it went silent. After that, Keigo didn't call again.

◆

What she remembered was his big form and gentle voice.

Look, look! I drew a picture of you at school today, Daddy!

Wow, this is me? I look very handsome in that suit. This box next to me, is it a computer?

Yes! It's a picture of you working! When I told my teacher my dad is a sis-tims engine-ear, she said "Wow!"

She loved her father's big hand when he ruffled her hair, and his arms when he lifted her up, light as a feather. But what she loved most was his smile.

"Today, Teitou Bank announced that hackers gained access to the account information of two hundred thousand customers. The bank is looking into the matter urgently, since there is a possibility the leak included customer account numbers and passwords. Investigators suggested that a vulnerability in the system's security may be to blame for the incident…"

Nagi was thirteen when a large-scale data breach occurred at Teitou Bank, one of the top banks in Japan. The public was in an uproar to learn of system vulnerabilities at a bank they had assumed was absolutely safe. Two days after the discovery, the bank's president and staff apologized at a large press conference. Nagi's father was among those subjected to the flashbulbs and scathing questions of the media. He had worked as head of system development at Teitou Bank, and his department was responsible for the breach. Ultimately, the bank's president took responsibility by resigning, and the company was taken over—or "merged," as they politely put it—by another megabank and essentially went bust.

Mom, why is Dad always at home now? Why doesn't he go to work...?
Dad lost his job. He's going to take some time off.
Her father had always headed to work dressed in a suit, but now he didn't so much as venture outdoors. He spent most of the day sleeping and never changed out of his pajamas. When he was up, all he did was stare at the TV or robotically eat the food Nae cooked. Eventually, he stopped eating and began to grow visibly gaunter. Around that time, he started waking up in the middle of the night screaming more often, and Nagi frequently heard her mother trying to soothe him through the wall between her room and theirs. Before long, he was admitted to the hospital.

Don't become a systems engineer. You're a girl, so you ought to choose an easier path where someone else can protect you.
Once, when Nagi stopped to see her father at the hospital on the way home from school, he had told her that. He seemed much calmer than when he'd been at home, but he also seemed as if his soul had fallen out of his body, leaving his physical form to go mechanically through life. Behind him, the September sky was a clear blue. Nagi remembered vividly how beautiful the sky was that day. Those were the last words she ever heard her father say. On September 17, the day she turned fourteen, he left this world.

From now on, every September seventeenth, let's go to that restaurant we always used to go to together.

It was a year after her father's death when Nagi's mother made that suggestion. Her fifteenth birthday was a month away.

We'll have them set a place for your father and bring him food, and we'll have a nice party. After all, it's your birthday. Your father would have wanted to celebrate with you.

Nagi wasn't sure that was true. For Nagi, September 17 was a day for solemn mourning and most definitely not a day to celebrate.

Nagi, please don't hate your own birthday, Nae had said kindly. *It makes me sad to see you looking so depressed every year.* Nagi, however, felt no enthusiasm for the plan.

It's a special day—the day you came into the world.

Even now, Nagi hated that "special day" more than anything.

◆

The first thing she was conscious of was a horrible pain all through her body. Her arms and shoulders stung with pins and needles, and her hips were stiff and sore.

"Ugh…"

She felt like she'd dreamed about the past. A dream about when her father was still alive. She stood up slowly, her sleepy head sensing that something was very wrong. She'd just woken up, so why wasn't she in her room? Her monitor was centimeters from her nose. The date and time glowed on the login screen.

Saturday, September 17, 11:05 AM

For a few seconds, it didn't register. But the instant she realized what had happened, a shock ran through her body.

"That can't be right!"

She sprang out her seat and gripped her head, trying to remember the events of the previous night. She recalled that, after her phone call with Keigo, she'd worked until midnight. But beyond that, she had no memory whatsoever. Going by circumstantial evidence, she must have fallen into an unbelievably deep, long sleep.

How could she have done that? She'd wasted eleven precious hours! This was worse than awful. The only possible explanation was her recent lack of sleep. She hadn't gotten a good night's rest in weeks, so she'd simply passed out. But why now, of all times?

"I—I have to…go on…"

If she didn't get back to work, midnight would come before she knew it. She sat down in a panic at her desk, but she was too rattled to think straight. What now? What now? She'd never finish!

"…"

The display in front of her slowly began to blur. She'd held it in all this time, but now memories of her father's words and her mother's sad face came flooding back, and she couldn't help crying, full of regret and frustration. Everything was her own fault. Fleeing from the stress of job-hunting into work as a systems engineer, going along with what Kojima said, sending Saotome and Saiga home early, turning down Keigo's offer of help, being unable even to mourn her dear father on the anniversary of his death—all of it, it was all her fault.

As she began to cry uncontrollably, she suddenly heard the office door open. She frantically wiped away her tears and glanced toward the door.

"…What? Yoroizuka?"

"Mr. Kojima…?"

She couldn't believe it was him. He was wearing sloppy weekend attire rather than his usual suit and looked slightly surprised to see her, but he nevertheless raised one hand and nodded. Her mood lifted slightly from the depths of despair. Could he possibly have come to help?

"Is something the matter?" she asked, clinging to a faint ray of hope.

"I forgot my wallet here," he answered.

The ray of hope blinked out. He strode past her to his own desk.

Opening the drawer, he muttered, "Ah, there it is!" and pocketed his wallet.

"Oh...ha-ha, did you?"

Her excitement deflated like a punctured balloon. What an idiot she'd been to expect anything from him.

"The question is, What are *you* doing here? Let me guess— still working on Yummy Foods? I thought the deadline was yesterday!"

Having accomplished his goal, he peered rudely at her screen.

"For various reasons, the deadline was extended to tonight," she said.

She silently praised herself for not telling him the real reason. Kojima snorted, then surveyed her smeared makeup and unchanged clothes.

"Don't tell me you've been here since last night," he said in shock. But Nagi saw his lips curl into a smile. There was no sign of worry or apology in his expression—only ridicule.

"Um, yes, I have."

"Sheesh. Instead of pulling all-nighters, you ought to divide the work better during the week. You've always been terrible at planning."

Fury swelled inside her and nearly exploded. Her vision went bright red, and she was overcome by an impulse to punch Kojima just so he would feel some pain. But as quickly as the urge arose, it withered. There was no point in punching Kojima. A sense of futility overtook her. All she could muster was a dry laugh.

"Ha-ha...I suppose you're right."

This whole thing was ridiculous. She didn't know what she was doing anymore. Why was she even here?

"...Pardon me!" someone called cheerfully, banging open the office door.

Nagi and Kojima both looked toward the voice in time to see a man enter the room. He was tall and dressed in a dark-gray suit, with short black hair pushed up off his forehead. He glanced around the office with his long, narrow eyes and quickly settled on Nagi and Kojima.

"Ah, there you are."

Nagi stared open-mouthed as he strode briskly in her direction. It was the last person she expected to see—her old friend Keigo Yuuki.

"Hey, aren't you from Systems Development Division Two?" Kojima asked suspiciously.

"That's right. My name is Keigo Yuuki."

He bowed to Kojima, then turned to the stunned Nagi.

"Ms. Yoroizuka, I'm sorry to bother you while you're working, but may I have a moment of your time?"

She nodded, flustered by his formal language.

"Actually, I have a message for you from the president."

"...What? From the president?"

"Yes. It's about Yummy Foods."

She felt the blood drain from her face. A message from the president about Yummy Foods at this moment could only mean bad news. There were so many reasons for him to be mad at her about the situation. Depending on how angry he was, he might lower her salary. Or even worse, fire her—

"He would like you to know that the Yummy Foods project has been completed."

It took a few seconds for Keigo's words to reach Nagi in the depths of her despair.

"...............He what?"

And even when they reached her, she didn't understand what he meant.

"It seems the president came into the office this morning, fixed the source code, and ran all the tests."

"My u-uncle...I mean, the president did that...? Really?"

She'd never heard of a company president taking on such petty work. She was so shocked she forgot to use polite language when she answered. Keigo nodded.

"I believe the repaired code and testing specifications have been uploaded to the server. Would you like to have a look?"

Flustered, Nagi logged on to her computer. She was highly skeptical of this whole story, but when she checked the server, she was stunned speechless. Keigo was telling the truth. The fixes she should have been working on that day were all neatly finished.

"Does everything look all right?" Keigo asked as she stared at the screen.

"Yes, it all looks good…"

She nodded in disbelief. Not only the code but the testing specifications were perfect, to the point that there was nothing left for her to do. She should be able to deliver the project immediately. Nagi felt relief permeate her body. She didn't understand how or why, but she really had been rescued. She had somehow escaped the worst-case scenario.

"By the way, Ms. Yoroizuka. Don't you think it would be a good idea to deliver the project now?"

Keigo's words snapped her out of a haze of teary relief. He was right. The system manager at Yummy Foods was waiting for her.

The sooner she got him the project, the better. She grabbed whatever her hand touched first and stuffed it into her bag, then hurriedly stood up.

"Thank you so much for delivering the message! I'll head out now!"

She bowed her head to Keigo and ran toward the door.

"Be careful!" he called as she dashed headlong out of the office.

◆

The sound of Nagi's footsteps faded from the other side of the door.

"I swear, that woman is always running around like a chicken with its head cut off."

"She must be busy."

Left alone in the office, Kojima and Keigo continued talking.

"Busy? Nah, just inexperienced," Kojima said, sounding exasperated.

"Is that so? I often hear people in my department say Ms. Yoro-izuka has a good reputation with clients."

"Her?" Kojima snorted. "I mean, I know there were a lot of additional requests with this project, but she knew that days ago. The fact that she cut it this close to the deadline is a sign of poor time management."

Keigo responded to this harsh assessment with an impressed "Ahh."

"That does sound like something you'd say, Mr. Kojima," he replied. "In fact, your own time management is quite famous in my department."

Kojima scratched his head, looking pretty pleased with this compliment.

"My reputation has spread that far? You're making me blush," he said.

"Oh yes, everyone talks about you," Keigo answered, smiling slightly. "They say you make schedules like you think programmers are livestock."

Silence.

"...Huh?" Kojima said after a moment, his cheek twitching. He didn't seem to fully grasp what Keigo had just said.

"Is something wrong?" Keigo asked innocently, tilting his head. Kojima looked increasingly flustered.

"No, it's just..."

As he backed away, his hand bumped Nagi's mouse. He looked at the screen as if to escape Keigo's gaze. The code for Yummy Foods, supposedly written by the president, was still pulled up.

"..."

Something seemed to catch his attention. He scrutinized the screen, then finally muttered, "...This can't be. All the code I wrote...has been completely rewritten."

He grabbed the mouse and began navigating the document.

"Here, and here, too… This is unbelievable. What's going on? The original code was here last night. I could understand a few corrections, but there's no way the president could have written all this himself…"

He scratched his head, then suddenly fell silent. After thinking for a few moments, he quietly continued.

"…Hey, did the president really write this? I thought he had practically no programming experience…"

"I believe that's true," Keigo said nonchalantly.

"Then who wrote the code for Yummy Foods?"

"I wonder," Keigo replied, shrugging. Kojima gasped in realization.

"Not…you?"

He stared at the preternaturally calm Keigo.

"I originally planned to do just the bare minimum," Keigo said. "But you'd written such awful spaghetti code, I couldn't bear to leave it, so I ended up rewriting the whole thing."

"Wh—…? In one day…?" Kojima said after a moment, fury flooding his face. "Who the hell do you think you are, coming in from another department and doing this?"

"I'll admit I broke some rules."

"Then…!"

"But my misdeeds are trivial compared with yours."

Slowly, Keigo withdrew a sheet of paper from his suit pocket and held it out to Kojima.

"Have a look at this."

Kojima took the paper and cautiously unfolded it. As he looked over the contents, the blood drained from his face.

"…What is this?"

"It's a log of the dating and adult websites you've accessed from company computers during work hours. I would've thought you had a lot of work as a manager, but it seems you spend most of your time on sites that have nothing to do with our industry. You're quite good at time management, I see."

Kojima flinched at Keigo's biting sarcasm like he'd been punched.

"H-how did you get this…?"

"Actually, the president appointed me manager of our internal network. We've had a suspicious increase in traffic to illegal foreign websites, so he asked me to look into it."

By now, Kojima's face had lost all trace of color.

"I believe you know which of us is in the more awkward position," Keigo said with a grin. "Well, I'll be going now."

He bowed and turned away. Just before he got to the door, he looked back one last time at the stunned Kojima.

"Oh, I almost forgot," he said. "It seems my old friend has been working under you quite frequently."

His smile had vanished entirely now. Cold anger and scorn filled his narrowed eyes.

"I will be informing the president of your obvious workplace harassment of Nagi Yoroizuka when I tell him about the present incident."

With that, he nodded politely and walked out the door.

On Monday morning, Ryou Yoroizuka, the president of Sync.System, stared at his computer screen in disbelief. Slowly, he picked up his phone and dialed an internal number.

"Yuuki speaking."

"Morning. I'd like to ask you a few things about your e-mail. Can you come to my office?"

"Of course, I'll be right there."

As Ryou read through the e-mail again, there was a knock on the door.

"Come in," he called.

Keigo walked into the familiar room and strode to Ryou's desk. "Can you explain what this is all about?"

He swiveled his screen toward Keigo to show him the message and attached file. Keigo looked at the screen, then shrugged calmly.

"What else can I say? It's a log of adult and dating websites accessed during work hours by Mr. Kojima in System Development Division One."

"That's not what I'm asking. How did you get access to Kojima's log—?"

Ryou's voice was drowned out by the ringing of his phone.

"Go ahead," Keigo urged, and he picked it up.

"Hello, this is Yoroizuka," his niece, Nagi, said briskly on the other end.

"Oh, good morning, Nagi."

At the office, he interacted with Nagi like he did with all the other employees, and they almost never talked on the phone.

"Is something wrong?" he asked, slightly surprised by her call.

"Thank you so much for your help with Yummy Foods. You got me out of a tough situation."

"…What are you talking about, Yummy Foods?"

"I had no idea you could write such beautiful code. You're amazing," she went on.

"I'm sorry, Nagi, I don't know…"

Before he could finish his sentence, he noticed Keigo flapping his hands at him. As Ryou made some vague statements to stall the conversation, Keigo grabbed a piece of paper on his desk and scrawled Go along with her. Ryou abruptly changed direction.

"Oh, right…Yummy Foods. It was nothing."

"You're too modest. Anyway, I'm truly grateful. Please let me repay you in the future," Nagi said enthusiastically, then lowered her voice to a teasing whisper. *"I know you don't need money, so how about I cook dinner for you? Just don't expect anything gourmet!"*

She returned to her normal voice and continued.

"I'm sorry for interrupting your work."

"Not at all. Thanks for taking the time to call."

After setting the receiver back down, Ryou turned slowly to Keigo.

"Thank you for playing along," Keigo said. "You really saved me there."

Ryou smiled wryly at the other man's easygoing expression.

"Now," he said, addressing his niece's childhood friend, "will you explain to me what's going on?"

"…Ah, so that's what happened," Ryou said when Keigo had given him the whole story. He leaned back in his chair and let out a long sigh. "Now I understand why you suddenly wanted to become the network manager."

The truth was, hardly anyone liked that kind of work, so Ryou had said yes without so much as asking Keigo's reason. He never would have guessed it was because he wanted to dig into Kojima's work log.

"And to top it all off, you rewrote Kojima's source code in a single day? He lost face big-time with this one."

"I'm sorry for using your name without asking first," Keigo said.

Ryou smiled wearily. He had doted on Nagi's friend just as he had his niece ever since they were children. Nagi's and Keigo's parents had been friends, and he'd been like an uncle to both of them since they were toddlers. Seeing the fine young man Keigo had become made him think about how frighteningly quickly time passed. Keigo had always liked computers and often created simple systems on his own. Ryou's older brother—Nagi's father—was a systems engineer and had praised the boy for his work, calling him a genius. Ryou agreed with his brother's assessment. Despite all that, Keigo was an honest boy who never boasted about his talent. That was exactly why Ryou had asked him to join Sync. System. And Keigo had exceeded his expectations, earning company MVP three years in a row. But he had one flaw.

"You're right that I can't let Kojima get away with this," Ryou said. "I'll handle that end of things. And this time, I'll overlook the fact that you performed work in a different department without permission."

Normally, that sort of thing was prohibited because of confidentiality issues, but given the situation, Ryou couldn't very well punish Keigo. That said, far from being contrite, Keigo was trying so hard to contain his laughter that his shoulders were shaking.

"Actually, I think I did you a favor here. I'm fairly sure we have a long-standing relationship with Yummy Foods, and they've been a steadfast client. If I hadn't stepped in, we'd probably have missed the deadline or handed over a system full of bugs. It's a good thing this wrapped up without negatively impacting our company's reputation."

Unfortunately, there was nothing Ryou could say to that.

"Fine, fine. I'll buy you dinner sometime. Now stop harassing your elders," he said, raising the white flag.

Keigo shook his head.

"You don't have to get me dinner. I'd rather you do what I asked before."

"You mean…the transfer?"

"Yes."

"Are you sure that's what you want?"

"It's exactly what I want," Keigo said decisively.

"All right." Ryou nodded.

"Thank you very much," Keigo said, bowing. Then he muttered coldly, "If you don't do it quickly, someone like Kojima will make a pass at her. The thought alone makes my skin crawl."

With that, he nodded and left Ryou's office.

"…I wouldn't want to make an enemy of that guy," Ryou mused.

Keigo Yuuki's sole flaw was that when it came to his childhood friend Nagi Yoroizuka, he had a tendency to go a bit overboard.

Third Try

Keigo had always been the type to stick with things and keep his possessions for a long time. He'd played the RPG game his parents bought him in elementary school more times than he could count. The computer he'd bought for himself in junior high using his saved-up New Year's money was still working, albeit with a lot of the parts changed out. As for programming, which he'd first learned about in elementary school, he still loved it now that it was his job, and he wanted to keep doing it for the rest of his life. He didn't have a reason for loving these things. A combination of his inborn personality and childhood experiences might have played a role, of course, but basically, he liked things because he liked them. Now, at the age of twenty-seven, he was still holding on tight to his love for the one thing he irrationally adored more than anything else: his exceedingly oblivious childhood friend.

"Let's all raise our glasses to congratulate Yuuki on his transfer! Cheers!"

The division head's toast was followed by a chorus of cheers and the clinking of beer mugs. It was seven thirty at night, and a welcome party was underway at a bar near the office. As his new coworkers came up one after the other to offer him boisterous toasts, Keigo tried to drill their faces and names into his memory.

"Looking forward to working together!" he answered again and again.

A week had passed since his transfer to System Development Division One. After the incident with Kojima, the president had immediately submitted the necessary paperwork. However, since it was unplanned, the actual move took another few days, and by the end of the hellish storm of related trainings and documents, everyone was very ready for it to be done.

When the dust settled and the day of his transfer finally arrived, the division head introduced him during the morning announcements. When she saw him, Nagi nearly jumped out of her skin. Considering his transfer had been kept secret until then, her reaction was only natural. Seeing the look on her face was reward enough for Keigo, but it seemed Ryou had taken the additional thoughtful step of assigning him to Nagi's team. That was how he ended up working with her directly. Although he still had a lot to get used to, there seemed to be no shortage of good folks in his new division, which was a relief.

Just when Keigo thought he had been introduced to everyone at the party, he heard a familiar voice behind him.

"Good job today, Keigo."

If he had to liken that voice to a color, he would choose orange. It was smooth and kind but, at the same time, lively. He turned around, his heart thumping.

"Nagi."

Her olive-greige hair was trimmed neatly at the nape of her neck, and she was quite tall for a woman. She had a cool gaze, but he knew well that when she smiled, her eyes would gently soften.

She clinked her glass against his.

"Same to you," he said.

Just then, a much smaller woman who had been hidden behind Nagi until now leaned her head out to the side and said with a friendly smile, "Yes, thank you for all your hard work!"

"I think you two have already met," Nagi said. "But this is Ai Saotome. She's on our team."

"It's a pleasure to meet you," Saotome said gently. She was the polar opposite of the brisk Nagi, but from what he could tell from the past week of work, she was very efficient.

"The pleasure's mine. As a junior team member, I'm looking forward to learning from you."

"Ha! I'm not sure I have much to teach, but I'll do what I can," she answered modestly. Nagi rested her hand on the other woman's shoulder.

"Saotome is extremely good at her job!"

"Please stop. I'm just starting out. Mr. Yuuki is much more impressive than me," she said, clinging shyly to Nagi's arm. Watching them, Keigo thought about how lucky women were. *They get to hug in public without being accused of sexual harassment. Wonder if they'd punch me if I asked to join in. Probably. Especially Nagi.*

"I'm looking forward to working together," he said instead.

"So am I," agreed Saotome.

Apparently having had their fill of joking around together, the two women waved at him and returned to their seats. *Now, time to chow down*, Keigo thought. But just as he was lifting his chopsticks, a young man approached him.

"...Welcome to the division."

"Oh, hi, Saiga. Thanks."

Keigo hadn't spoken much yet with Takumi Saiga, his other new team member, so he didn't have a grasp on his personality. But from observing the general situation, Keigo got the sense he didn't get along very well with Nagi. That said, given that he'd made a point of coming over to say hello, he probably wasn't a bad kid. They clinked glasses and tossed back their drinks.

"Remind me how old you are," Keigo said to Saiga, who looked vaguely uncomfortable.

"Twenty-three."

"You just started at the company this year, right? I wish I was still that young. You have all that potential ahead of you."

"I might have potential, but I'm still useless."

Keigo felt the atmosphere chill noticeably. *What's the deal, Saiga? You're being too negative.*

"H-hey…that's not true. I heard you studied programming in university, right?" Keigo said, urgently trying to lighten the mood.

"Yeah, I did. I was an information sciences major."

At first, Keigo feared he'd already gotten on the kid's bad side, but Saiga responded normally to his question, which reassured him.

"What kind of stuff were you working on?"

"I was totally focused on programming."

"Ha-ha, sounds like me. That's about all I did. I even participated in some contests."

Saiga's expression changed visibly at Keigo's casual remark.

"Really, you did? What did you make?"

Maybe it was Keigo's imagination, but Saiga's eyes seemed to glitter, and he leaned forward.

"I created my own search engine. I've still got an app version on my phone. Wanna see it?"

"I'd love to!"

Apparently, Saiga really liked programming, and he went on to barrage Keigo with more questions. Even people employed at IT companies rarely did programming in their spare time, too. Keigo, one of the few who did, had never talked so much with a coworker about this hobby, and the conversation flourished.

"—That sounds so fun!"

As they were talking about the computer Keigo had recently built, someone interrupted them. It was Saotome.

"Saiga, the department head wants to speak with you," she whispered, turning to the man in question.

"What? To me?"

"Yes. Since you've been in the department for six months now, it seems he wants to know if everything is going okay. We're at a party, so you can probably just casually go over and pour him a drink."

Saiga reluctantly stood up.

"Well, then I guess I'd better go," he said, looking at Keigo like he'd rather stay. "Mr. Yuuki, I hope we can continue this conversation in the future."

"I'd like that. We could get dinner or something."

"I'll hold you to it," Saiga replied. Keigo watched him as he walked over to the department head.

"Would you mind if I sat down?" Saotome asked with a slight tilt of her head as she took a seat next to Keigo. "It seems you're very popular, Mr. Yuuki."

"I rarely get a chance to bask in the spotlight, so I'm enjoying it while I can."

"Ha-ha. You stand out, so I'm sure you're always in the spotlight."

Saotome giggled, then suddenly stared at him.

"...What?" he asked, embarrassed by her prolonged gaze.

"Oh, I'm sorry!" she said, pressing her cheeks with both hands like she was flustered. "I was just noticing how tall you are. How many centimeters are you?"

"A little over a hundred and eighty, although I haven't measured myself lately."

"Wow, that's amazing! I'm a hundred and fifty-five... That's almost a thirty-centimeter difference!"

It was true—if they stood next to each other, they would look like an adult and a child.

"I wish I was taller," she said.

Keigo figured she must have a complex about it.

"I mean...," she went on. "The perfect height difference for kissing is about fifteen centimeters."

Keigo nearly choked on his beer and slapped his hand over his mouth to avoid spewing it all over. He glanced at Saotome in disbelief, but she was still gazing up at him.

Is she making a move on me?

"Uh..."

As he glanced around looking for an escape, his eyes fell on Nagi, chatting happily with some coworkers a distance away. Under no circumstances did he want Nagi to know about this conversation. *Should I just laugh and muddle through? But on the off chance she's not joking, would that be rude?* Remembering how affectionate Nagi had been with her earlier, he floundered for a good response.

"Mr. Yuuki? What are you looking at?"

Saotome craned her neck curiously.

"Yuuki! What's the star of the show doing off in a corner?"

A senior member of the sales team he was already acquainted with wrapped his arm around Keigo's shoulders. *Thank God!* he thought. As he chatted casually with the man, Saotome quietly vanished.

The party had been going for two hours. Voice hoarse from talking too much to too many people, Keigo headed to the restroom partly to take a break. Thanks to not enough food and too many people pouring him drinks, he was drunker than usual. As he rounded a corner in the hallway on unsteady feet, he bumped into someone.

"Oh!"

His heart skipped a beat. It was Nagi. She seemed to be on the way back from the bathroom.

"Oh, Keigo, it's you. Are you enjoying yourself?"

"Yeah, everyone's been great."

"I'm glad," she said, smiling. Then she suddenly stared at him with a serious expression. He didn't know how to put it exactly, but it felt like she could see right through him. Ever since he was little, he'd had a strong impulse to look away whenever she stared at him.

"Drank a lot tonight?"

He tensed, and she grinned as if she knew exactly what he was thinking.

"Why…? Is my face red?"

"No. It's normal—but see here?"

Nagi reached out one of her long, thin fingers toward him. Her nails were trimmed short so she could type more easily. Her natural, unadorned finger gently touched the corner of his eye.

"Your eyes are slacker than usual."

From the point where her finger touched his skin, an amorphous joy poured into him and filled his heart. This feeling of pure happiness, however, was instantly engulfed by a conflicting feeling of loneliness. He knew why. It was because being this close to her made him feel further away than ever.

"My eyes are slacker? What's that even mean?"

Keigo flashed her a wry smile, and Nagi giggled in amusement. That's when they heard it.

"…Really? You mean Yoroizuka was behind what happened with Mr. Kojima?"

The two of them froze at the sound of a man's voice accompanied by multiple sets of footsteps coming their way from down the hall. Not good. Keigo grabbed Nagi's hand and pulled her away from the approaching voices. Slipping into a semiprivate room that happened to be open, he covered her mouth as she shot him a confused look. They peeked through the curtains hanging in the doorway. Two men from System Development Division One were passing the room where they were hiding, probably on their way to the bathroom.

"That's what everyone's saying. Anyway, he was obviously harsh on her."

Nagi's shoulder twitched. After all the drama, Keigo had heard that Kojima voluntarily resigned, leaving the company just as Keigo entered the department. The company had found a new job for him, so he probably wouldn't end up dead in a ditch—but unfortunately, since only the president and Keigo knew the real reason he'd left, everyone else was curious about it.

"Honestly, though, he was useless. I'm glad he's gone. I bet the president had something to do with it."

"It's probably a warning. Mess with Yoroizuka, and you're out."

"She's so lucky. I wish I worked at a company run by my relatives."

They laughed as they passed the room. Keigo remained frozen in place.

"...Keigo, I can't breathe."

Returning to his senses at the sound of Nagi's voice, he realized he'd been pressing her to him.

"Sorry!"

He abruptly let her go but couldn't think of anything else to say. Nagi burst out laughing.

"Oh, don't worry about them. They've been drinking, and anyway, they didn't say anything bad about me."

She might be able to laugh it off, but he couldn't bring himself to share her attitude. True, they hadn't trash-talked her, but hearing them say such things must not feel very good.

"...Do people say stuff like that to you a lot?"

She might be the president's niece, but she would never take advantage of it. To the contrary, she was the type who genuinely hated when people walked on eggshells around her because of who she was. He'd assumed she'd handled the situation with skill and built good relationships with her coworkers, but now he wasn't sure.

"People hardly ever say it to my face," she said.

She was being evasive, but her words suggested the incident just now wasn't unique.

"I know I got this job through family connections. It's fine. Actually, it's a good thing, because when people realize I can actually do the work, my reputation shoots up," she joked.

He knew she didn't want him to worry about it, so there was nothing more he could say to make her feel better.

Fourth Try

"...*Yawn*, I need a nap."

It was Friday morning, a week after his welcome party. Keigo took advantage of the fact that no one nearby was in the office yet to yawn theatrically at his desk. Work didn't officially start for another half hour, and with only a scattering of employees present, the office was hushed. He'd woken up earlier than usual that morning and decided on a whim to head in. Now, he was scrolling through an IT magazine online with a coffee in hand. As he read through an article on a recent spate of ransomware attacks, a floral scent reached his nose through the faintly bitter steam of his coffee.

"Good morning. You're early today!"

He looked up from his monitor in surprise. Saotome, who had arrived at the office without his noticing, was standing next to him.

"Oh, morning."

"What are you reading? Oh, IT news?"

She casually leaned toward his screen. The sweet aroma intensified, and he reflexively moved his chair back to escape her.

"Yeah, something like that."

"Wow, you sure are passionate about your work."

He smiled politely, pretended to find an article that interested him, and stared intently at the screen. But because Saotome was peering at him from close range, not a word reached his brain.

"...What?" he finally asked, unable to ignore her any longer.

"Nothing, I was just noticing how long and shapely your fingers are," she said, gazing at his hand gripping the mouse. "I like men with nice hands."

Keigo realized he needed to end this conversation immediately.

"Ha-ha… Oh yeah…I just remembered I have something I need to do."

"You do?"

"Yeah. I'll be back in time for the morning announcements."

Knowing it was a lousy excuse, he rushed out of the office, leaving the surprised Saotome behind. Only when he made it to the empty break room did he finally let out a sigh of relief.

Maybe, just maybe, Saotome had a thing for him. He wanted to punch himself for even considering it, but what else could he think when she kept speaking to him like that?

Ever since she'd said that thing about "the perfect height for kissing," he had actively avoided talking to her. You never knew who was listening in on conversations at work. The one scenario he wanted to avoid was a rumor making its way to Nagi. Still, Saotome hadn't come out and declared her feelings. Since it was entirely possible he was imagining everything (and he hoped he was), he figured he'd just have to wait and see what happened.

"…Hey, is that you, Keigo?"

Keigo jumped at the unexpected voice behind him. Nagi was standing with her purse in one hand, peering at him curiously.

"Uh, yeah…hi."

"Good morning. You're awfully early today," she said, choosing a drink from the vending machine.

"I woke up early for no reason."

"Impressive! I'd definitely lie around in bed if that happened to me."

He smiled, sensing his emotions settle back into place after being stirred up by Saotome. As he absently watched Nagi lingering in front of the vending machine, he noticed something.

"…Hey, you look different today," he said.

She turned toward him. Typically, she dressed in casual dark jackets and slacks, but not that day. A silver necklace peeked out from her tastefully revealing dark-brown top, below which she wore an off-white skirt. That was unusual. Upon closer inspection, he noticed that her short hair, which she usually wore nearly straight, was lightly curled. What was this? He liked it.

"Going on a date?" he joked casually.

"Very observant."

That was unexpected. His smile vanished. What? He hadn't been serious!

"Oh… Really…? I'd better start saving up for a wedding gift…," he said, too upset to be coherent.

"Don't get ahead of yourself," she said, laughing. "Anyway, it's not officially a date. It's just dinner with a guy I've been texting."

Keigo's heart bounded up from the pit of despair it had been languishing in.

"So…what's he like?" he asked, pretending to be calm as he prodded for information.

"Wanna see?" she replied, pulling out her phone. "This is him."

On her screen was a profile photo from a messaging app. Interesting. He was handsome and fresh-faced, like a guy in a cider commercial or something.

"His messages are super polite and thoughtful, and after texting for five months, he finally suggested we meet. I think it's a good sign he doesn't rush into things, don't you?" she said happily.

Shit. Why couldn't this guy be a player? Isn't that what handsome men were supposed to be like?

"I'm glad he seems nice," Keigo said noncommittally.

"Yeah," she answered bashfully.

As he watched her smile, he noticed her makeup had been applied more carefully than usual. It dawned on him then that she never did such things when the two of them hung out.

"…Oh, and I almost forgot!" she said, just as his emotions were hitting rock bottom. "His birthday is tomorrow… Do you think that means something?"

"What? His birthday?"

"Back up, dude!" she said, leaning away from him. He'd moved in close without even realizing it. But he didn't ease up his interrogation.

"He was the one who invited you? And it's just dinner?"

"For now…"

"What time are you meeting? What restaurant?"

"…Does that have anything to do with my question?"

"………No."

"I didn't think so."

Forcing himself to calm down, Keigo stepped slowly away from her. She gave him a suspicious look but nevertheless went on.

"Anyway, do you think I should give him a present? I don't have any ideas. Do you think it would be off-putting to get a present from someone you've just met? But it's probably not a good idea to ignore it, either. I wish I at least knew a little about his tastes…"

She was practically talking to herself by this point. There were countless guys out there willing to use their birthday as a pretense to invite a woman to a hotel. Mr. Cider Commercial was probably no exception. Keigo wished he could break into her ruminations and shout "Blow him off!" But he was nowhere near that brave.

"What a pity. If you stuck closer to home, you wouldn't have to go through all of this," he said, forcing a smile.

"What do you mean, closer to home?" she asked.

"You could date me."

There was a second of silence, and then they both broke out laughing.

"Ha-ha. Oh, you're hilarious. Thanks. I feel a lot more relaxed now."

Evidently done laughing, she caught her breath. That was odd. He hadn't intended to help her relax at all.

"Oh, it's almost time for morning announcements. I'd better get going," Nagi said, checking her watch. She quickly bought a bottle of mineral water and glanced back at him. "We've got that meeting with Acsis this afternoon. Don't forget!"

Following his transfer, he'd been given only odd jobs and easy programming tasks, but that day, he was supposed to accompany Nagi to a meeting with Acsis, an apparel shop whose account she handled.

"I won't," he said.

"Good." She smiled and walked out of the break room with what looked like a bounce in her step, although he might have been imagining it. The second the door closed, he drooped like a wilted flower.

◆

"You're kidding! You still have a crush on Yoroizuka?"

Keigo was eating at a crowded restaurant that served set lunches with his university friend Yuuma Saeki. Yuuma worked at a nearby company, so they sometimes met for lunch when they both had time.

"...What's wrong with that?"

Keigo glared at Yuuma over his bowl of miso soup.

"I didn't say anything was wrong with it," Yuuma said, shaking his head. "It's just when you're that dead set, it looks kind of obsessive, like you're a late bloomer, or kind of girlie or something. It's a little weird... Okay, I'll admit—she was pretty hot in high school. Tall, with a nice body, though her boobs were a little small. But if she's still not into you, maybe it's time to give up..."

"Hey, butt out!" Keigo snapped.

Yuuma shrugged. He and Keigo had been in the same class in high school along with Nagi, and he knew her well.

"Anyway, so your darling Yoroizuka is going on a date with another guy tonight, huh?" he said, lifting a piece of grilled pork with ginger between his chopsticks.

"It's not a date. They're just having dinner."

"Same difference. Dinner the night before his birthday."

Keigo didn't have a comeback for that. Yuuma had found the weak point in his argument, and he was right. Keigo didn't want to think of it as a date, but by the conventional definition of the word, it was *definitely* a date.

"...Want me to introduce you to someone?"

Yuuma gazed at Keigo, who was clearly in agony, with pity in his eyes.

"I'll take the sympathy and pass on the intro," Keigo answered instantly. The emotion in Yuuma's eyes only deepened.

"You never stay in relationships long, do you? You don't smoke or gamble, and you're basically a good guy...so I wonder why that is."

Keigo had dated a couple of women in the past in an attempt to forget Nagi, who showed no interest in him. Thankfully, all of them had been the type to make the first move, and he'd tried to cherish them in his own way. But inevitably, within a week to a couple of months, they would leave him. He, more than anyone, wished he knew why.

"Well, they say women are perceptive," Yuuma remarked, shoveling up the shredded cabbage left on his plate. "They probably pick up on the fact that you're not really into them. That female sixth sense, man, it's terrifying."

"Then why doesn't Nagi ever notice I like her?"

"Probably because she's not interested."

".........I hate you," Keigo said, collapsing onto the table. Yuuma howled with laughter. *He wouldn't be laughing if he was in my shoes!*

"Seriously, though, it'd do you good to check out some other women," Yuuma said, turning solemn now that he was done laughing.

An image of Saotome popped into Keigo's head. What if he wasn't imagining things and she really did like him?

"Listen, Keigo," Yuuma chided. "I know you're in love with Yoroizuka, but do you really think she can see you as dating material after being your friend for twenty-eight years?" Keigo, still deep in thought, knew his friend was right. He and Nagi knew everything good and everything bad about each other. They were practically family. Novelty was essential in love. Not having any surprises to offer was a huge disadvantage. He knew that. He knew it painfully well. But still.

"It's been twenty-eight years. For your own sake, why don't you try looking for a more realistic option?"

Keigo had grown into adulthood holding his love for Nagi in his heart. It was the one thing he couldn't give up.

◆

"So in a nutshell, that's the initial plan we've come up with," Nagi said, wrapping up her presentation in an office crowded with clothes racks and cardboard boxes.

The proposal she had brought was spread on the table in front of her, marked up all over with scribbled notes. She and Keigo were visiting an Acsis shop a short distance from the station to present their plan for transitioning the company to a new e-commerce site.

"It looks good to me. It's very close to what we envisioned," the owner said, looking over the proposal carefully. As might be expected for the owner of an apparel shop, his hair and clothing were simple but elegant. Judging from his response, he liked Nagi's proposal.

"I have a question," said the shop manager, who was sitting next to the owner and looking through some documents. His fashion sense was a good deal more cutting-edge and quirkier than the owner's. "Can you use COBOL to make this?"

Nagi and Keigo both blinked. Just like Japanese, English, French, and Chinese existed in the real world, various languages existed in the programming world. Code was written differently in each one, and certain languages were better suited to certain systems. COBOL was one such language.

"COBOL...?" Nagi echoed.

"I don't know the details," the manager said, "but it's a famous language, right?"

"It's true that it's famous, but it's not used as widely these days. I can't say I recommend it for this project...," Nagi answered hesitantly.

Programming languages, like clothes, go in and out of fashion. COBOL was once used in many industries, but that was before the year 2000. As Nagi had said, unless there was some special reason to use it, it didn't make sense for new systems. But before she could explain, the manager scowled.

"I'm asking if you can use it or not," he said in a nasty tone.

The owner seems mellow, but this guy is harsh, Keigo thought. He considered stepping in, but Nagi was the project manager. As he was debating whether interfering would be a mistake, Nagi responded apologetically.

"I'm terribly sorry, but our company does not have experience in COBOL, so I can't give you an answer immediately... Would you mind if I get back to you after discussing the issue at the office?"

Very few programmers in their generation had experience using COBOL. It happened that Keigo had come across it while pursuing his programming hobby, but he'd never used it at work, and he doubted Nagi had ever used it at all.

"Are you serious? You're a systems engineer, and you can't answer my question?"

"I'm very sorry I don't have more knowledge in that area."

The manager snorted and stroked his chin, looking down at the back of Nagi's head as she bowed apologetically.

"I'm starting to worry about hiring you for this job. If you were a pro, you'd be able to answer whatever question a client threw at you."

"You're right," Nagi said.

"But actually, I was worried to start with. Women never seem to know as much about IT as men do. And you never know when they're going to up and quit for maternity leave. How do I know you won't do that?"

"Excuse me, may I say something?" Keigo interjected, unable to restrain himself any longer. "It's true that since COBOL has high maintainability and performs calculations accurately, financial and securities firms still sometimes use it. But it lacks flexibility. I see it as a poor fit for your company, given that you have to adjust your pitch to customers on a daily basis depending on your marketing plan."

"…Oh, is that right?"

The manager looked somewhat surprised by Keigo's sudden interruption.

"Yes." Keigo nodded, continuing so quickly the manager couldn't squeeze in any objections. "I'd like to suggest Python for this project. Python is well known for its use in AI development. So for example, by incorporating AI into your e-commerce site, we'd be able to change the featured items displayed on the home page depending on a registered user's gender or age. The site would also be able to sense when a user is hesitating over a purchase and display coupons or banners to encourage the sale."

"Really? That sounds great."

"I've heard AI is the trend these days. I'd like to know more," the owner said, immediately latching on to Keigo's suggestion. It seemed he'd managed to divert their attention.

"We'd be happy to prepare a revised proposal for you incorporating that technology. Would next week—?"

"Wait, could you e-mail it to me by tomorrow? Headquarters is pushing us to get this done fast," the manager interrupted.

"Tomorrow…?" Keigo said, glancing at his watch. It was already after five. Drawing up a new proposal from scratch would take more than an hour or two, even for him. But before he could answer, Nagi spoke up.

"Yes, we can do that."

"Really, you can?"

"Yes. The proposal will be in your in-box by tomorrow morning," she said with a cheerful smile, ending the meeting.

"Um, Nagi?" Keigo said in confusion. He was trying to keep up with her as she speed-walked away from the Acsis shop. "Finishing that proposal by tomorrow is gonna be impossible."

"Don't worry. I can finish it if I stay late."

"But you're going out to dinner tonight."

"I'll tell him I can't make it. Work is more important."

Her tone was so blithe he didn't know what to say.

"But you…"

"It's fine," she said, gently cutting him off.

He sensed a finality in her voice. *It's fine* was a phrase she'd said often even when she was young. She'd used it to turn down his offer to help with the Kojima situation, too.

"I don't want people to blame my lack of ability on the fact that I'm a woman," she said, looking straight ahead.

Keigo began to understand what she was getting at. Women were far outnumbered in the IT industry, and there were probably still plenty of people clinging to the same stereotypes as the Acsis store manager. No doubt she'd put up with plenty of shit in the past. When he didn't say anything, she glanced back at him with a bitter smile.

"Anyway, I'm sorry. I feel bad you had to help me out of that situation even though you just joined our team… Oh! I'd better text Kousaka…"

She pulled her phone out of her bag. She was probably going to tell Mr. Cider Commercial that she wanted to cancel dinner. He grabbed her hand.

"I'll write up the new proposal. You go home."

She looked at him in shock.

"No way, what are you talking about? I'll do it."

"I'm the one who brought up AI in the first place. Anyway, I did something similar back in the other department, so I'll be able to do it faster."

"That's... Well, maybe that's true, but..."

As her eyes darted around, Keigo noticed the lovely shade of brown eye shadow tinting her eyelids. Then he noticed her pale lipstick, the silver necklace peeking out from her blouse, and her carefully curled hair. Not a strand of it was for him. He knew that. But still.

"You've been messaging for five months, and today is the day you're finally having dinner, right? It's an important day. Go. Anyway, I'll be done before midnight if I start now. Okay?"

He was supposed to be convincing Nagi, but it was more like he was soothing himself. His heart throbbed painfully. He'd felt this same pain hundreds of times. He was used to it. It wasn't a big deal. It was the agony that came from not being able to do anything but look on in silence whenever she got interested in someone else or started dating them. That was his lot in life.

"But..."

"Please go and don't worry about the proposal. If you stay, I'll die of guilt for butting in and suggesting the AI idea."

He pressed a hand to his chest theatrically. She hesitated. She had a weak spot for lines like that. After thinking for a few moments, though a little reluctant, she finally nodded. Just as he'd predicted she would.

"...All right. I'm sorry, Keigo."

See? That wasn't painful at all.

"Great. Now go and have fun."

"Really, I'm sorry... Thank you..."

"Don't worry about it."

As he gave her a light pat on the back, his phone buzzed. It was a colleague from System Development Division Two. He had a bad feeling about this.

"Yuuki, help me!" came a tearful voice the moment he picked up.

"You were in charge of that senior welfare resource system, right?! Believe it or not, the client messed up and erased all the data…"

"Erased the data?" Keigo shouted. Nagi flinched in surprise. He gestured apologetically to her and took a few steps away to hear the details. According to his colleague, the situation was hanging by a thread. The data could still be retrieved, but at any moment, it could be gone for good.

"…I understand. I'm not far away. I'll head right over."

Fortunately, he happened to be fairly near the client's office. It would probably take about fifteen minutes by train. He hung up and walked over to Nagi with a worried expression.

"Sorry, Nagi. There seems to be some trouble in my old department. I've got to go take care of it. Head back without me, okay?"

"Uh…is everything all right?"

"Oh, it's totally fine. Now hurry up. Dinner's at seven, right? You better not be late."

He waved good-bye and headed in the opposite direction from Nagi.

◆

"…Whew."

Keigo was utterly exhausted. After rushing to the client's office, he'd managed to avert disaster. It had been an awful situation, but it would have been a lot worse if he hadn't fixed it before the date changed. His colleague offered to take him to dinner as thanks, but he said he had work to do and dragged himself back to the office.

I'm beat. He let out a long, long breath as he walked down the dark hallway. Glancing at his watch, he saw it was already past eleven. He wondered how long it would take him to redo the proposal. He could feel his body grow twice as heavy just thinking about it. Right now, Nagi was probably living it up at her dinner with Mr. Cider Commercial. By this time, they might even be at their second or third bar. Or maybe even—

His stomach twisted at the thought of the worst possible scenario. Should he have told her not to go?

He opened the office door glumly and instantly noticed something was off. A light was on in the office when it should have been deserted.

"Oh, hi, Keigo," said the one voice that couldn't possibly be saying his name.

"...Nagi?"

There she was, all alone in the otherwise desolate office.

"Welcome back. Did everything go okay?"

Her caring voice brought him back to his senses.

"Forget that—what the heck are you doing?!"

He pulled a chair up to Nagi's desk and looked at the monitor. "That's not...the proposal, is it?"

"It is. It's taken me a while 'cause I had to look up some info on AI...but I'm almost done."

Her words were so unexpected he couldn't process them. Maybe this was all just a happy dream created by his overly exhausted brain.

"Wh...what about dinner...?"

"Oh, that? I felt bad, but I canceled," she said casually. Keigo was in shock.

He thought he knew Nagi better than anyone else, but at the moment, he couldn't make any sense of her actions. Why, on this day of all days, had she made such a clearly incorrect choice—a choice that, at the same time, worked out so well for him?

"After all," she said with a cynical laugh, "I could hardly run off and enjoy dinner when you were in such a tight spot."

"Wait, but you...!"

"It's fine," she said, just like she had earlier that day. But this time was different. She was looking him straight in the eye and saying it for him alone. "You're way more important than any of that."

She could have easily left him to his own devices. What did she want with a guy who just stood there watching her from behind as she walked forward in life? But instead, she'd turned back and reached out her hand. She always did. Her hands were as warm and gentle as a pool of sunshine. Every time she did that, idiot that he was, he gave up on giving up all over again.

"…"

He couldn't tell if it was pain or joy surging in his chest.

"What's wrong? You okay?"

Nagi peered at his downturned face in surprise. Her eyes were filled with worry.

If Saotome was right about there being a perfect distance for kissing and all that, then he was certain it wasn't the distance that made kissing easiest. Instead, he thought it must be the distance that made you want to kiss someone. Nagi was so close that if he bent down just a little farther, their lips would have brushed. What would hers taste like? How soft would they be? His mind filled with those thoughts, he reached out his hand.

"Ah!" she gasped, flinching in surprise.

"…Thanks, Nagi."

He ruffled her hair. For a moment, she looked caught off guard by his heartfelt gratitude. But a second later, her eyes crinkled in a smile.

"It's nothing."

Once again, he felt his love for her overflow. He smiled back. He'd always been the type to stick with things and keep his possessions for a long time. The same held true when it came to his childhood friend Nagi Yoroizuka. He couldn't even remember how long he'd felt this way toward her. There were lots of great things about her. Her ability to understand another person's feelings. How she never ridiculed others. Her competitive streak. Her optimism toward her own situation. How hard she worked. He could go on forever listing reasons he loved her, but if he had to choose one—

"It's you I should be thanking, Keigo."

—it would be her smile. He had a tremendous weakness for her smile.

Fifth Try

Nagi had been restless all day. It wasn't because she was wearing a brand-new dress, or because she'd curled her hair for the first time in ages, or because she had a necklace on. It was because she was finally going to have that long-awaited dinner with Kousaka. Two weeks earlier, when she'd canceled their dinner plans the night before his birthday, she'd done so knowing he might hate her for it. But not only had he graciously accepted her change of plans, he'd even wished her luck with work. It would be no exaggeration to say their date that day, which she'd managed to reschedule with him, would impact the rest of her life. No matter what, she couldn't screw up this time.

As she was powering through her work with demonic speed so she wouldn't be late to meet him, her eyes stopped on a particular spot in a system specification document. Something was strange about it. When she checked who had written that section, she saw it was Keigo.

"Hey, Keigo," she called out, stretching her neck to look over her monitor.

"What do you need?" he asked, raising his head.

"I looked at the specifications for the product details page, and it looks like the changes haven't been incorporated."

"Really?! My bad. I'll look it over right away!"

Keigo carried out his work with almost robotic perfection, and it was unusual for him to make even a small mistake like this. Maybe it was her imagination, but that day, he seemed to lack his usual drive. Now that she thought about it, she felt like he'd started acting weird after seeing her outfit that morning and asking if she had a date. Maybe he was sick or something.

He called to her once more through the gap between their screens.

"Sorry about that, Nagi! I fixed the specifications."

"Got it, thanks."

As she was rechecking the document, he quietly stood up and walked out of the office. Ever since they were young, he'd been prone to colds—unlike Nagi, who was almost *too* healthy. It had always been her job to bring him printouts and school-lunch desserts when he stayed home, since she'd lived across the street. Now that they were adults, he didn't seem to get quite as many colds, but she worried about his health. Knowing how absent-minded he was when it came to himself, she figured he might just buy an energy drink and go on with his day. Slightly worried, she got up to follow him.

"Ms. Yoroizuka."

But before she could fully stand up, Saiga called her name.

"...Yes?"

"...I can wait, if you're busy," he said with a dubious glance at her awkward half-standing posture.

"No, it's completely fine! What's going on?"

Their relationship hadn't improved at all, and Nagi couldn't shake her habit of acting a little stiff around him.

"I finished the work you asked me to do, so I wanted to let you know."

"Oh, thank you!"

As she opened the schedule on her computer and updated his progress, she let out a reflexive "Ooh!"

"Saiga, you're working faster! Impressive!" she said excitedly, forgetting for a moment that he didn't like her. Maybe because he was getting used to the work, his pace had improved markedly compared with a few months ago. He looked down, seeming embarrassed.

"...Thanks."

His tone was curt but a little shy. Happy that his development was going so well, Nagi turned back to the schedule in high spirits.

"So your next task will be..."

She scrolled down, pondering what to assign him next. Should she ask him to program a slightly more difficult section than she'd originally planned? That would make Saotome's work easier, which would allow her to help out Nagi, opening up time for Nagi to work on other things. But she didn't want to place too much of a burden on a new employee. Right, she'd better go with the original, easier assignment.

"How about this? It's not difficult at all, so you don't need to wor...ry..."

She glanced back at him as she pointed to the schedule, then froze. Where was that shy expression from a minute ago? He was glaring at the schedule on her screen with an obviously grumpy look on his face.

"What's...wrong...?"

"...Nothing. Nothing at all. I understand," he said curtly, turning to go.

"Wait!" Nagi said, scrambling to stop him. "What's going on?"

"Nothing, it's just..."

Nagi was completely confused. She had tried her best to prevent him from disliking his work. She'd given him the easiest jobs possible, and whenever he'd had difficulty finishing something, she'd stayed late to do it for him. So why did she have to put up with such overt loathing?

Wait, maybe she had it all wrong. She hurriedly rejected her childish reaction. She may have "tried" to take his best interests into account, but that was only her perspective. He was an independent person, and he was free to dislike what she had intended as thoughtfulness. And as the senior employee, it was on her if he felt that way.

"...Saiga, would you mind coming with me to the meeting space?"

She forced herself to speak calmly to him, and he followed obediently. She sat down across from him, took a few deep breaths, and plunged in.

"If there's something I've been doing that bothers you, I'd like you to tell me. I want you to feel at ease here. To be honest, I should probably have figured out the issue without you having to tell me...but I'm still inexperienced as a leader, and if you're willing, I want to work together to make this team better."

She still found it difficult to interact with him, but what she'd just said was the truth. She wanted to create the best environment she could for Saotome and Saiga, who were working so hard under her inadequate leadership, so that they would stay on for a long time. Having clearly laid out her case, she waited tensely for Saiga to respond. Quietly, he raised his head and looked straight at her.

"Can I say something?"

"Of course," she said, nodding firmly. Never very talkative, he took his time before speaking.

"I'd like to be assigned to a different team."

Nagi's mind went blank in disbelief.

"You...you mean...?"

"I don't want to be on your team anymore."

His point-blank rejection stabbed her right in the heart. She'd heard once that when people were truly shaken, they stopped speaking. Maybe he ran out of patience with her dazed silence, because he stood up with a sigh.

"I know it's probably impossible, so don't worry about it. I don't expect anything from you, anyway."

After Saiga left, Nagi remained rooted in place. She was still in shock. Eventually, she stood on wobbly legs and left the office. There was no way she could focus on her work right now. She wanted to find a place to be alone.

I don't expect anything from you, anyway.

As she walked aimlessly forward, Saiga's words played over and over in her head.

What kind of expectations did he mean? If he'd expected something, she wished he'd have told her. Then she would have been able to act closer to how he'd wanted. But it wasn't too late. She could talk with him again, and—

"…No."

She shook her head. It was pointless. If he disliked her that much, it would be impossible to repair the relationship. She was nearly in tears, but at the same time, her mind was rationally planning the next steps she had to take. The department head was on a business trip that day, but she could talk to him early the next week. She could admit she'd made a mistake in leadership and ask him to find a placement for Saiga that suited him. But if the team makeup changed, what would she do about the work she'd planned on assigning to Saiga? Oh well, she could do it herself with a bit of overtime. And then—if he would let her, she wanted to apologize to Saiga.

Just then, she heard voices from around the corner in the hallway.

"…Okay, okay. How about dinner tonight?"

"Really, can we?"

It was Keigo and Saotome. Thinking they were an odd pair, she peeked around the corner.

"Sure. I'll find a place."

"Thank you so much! I can't wait!"

From where she was standing, Nagi couldn't see Keigo's face, but she had a perfect view of Saotome's delighted expression. Huh? Were the two of them that close?

Frozen in place, she didn't realize how far around the corner she'd leaned.

"Oh!"

Saotome, who had been looking at Keigo with a smile practically overflowing with joy, suddenly shifted her gaze toward Nagi. Keigo glanced over his shoulder as well. His face tensed.

"Nagi…"

If she were to put a caption to his expression, it would be "Oh shit." Like he'd been caught doing something he'd wanted to keep secret. In that instant, something dawned on Nagi.

"Oh, s-sorry! I didn't mean to listen in…! I didn't know you two were seeing each other! I'm so sorry for not realizing!"

"Wait, Nagi…"

Keigo tried to interrupt her, but Nagi drowned him out with shouts of "It's fine, it's fine!"

"Don't worry—I won't tell anyone!" she continued quickly. "Um…Saotome! Keigo is an old friend of mine, but he's like family, and I don't see him any other way, so please don't worry about me! Okay then, the intruder will leave now! Excuse me!"

Bowing energetically, she made a U-turn and retreated full speed the way she'd come. She thought she heard Keigo calling after her, but she pretended she hadn't and kept running. She ran right past her own office and only stopped after ducking into the women's restroom on the far side.

"Whoa… I had no idea…"

She clasped both her hands to her cheeks, pressing her arms against her pounding heart. In her wildest dreams, she never would have imagined Keigo and Saotome together like that. She'd hardly ever heard Keigo mention women in the past, so she'd assumed he wasn't very interested in romance. But maybe it was a different story if the woman was Saotome. It was only natural that even Keigo would fall for her.

"I see…"

She was oddly filled with emotion. If the two of them were dating, that was wonderful. As team leader, she knew she should congratulate them heartily. But now that Saiga was leaving, she realized sadly that she would be the only single person on the team.

She felt kind of down, but she knew she couldn't sit in the bathroom avoiding her problems forever, so she steeled herself to go back to her desk.

"Huh…?"

Suddenly, she became aware of an odd sensation in her chest.

It was as if her heart was a piece of paper that had just been scrunched up into a ball. It must be shock from the combined bombshell of Saiga's request followed by her discovery of Keigo and Saotome's relationship.

"…Time to get back to work."

Massaging the area above her heart, she pulled herself together and left the bathroom. She had to set aside Saiga, Keigo, and Saotome for the time being and focus on her job. After all, it was a very important day for her. But no matter how much she tried to psyche herself up, the strange feeling in her heart refused to go away.

◆

Nagi shivered and pulled her Chesterfield coat tight as the cold mid-November wind pricked her cheeks. It was Friday, and the street lined with bars and restaurants was packed with workers off for the weekend. Her hair was in place, and she'd fixed her makeup in the bathroom before leaving the office. She was as ready as she could be. As she waited nervously, someone stopped in front of her.

"Uh…are you Ms. Nagi?"

She looked up. A man wearing a gray coat over his suit was peering at her. She had looked at his photo enough times to know right away that it was Nao Kousaka. He was as handsome as his picture—no, even more handsome in real life.

"Kousaka…right?"

"Yes. Good to meet you."

Their greetings were stiff. She was hearing his voice for the first time. It was lower and gentler than she'd imagined.

As Kousaka headed toward the nearby restaurant where he'd made a reservation, she stayed half a pace behind, glancing at his tall form as he walked. She'd worn low heels just in case, but this precaution turned out to be unnecessary. She couldn't care less herself, but apparently, a lot of guys saw her height of almost 170 centimeters as a deterrent to dating. She'd been dumped a number of times for just that reason. But she didn't need to worry about that with Kousaka. As she let out a sigh of relief, he paused.

"Here we are."

They were standing in front of a bustling, steam-filled bar. Beyond the timeworn door, customers were packed shoulder to shoulder, happily downing their beer and food. At a counter lined with an abundant selection of *shouchuu* and *nihonshuu*, someone who looked like the owner was grilling chicken with a practiced hand. What was this place? It was too good to be true!

"I had no idea a place like this was tucked in back here! I absolutely love bars like this where all kinds of people rub elbows—"

Suddenly, she stopped her excited flood of words. Kousaka was blinking in confusion.

"Um... Ms. Nagi, not that place. I meant the one next door."

Nagi slowly looked around and belatedly noticed the elegant French restaurant sitting quietly to the right of the bar.

"...S-sorry..."

"No, I'm the one who should apologize. Now I know you like bars. Next time we'll do that," he said kindly, with a wry smile. She apologized again and followed him into the restaurant. Calming classical music was playing in the dim dining area. Shrinking at the refined ambiance, she sat down carefully in the chair the waiter pulled out for her.

"It's prix fixe. Will that be all right?"

Nagi, who had been glancing around for a paper menu, looked up in surprise at Kousaka's words.

"O-of course."

"Great. What will you have to drink?"

Reading over the drinks menu he handed her, she recoiled in shock at the astronomical prices. She occasionally went out for French food, but the prices here were a step up...no, two or three steps up.

"Ms. Nagi, may I suggest the champagne? They've got some good ones here," he prompted considerately as she sat frozen in front of the open menu.

"Oh, yes, that sounds good." She nodded.

Kousaka called the waiter over and ordered a brand of champagne she'd never heard of. When the man returned with their glasses, the liquid inside was a lovely, appetizing golden color. Unfortunately, the quantity, too, was elegantly restrained.

"Cheers."

When she brought her lips to the rim of the glass, Nagi took great care not to drink down the entire contents in one gulp. As one would hope when paying such a high price, it was delicious: not too sweet, but dry and refreshing.

"I hope our dinner isn't interfering with your work. You seem to stay late a lot," Kousaka began after carefully setting down his glass.

"Oh, not at all! I finished up at top speed today, so everything's fine!"

"That's good," Kousaka said with a smile, but then the conversation stalled. Nagi had been genuinely looking forward to meeting him, but now she was so nervous she had no idea what to say. When she was with other women, she could talk about makeup or clothes or something, but that didn't work with men. Although the conversation never dried up with Keigo.

"Mademoiselle, your appetizer."

The waiter broke into her restless thoughts with a plate of food.

"That looks delicious!" she said. *Thank goodness*, she thought as she took a bite.

"By the way," Kousaka said. "It's gotten colder lately, and it seems we're already at the end of the year. How do you usually spend the New Year?"

Nagi thought back to the previous winter.

"Well…last year, we got together at my mom's house with some neighbors and watched boxing on TV."

Keigo's family had come over on New Year's Eve, and they'd all been shouting and cheering over the heated match. Maybe because their parents were such good friends, they usually spent the holiday at one or the other's family home.

"…Do you like boxing, then?" Kousaka asked. She didn't notice the slightly subdued tone of his voice.

"Oh, I love it!" she replied. "Do you follow any sports?"

"I don't watch much…although I do enjoy snowboarding and rock climbing."

She hadn't tried either, and she racked her brain to think of something else to ask him about. She had to find a shared interest! What did men like to talk about anyway? If she were talking to Keigo—

Suddenly, his face popped into her mind.

"Oh, that reminds me. Last year on New Year's Eve, we all played mahjong!"

He looked surprised.

"You play mahjong?"

"Yes, although I'm not very good."

Keigo's father loved the game and always suggested they play. It was another annual tradition for Nagi, Keigo, and his mom and dad to sit around the table until dawn. Keigo's parents usually won, while Keigo and Nagi competed for last place.

"When we play," she went on, describing the happy memory, "the rule is that the two in last place have to drink *nihonshuu*. Last year, me and Keigo…oh, he's my childhood friend…anyway, we got crushed and ended up drinking a whole bottle between the two of us."

Slowly, the smile faded from Nagi's face.

"Huh… That sounds fun."

Kousaka didn't look like he thought it sounded fun at all. *Crap.*

"H-how do you spend the New Year?" she asked in a panic.

"Well…last year, I watched the fireworks at Disney World in Florida with some friends."

She almost spat out the champagne she was so cautiously sipping. What kind of a poster child for success was this man?

"Um…did you grow up in a good family…?" she asked, a bit embarrassed. He chuckled.

"Not at all. I like having fun, so that's what I spend my money on."

"Having fun…you mean like traveling?"

"Yes. Last year I went to Bali and Hawaii…oh, and Australia. After all, when else in our lives will we be so free to use our time as we please? I think it's such a waste to just sit around and let the clock tally up our precious hours. That's why I always strive to be active."

He lifted his glass and grinned. For Nagi, who preferred to hibernate in her apartment on her days off, his words sounded like a foreign language.

"Do you like to travel, Ms. Nagi?"

This was the question she had been dreading. Her heart pounded.

"Um, well, I suppose… Ah-ha-ha…"

Traveling was fun, but it was also exhausting, so she didn't much like it. If she was going to go anywhere, it would probably be to a hot spring resort where she could relax.

"Ah…I see."

Her answer must have been too negative, because he didn't say anything else on the subject. As they finished the appetizer and waited on the next course, the conversation continued to stall. Nagi was getting the sense that their interests didn't match, and

Kousaka probably was, too. Neither of them wanted to risk opening up a new topic.

◆

After finishing her flavorless French meal, Nagi walked back to the train station accompanied by Kousaka.

"Thank you. That was very nice," she said.

"It was my pleasure," he answered.

They delivered their social niceties and bobbed their heads politely. She probably should have gathered her courage and suggested they go to a bar, but she didn't have the requisite nerves of steel, and anyhow, she desperately wanted to go home.

"Well…good-bye."

They each gave a lukewarm wave and parted at the ticket gate. Nagi boarded her train and collapsed into a seat.

What was all that about? She felt like she had just wasted a lot of time and energy. How strange. It wasn't supposed to go like that.

She glanced at her phone. It was only just past nine. They had been exchanging messages daily for months. She'd never dreamed it would all fall apart in less than two hours. She felt like the world was ending. The train rocked her along to her station, where she stepped off with leaden feet. Just outside in the street, the delicious aroma of broth tickled her nose. It was coming from a little *oden* shop she stopped at sometimes after work. Sucked in by the good smell, she sat down at the scratched-up counter she knew so well.

"Evening."

Without her having to say a word, the familiar owner brought her a hot towel and a beer.

"Daikon, beef tendon, and hard-boiled egg…and fish cake, please," she said.

"Coming right up," he answered. A moment later, the steaming bowl of broth with her requested items floating in it was set on the counter. She picked up her disposable chopsticks, took a sip of the broth, and let out a long sigh. *Ahh, delicious!* The flavor seemed to seep into her very bones. She had just finished half her beer in one go when her phone buzzed on the counter. She casually picked it up and nearly choked. It was a message from Kousaka. With great trepidation, she opened it. There was a neutral greeting, and then at the end:

...I hope we can continue to be good friends.

So it was over. She set the phone down softly and flopped over the counter in sorrow. She wanted to punch herself for being so stupid.

"...Haaah."

Listlessly sitting back up, she typed out a reply. It was pure boilerplate, a thank-you-for-tonight followed by an I'm-glad-we-met. She wrapped it up with Yes, let's stay in touch. Before hitting Send, she scrolled up and reread his old messages. They'd exchanged a lot. It had been fun. And pointless.

She reluctantly sent the message, then slipped her phone into her bag, chugged down her slightly warm beer, and asked for another. As she lifted a bite of the broth-soaked radish to her mouth, her second beer in hand, a feeling of inexpressible emptiness overwhelmed her. *It's all in the past. No use worrying about it now.* She forced Kousaka out of her mind, but one negative thought tends to bring another, and Saiga popped up to fill the space Kousaka had left.

I don't expect anything from you, anyway.

The remembered words were like a knife to her heart. She'd have to tell the department head about the situation on Monday. Crushed by melancholy, she flopped back down on the counter. Work was a disaster. Love was a disaster. Everything was a disaster. Was there anything she was good at?

She thought about that question seriously for a while, but all she could come up with was turning oxygen into carbon dioxide. She hated this. She was exhausted. Her body and mind both felt heavy, and she didn't have the will to keep fighting—

Suddenly, someone tapped her shoulder, and she shot upright.

"Wh—? …Erk!"

As soon as she turned around, the person poked her in the cheek.

"Gotcha!" he said, laughing.

Nagi froze.

"K…Keigo?! What are you doing here?" she asked, shaken. He sat down next to her.

"I saw you as I left the station, so I thought I'd come mess with you."

He might live near the same station as her, but it was still odd to bump into him here. He ordered a beer. As she peered at him in surprise, she suddenly remembered something.

"What happened with Saotome?! Didn't you two go to dinner tonight?"

"I walked her to the station. She's probably getting home about now."

It was only nine thirty. She was hardly one to speak, but wasn't the time for romance just starting? Since she couldn't bring herself to ask him about it, and his beer had just arrived, they clinked glasses. After taking synchronized swigs, Keigo said, "Did something happen tonight? Your back looked really sad when I was walking up."

Her back looked sad? It was too much of a hassle to ask what that meant, so she silently sipped her beer.

"Things didn't go well with the guy?"

"…I don't think so," she answered hesitantly.

"You don't think so?" he echoed with a wry smile. "Well, if you feel like telling me later, I'm all ears."

He paused for a second, then asked, "Can I eat your fish cake?"

"Sure. Just not the beef tendon."

"Thanks."

She watched him scarf it down in two bites with an appreciative "Yum." He sure could eat. She supposed that since he was so tall, he had to have more or else he'd get hungry.

"How much have you had to drink?" he asked her.

"Not that much. Three glasses of champagne, and this is my second beer."

"So you can have five more. I'll take you home, so drink until you've had enough. But no more than that. You'll pass out and be totally unable to wake up," he teased. She pouted.

"I don't pass out outside. Anyway, you're the one who's impossible to wake up."

"Not true. I never drink recklessly."

"Listen to you! Who passed out in my mom's flower bed on New Year's?"

"You mean when we got thrashed at mahjong? Man, when I woke up freezing cold in a field of flowers, I seriously thought I'd died and moved on to the next life."

Nagi roared with laughter, feeling slightly better. There wasn't any refined classical music playing, the food wasn't fancy, and the counter was covered in scars and a little greasy. But the conversation was light and easy, and before she knew it, Saiga and Kousaka had vanished from her mind.

"...So what do you think I need to work on?"

Happily drunk, she set her mug down with a clatter. She was talking more openly now and had just finished explaining to Keigo what her dinner with Kousaka had been like. He listened with a look halfway between sympathy and amusement.

"Poor Mr. Cider Commercial..." He sighed.

"Mr. Cider who?"

"Oh, nothing. Anyway...maybe you could tone down your old-man tendencies."

"But you like to watch boxing and play mahjong, too!"

"We just happen to have similar hobbies. As far as I can tell, this Kousaka is a completely different type."

Nagi had been leaning in toward him, but at this candid comment, she backed away meekly.

"Now I've done it... I was an idiot to use you as a standard."

She held her head in her hands, thinking back over her many missteps.

"Don't you have anyone else to use?"

"I mean, I know everything about you, so you're the easy choice," she said without thinking too much about it.

There was an abrupt silence. Finding it odd he wasn't saying anything, she looked over at him. He was staring into his mug.

"Everything, huh…?"

He let out a short breath that could have been a laugh or a sigh, then turned slowly toward her.

"If you know everything about me, what am I thinking right now?"

"You want me to play a guessing game?"

"Just give it a shot."

She thought for a minute, then said, "I know!" and looked at him. "Nagi sure looked cute today! Not. Ha-ha."

She laughed at her own joke, then gradually fell silent. Keigo wasn't even smiling. To the contrary, he was staring at her. *Hey, you were supposed to laugh!* Just as she was about to make a follow-up comment, he spoke.

"You're right. That's exactly what I'm thinking."

Her thoughts blurred. She had to think hard about what he meant.

"Um…well…"

Maybe she'd drunk too much. His strangely ardent gaze was focused directly on her. She knew she was shaken, and she knew he could tell. Still, she couldn't look away. Even though it was Keigo sitting next to her, in that moment, the mood swirling around them felt completely different.

"…Ha-ha, got you!"

His lips curled up. When she realized he was messing with her, she pinched his side.

"Ow!" he said, squirming away.

"You're drunk!" she said, giving him a hard stare.

"Am not."

"Are too. This is how you act when you're drunk."

She pouted and tilted back her mug. After swallowing some of the slightly watery highball she'd ordered, she noticed her throat was horribly dry. Keigo had always been like this. When he got drunk, he sometimes teased her and said things like he'd done a moment ago. He'd have on a dead serious expression, too, which made it even worse.

"Why don't you try that line on Saotome?"

"...Why Saotome?"

He frowned, and so did she.

"You're dating her, aren't you?"

For some reason, a look of blatant disgust came over his face.

"...So you *did* take that the wrong way. I didn't think you would."

"What? You're not dating?"

"She told me she wanted to ask my advice about something, so we went to dinner. That's it. We're just coworkers, I swear."

"Oh, okay. I was so sure..."

"I was going to tell you, but you ran off before I could say anything."

It was true she'd rushed off just as he tried to speak.

"Huh..."

She felt vaguely deflated as Keigo peered into her face.

"Anything else you want to talk about?"

This surprised her a little, but then again, he was her oldest friend. It was only natural he'd be able to guess she had something on her mind other than Kousaka.

"...There's an issue at work," she said quietly.

"Oh yeah?" he replied, nodding gently.

He set down his chopsticks and took up a listening position, and she told him about Saiga.

"Ah, I see...," he said when she was done, sinking into thought. Keigo was considerate enough not to criticize Nagi *or* Saiga—he probably knew she didn't like to be viewed as whiny. She sipped her highball, the ice now totally melted, and waited for him to respond.

"Saiga likes challenges," he said finally. "I think he might respond better to being left to his own devices than to being coddled."

"He likes challenges…?"

"Yeah. He told me he studies programming at home and makes his own systems and stuff. He's really passionate about learning."

She'd had no idea. She listened in surprise as Keigo went on.

"I think he's got the skills to figure out a more difficult assignment if you gave it to him. Of course, it would take some time at first, but it might be good to let him work on something like that until he's satisfied."

As she listened to his advice, she grew increasingly ashamed of herself. She'd been trying not to overburden him. But had she ever once asked him what he wanted?

"…Thanks, Keigo. I'll try talking with him again on Monday."

I can understand why he's fed up with me. Who would want to follow a leader who's rushing forward headlong all by herself? Instead of trying to get him to like me, I should be trying to get to know him. Keigo smiled at her as she made this small resolution.

"Yeah, go for it."

He reached out his hand and lightly stroked her head. Then he moved his hand back and gently ruffled the hair behind her ear. His hands were so big. He didn't just tease her when he drank; sometimes he also petted her like she was his beloved dog. When he touched her with his big hands, she felt like she understood the happiness dogs must feel when their owners pet them. She sat quietly and let him continue as long as he wanted. He must have finally had enough, because he moved his hand away.

"…Shit, it's already two," he said, looking at his watch. She was flabbergasted. They'd been talking for over four hours.

"Should we head home?"

The minute they opened the rickety door after settling the bill, a biting wind mercilessly pricked at their cheeks.

"It's freezing!" Nagi yelped as they walked along. Finally, they came to the place where their paths home diverged.

"Thanks for hanging out with me tonight. See you at work… Um, Keigo?"

He was still striding forward, ignoring her. Not toward his house but toward hers. Apparently, he was bent on dutifully seeing her home.

"I'm fine, okay? My house isn't that far," she said, running after him, but he showed no sign of stopping.

"Oh no. My legs are moving on their own. I can't stop them," he said in an exaggerated monotone. She laughed.

"…Thanks, Keigo," she said to his back.

"No biggie," he replied.

Responding to a sudden urge, she quickened her pace to catch up with him and pressed herself against his left arm. He pushed her away with his whole body, so she shoved him back. They jostled each other for a while, laughing, then walked along the dark streets pressed against each other. The warmth of his body felt natural, as if it were the warmth of her own.

"Man, it's cold. Wish I could go to a hot spring," Keigo said, his breath coming out white.

"Me too. Somewhere with a good local brewery."

"You're basing your choice on alcohol?"

"It's important!"

"It is."

Their laughter overlapped and melted into the cold, quiet air.

◆

The following Monday morning, Nagi woke up feeling fresh and energetic. It was like her heart had never even taken that beating on Friday night. She arrived at work an hour earlier than usual and revised the development schedule. Half an hour into the work day, she called Saiga into the meeting space.

"…And that's why I'd like you to work according to this

schedule," she said, holding it out. That morning she had rearranged the workloads so Saiga would have plenty of time to try a difficult section she had originally planned on assigning to Saotome. Saiga sat across from her, staring at the piece of paper, and she waited nervously for his reaction. Finally, he looked up.

"…Are you sure this is okay?" he asked.

She tensed, not having expected that response.

"You mean…?"

"I mean, are you sure it's okay for me to work on something this difficult?"

Finally understanding, she nodded enthusiastically.

"Of course! If you don't mind, that is!"

"…I don't mind."

His response was as curt as ever, but Nagi felt distinctly hopeful. She suspected that by *I don't mind*, he actually meant *I really want to do it*. She stretched, then made up her mind to say something else.

"Saiga, as team leader, I should have asked you what you wanted to work on, but instead I held back your potential. I mistakenly thought I was protecting you… I really messed up. I'm sorry."

She bowed her head deeply.

"No," he mumbled. "I knew you were trying to protect me… and I was happy about that part. I just wanted to try different kinds of work. You only gave me the easy stuff."

Nagi glanced up and caught her breath. Saiga was looking straight at her.

"You and Ms. Saotome are so busy, and here I was getting all the easy jobs. I felt like I wasn't needed on the team. I didn't even know why I was here…"

Regret washed over her. *What was I thinking? I'm the one who's been crushing his motivation!*

"…I'm gonna pile on the work mercilessly, so get ready!" she declared, half standing in her seat. "I'm going to have you program one tough system after another so you can load up on skills!

But if it gets to be too much, tell me! I can readjust the schedule whenever you need me to, and I can give you advice, as well. I'll be there for you whenever you need me! I promise!"

After she finished shouting, silence descended between them. Saiga stared at her face, dumbfounded—she must've looked crazy.

"Wow, you have some strong feelings there," he finally said, letting slip a wry smile.

Saiga smiled! As Nagi reeled in shock, he muttered her name.

"Ms. Yoroizuka, I'm sorry. Please forget about me wanting to be on a different team."

"Huh?" she blurted out in surprise. "Are…you sure?"

"Yes. I'm looking forward to working with you in the future."

Saiga bowed his head deeply. *In the future*—happiness surged in Nagi's chest at those words.

"Yes…yes, yes! So am I! Yes!"

She nodded over and over.

"You sure do nod a lot," he said with that same wry smile.

After that, they went over the details of the schedule. When they were finished, Nagi practically skipped back to her seat. Surging with newfound motivation, she was turning enthusiastically back toward her computer when Keigo poked his head out between their two screens.

"How'd it go?" he whispered. She gave him an elated thumbs-up. He grinned as if to say, "I'm glad," and she reciprocated with an ear-to-ear smile.

She was filled with gratitude toward Keigo as she started on her work. He knew what she liked, what she hated, and what she wanted without her having to say a word. And to top it off, he was her coworker, so he was able to give her advice about work. *Wouldn't everything be so easy if he was my boyfriend?* she thought.

She laughed dryly at this wild notion. They had been friends for more than twenty-five years. There was no way something like that would happen after all this time.

But if it did happen, what would it be like? Would they kiss and stuff?

No way, she couldn't. It was Keigo!

After imagining this and then laughing it off, she finally refocused on her work. But as it turned out, that morning was the last time she would be able to think about such things so casually.

"…I'm sorry, Uncle Ryou, what did you just say?"

It was one o'clock, and she was in the president's office. She had been utterly baffled when he summoned her a few minutes earlier.

"Huh? I asked if you've noticed anything peculiar between Ms. Saotome and Keigo," Ryou said, equally confused.

"Not that! What you said before!" Nagi shouted.

"Well, like I said… Ms. Saotome came to talk to me, and she said Keigo tried to pressure her into going to a love hotel."

So she hadn't misheard him after all. Nagi pressed both hands over her mouth at this unbelievable news.

"If you don't know about it, I'll ask him directly. I'm going to call for him, all right?"

Nagi nodded, bewildered. Listening in a daze as he picked up the receiver, she put a hand to her head. Her mind was swirling. She wanted to deny the accusation with all her might, but the two of them *had* gone out to dinner the previous Friday.

Keigo had told her Saotome was "just a colleague"—but what if that was a lie?

No, this must just be some big misunderstanding, right?

Sixth Try

The shelves on the brick walls were lined with a wide selection of wines. The sizzling sound of food cooking in the kitchen mixed with the faint smell of garlic. Three other groups aside from Keigo and Saotome were seated in the cozy restaurant.

"Everything looks delicious!" Saotome gasped as the waiter set out colorful dishes of bruschetta and caprese salad. "I'll serve."

"Oh, okay, thanks."

As Keigo watched her divide up the food, he thought about the events of that morning.

Date tonight?

The fact that Nagi was wearing a dress, which was unusual for her, had raised his suspicions.

Yeah.

Finally, the day he'd feared had arrived. Her dinner with Kousaka had been canceled once, and he knew they would inevitably reschedule, but hearing her say the words had dealt a heavy blow. That was why he had made so many careless mistakes at work. For better or worse, no big problems had cropped up like last time. That meant that right about now, Nagi was probably enjoying her dinner with Mr. Cider Commercial. She'd called him "a good person," but would he really let their date end without trying anything? The very thought of it sent him into a frenzy of worry. And he had something else on his mind, too.

"Here you are," Saotome said, gently placing a prettily arranged plate of food in front of him. He thanked her, flustered. She smiled and waved dismissively.

Actually, I wanted to ask your advice about something at work.

She'd approached him when he'd stepped out of the office in an attempt to stop thinking about Nagi and focus on his job. In retrospect, it seemed awful of him, but he'd suspected she was using "advice" as an excuse to get closer to him—in a romantic way. He was wary of her and originally planned to turn down her request.

I wanted to ask Ms. Yoroizuka about it, but she said she has plans tonight, so...

In the end, when he saw the troubled look on her face, he couldn't bring himself to say no. Nagi had happened upon them just as they were making dinner plans, and when he'd tried to explain himself, she'd run off. He hadn't gotten another chance to talk to her since. The whole day had been one disaster after another. As he sat across from Saotome, he prayed nothing else would go wrong.

"So what kind of advice did you need?" he asked when they'd finished eating the main course and gotten through an appropriate amount of trivial chatting. She quietly set down her glass and parted her glossy, moist lips.

"Actually, I'm interested in someone at the office."

"...Huh."

He was too rattled by her unexpected confession to think of anything better to say.

"Do you think it's okay to date a coworker, Mr. Yuuki?" she asked.

He glanced away, unable to hold her serious gaze.

"I think it's fine. As long as the parties involved are okay with it, of course," he said noncommittally.

"You think so?" she asked, looking down. He was relieved to finally be released from her stare, but apparently, she wasn't finished talking. "Um...do you like anyone at work?"

He choked on his gin and tonic.

"Uh...*cough, cough*...do I like anyone...?"

He almost snapped back "Don't be ridiculous" but suddenly thought better of it. He didn't know what she was after, but it was probably better to contain the situation by being honest instead of fumbling a denial. He planted his hands on his knees and looked at her squarely.

"Yes, I do," he said nervously. He did not elaborate. She didn't appear surprised. Slowly, she looked up.

"May I ask who it is?" she said in an extremely quiet voice.

"I don't think the name would mean anything. It's not anyone you know," he said with a half smile. To avoid her accusatory gaze, he took another gulp of his gin and tonic.

"Is that all you wanted to ask me? If there's nothing else, then—," he was saying, trying to wind down their dinner, when she interrupted.

"I believe I know Ms. Yoroizuka quite well."

Her icy tone wove its way through the din of the restaurant to his ears. His hand froze midreach toward their check. He glanced at her, stunned.

"It's Ms. Yoroizuka you like, isn't it? I can tell. I've been watching you."

The expression on her face was uncharacteristically serious. Her tone was so decisive he didn't even think to argue back.

"Please. If I'm right, then tell me," she said earnestly. For an instant, he considered nodding. It would have been easy. Just a single movement of his head.

"No…it's someone else."

Instead, he flatly denied it. He was agitated, but his rational brain won out. Carrying the conversation any further could only hurt her.

"Let's get going," he said, standing up with the check in his hand.

"Thank you for dinner." Saotome bowed to him as they left the restaurant.

"You're welcome," he answered. It was such a relief to no longer have to sit across from her. "I'll walk you to the station. There are a lot of drunks around here. Which line do you take?"

"Thank you… Let's go this way. It's a shortcut."

They walked on in silence, just far enough apart to make it hard to tell if they were strangers or acquaintances. Keigo wished he could run at top speed to their destination to escape the exceedingly awkward atmosphere. But since Saotome was wearing heels, his only option was to match her slow pace.

It sure was going to be uncomfortable seeing her on Monday. Would it have been better to admit he liked Nagi? Keigo was so lost in his own worries, he didn't notice a couple stumbling drunkenly toward them.

"Eek!" Saotome squealed as she collided with the woman. Both of them tottered perilously.

"Be careful!" Keigo shouted, shooting out a hand to Saotome and pulling her close.

The woman apologized dully and continued down the street, latched on to the arm of her male companion. Judging by the way they were walking, both of them must have been plastered. Eventually, they whispered something to each other and slipped into a building. A signboard set by the entrance brazenly advertised cheap rooms alongside the suggestive name of the establishment in large, fancy script. Glancing around, Keigo realized this street was full of similar signs.

Shit. This area was extremely sketchy. He quickly removed the hand he'd placed on Saotome to stop her from falling.

"The station is this way. Let's get out of…here…"

He was in the middle of turning around when he stopped in his tracks. He could feel something soft on his back. When he looked down, he saw a slender arm wrapped around his waist.

"Mr. Yuuki…"

Somehow, her hot breath as she whispered his name seemed to penetrate his coat and caress his skin.

"What are you doing...?"

He glanced awkwardly over his shoulder and gasped. Two watery eyes were staring up at him from very close range, wavering helplessly. He couldn't tell if she was about to cry or get mad or ask him for something, but her expression appealed directly to his male instincts.

I don't want people to blame my lack of ability on the fact that I'm a woman.

Keigo suddenly remembered Nagi's words from before. It seemed to him like the disadvantages of being a woman could sometimes be turned into weapons. Right now was a perfect example. But there were women who didn't even know how to use those weapons, whose only option was to fight head-on. He thought of Nagi—her clumsiness and honest strength. That was just one of the reasons he loved her.

"Saotome, please let go of me."

He gently peeled away her arms, and she stood, unmoving.

"If you're having trouble walking, I can call a taxi," he offered.

She shook her head softly.

"...No, I'm fine."

"Then let's go. Just tell me if it gets hard to walk."

They started moving and didn't say a word until they parted. Keigo left her at the station, and about half an hour later, he ran into Nagi at the *oden* stand.

◆

"...And that's all that happened..."

Nagi and Ryou were watching Keigo with solemn expressions. He had just finished summarizing the events of the previous Friday night, after being abruptly called to the president's office.

"Is that the truth? You aren't lying about anything?" Nagi asked in an accusatory tone, her arms crossed.

"Of course not!"

He was the one who should have been angry. He had no idea

why he was being accused of such a thing, but it couldn't have been further from the truth.

"Nagi, I think he's being honest," Ryou said quietly. Up till then, he'd been listening in silence. "I think all of this can be chalked up to a simple misunderstanding between Ms. Saotome and Keigo."

He glanced sympathetically at Keigo. Ryou knew all about his long-standing, unrequited love for Nagi.

"...I suppose so," Nagi mumbled. She sighed, the crease fading from between her eyebrows. "I'm glad. I didn't think Keigo would ever do something like that."

Keigo's chest tightened as she turned to him with a relieved smile. He was sincerely glad they had both believed him.

"That said, Saotome still feels like her side of the story is true. We need to clear up the misconception," Nagi continued, pulling herself together.

"You're right." Ryou nodded. "Let's hear her side of the story. I think it would be best for you to leave the room, Keigo. I'll call her."

He picked up his phone and dialed her internal number. But when he set the receiver back down, he seemed bewildered.

"Keigo, Ms. Saotome says she would like to speak with you alone..."

Both Keigo and Nagi looked at him in surprise.

"Sh-she's okay with that...?" Nagi asked. Keigo had the same question.

"That's what she said, so I guess it's fine...," Ryou answered.

As the three of them exchanged confused looks, there was a knock on the door. All three pressed their lips shut.

"Excuse me," Saotome said as she walked into the room, back straight. As Keigo tried to pull his thoughts together, he sensed Nagi and Ryou glancing at each other.

"Um, well...we'll leave you two alone. We'll be nearby, so just call if you need anything," Ryou said. The two of them left, seeming worried. Keigo had only one way forward. He steeled his will and quietly turned to Saotome.

"Saotome. I'm sorry for making you uncomfortable."

He bowed to her graciously.

"As a man, I should have been more aware of the situation. But I want you to know that I truly had no intention of doing what you thought I was trying to do."

As Nagi had said, whatever the truth of the situation, if Saotome thought he'd done something inappropriate, then the first thing he had to do was clear up the misunderstanding. Plus, he might be partly at fault for putting his arm around her when she was falling, even if he'd done so reflexively.

"...Of course I understand. It was my mistake. I'm sorry," he heard her say as he continued to bow his head. "And you want me to say that to the president and Ms. Yoroizuka, don't you?"

Keigo looked up abruptly. There was a distinctly threatening smile on Saotome's face.

"What...do you mean?"

Saotome giggled at his failure to grasp the situation.

"I'd like something in return for putting things right."

Something in return. He finally understood what was going on.

"...Ha-ha, I see. So that's what this is about."

This had all been a trap. He didn't know how far back it went, but he was sure she'd set him up for this moment.

"I'm glad you're catching on so quickly, Mr. Yuuki."

She grinned. The complete lack of guilt in her smile was terrifying.

"I want you to promise that you will have no interaction with Ms. Yoroizuka outside of work," she went on blithely. He'd suspected as much. This had to do with Nagi.

"That won't be so easy. We've been friends since we were kids. I don't think I can make that promise."

Their parents lived across the street from each other, and their families occasionally socialized. Cutting off contact outside of work would be next to impossible. More importantly, he didn't have the slightest desire to do so.

"…Do you understand the position you are in?"

Perhaps grasping that Keigo had no intention of accommodating her demand, Saotome frowned.

"If you want to spread rumors about me, go right ahead," he answered. "Unfortunately for you, all I care about is whether the people who need to believe me do."

Since Ryou, the company president, knew it was a misunderstanding, his work was unlikely to be seriously impacted. More importantly, the one person in the world he most wanted to believe in him understood the situation. That was enough for him. But Saotome smiled calmly in the face of his resolve.

"Do you really think you'll be the only one affected?"

"…What?"

"You care about Ms. Yoroizuka, don't you?"

Her words were enough to freeze his heart.

"Don't you dare touch her!"

The instant he shouted, he realized what he'd done.

"Ha-ha. It seems you care for her quite a bit after all," she said with a snicker. He didn't have the energy left to deny it.

"…What do you want from me?" he asked cautiously.

She crossed her arms in triumph.

"I already told you. All I want is for you to have nothing to do with Ms. Yoroizuka."

Keigo was puzzled. He understood her request, but it seemed like she still hadn't gotten to the heart of the matter. Wouldn't it be typical for her to ask him to date her at this point?

"You look mystified. Let me take this opportunity to state my feelings clearly," Saotome announced. "I hate you."

She spat out her words, glaring at him all the while. After a pause lasting ten full seconds, he finally responded.

"………………What?"

"I said I hate you. I've hated you ever since you transferred to our department."

"...I'm sorry, did I do something to offend you...?"

He frantically thought back over their conversations. Unfortunately, he couldn't come up with anything that would make her dislike him this much.

"You didn't do anything. It's your existence I can't stand," she said, clearly irritated. "You're handsome, you're tall, you're good at your work, women think you're nice, and men think you're fun to be around. Who the hell are you anyway?"

Keigo pressed his temples, feeling dizzy.

"Listen to me!" he shouted. "...No one is that perfect! That would be scary! I may be tall, but that's it!"

"Your modesty is just one more thing I hate about you!"

It was impossible. Whatever he said, she was going to attack him.

"Enough of this! Hurry up and promise me!" she snarled.

"I told you. It's impossible for me to have nothing to do with Nagi—"

"Don't you dare call her by her first name. It's disrespectful!" she interrupted sharply.

He snapped his mouth shut. Saotome was more furious than she had been at any point so far. She stared at him relentlessly, rage burning in her eyes.

"Do not call her by her first name. Do not take liberties when you speak to her. And do not touch her."

With each word, she bore down on him, closer and closer.

"Hey now, Saotome...," he said, backing away.

"You may have known her for longer than I have. But right now, I know her better than you! So you can stop acting so full of yourself this instant!"

Her face was as close now as it had been on Friday night when she'd embraced him from behind. But her expression was so completely different that she was almost unrecognizable. It was like he'd killed her parents or something, and she was out for revenge...

"You don't...mean to say the person you like is..."

"That's exactly what I mean." She nodded. "I like Ms. Yoroizuka."

Now he was truly flabbergasted. After considering this new information thoroughly, he cautiously opened his mouth.

"Uh...I'm sorry. Just so I understand correctly, what do you mean?"

"What do I mean? Just what I said. And by *like*, I mean *love*. I want to hold her hand. I want to hug her, kiss her, and then—"

"I got it, I got it—you can stop now!" he interrupted, before frantically attempting to sort out his thoughts.

Saotome didn't like Keigo; she liked Nagi. And Keigo liked Nagi, too, and Saotome knew that, and—

"Oh... So that's why you don't want me to have anything to do with Nagi."

He clapped his hands together. Finally, the pieces were falling into place.

"You really are slow," Saotome said with a click of her tongue. She glared at him. "By the way, the only reason I'm telling you this is because it would have been irritating if you went on misunderstanding the situation. You can tell Ms. Yoroizuka if you want. We're both women, so there are plenty of ways to smooth it over."

"I wasn't planning on saying anything..."

Ignoring him, she placed her finger on the tip of his nose.

"Anyway! As long as you don't promise, I refuse to take back a single word I said about you."

She put extra emphasis on the phrase *a single word*. As Keigo gaped at her, she spun on her heels.

"That is all," she said, leaving and shutting the door behind her. He could hear Nagi calling her name and then the sound of approaching footsteps.

"I'm sorry... Mr. Yuuki said he couldn't remember what happened... He was very drunk, so I guess that's not a surprise..."

"Saotome..."

"If he doesn't remember, that's fine. But I...I was so happy when it happened...and it's so hard now..."

Keigo couldn't help being impressed by how perfectly miserable Saotome's voice suddenly sounded.

Women were terrifying when you wound up on their bad side. That was a lesson he wouldn't soon forget.

Seventh Try

Nagi was flummoxed. Completely flummoxed.

"Nagi, can I talk to you? I want to ask you something about the Acsis account—"

Keigo walked toward her seat, a document in his hand, then suddenly stopped. He was looking at Saotome, who was next to Nagi.

"I'm sorry, Keigo…," Nagi started.

Before she could say "Can we talk about it later?" Saotome interrupted.

"Would you mind asking her later?" she said more curtly than usual. "Ms. Yoroizuka is speaking with me right now."

"Oh…I see. I'm sorry to have bothered you."

Keigo quickly looked away and strode back to his seat. Saotome picked up where she had left off, smiling without a hint of discomfort.

For the past few days, Keigo and Saotome had been acting very strangely. It was clear they hadn't managed to resolve their differences when they spoke alone in the president's office. All Saotome would say was "Everything's fine," and Keigo kept telling her not to ask him about it. There was nothing she could do.

It was understandable that the atmosphere would be awkward. Saotome probably had feelings for Keigo.

If he doesn't remember, that's fine. But I…I was so happy when it happened…and it's so hard now…

That's what Saotome had said that day, quiet tears in her eyes. According to Keigo, they had gone out to dinner because she wanted his advice, but the fact that she'd asked him, rather than Nagi, who had known her much longer, suggested she was interested in him.

Nagi watched Saotome beside her, unable to shake off her worry.

"…Ms. Yoroizuka, can I talk to you?"

Saiga caught up with her that day as she was returning to the office from lunch. He glanced around to make sure no one else was nearby, then whispered, "Did something happen between those two?"

She knew immediately who he meant by *those two*. Unsurprisingly, Saiga seemed to have noticed the uneasy atmosphere within their team.

"Uh…well…kind of yes, kind of no…?"

She couldn't very well tell him everything that had happened, so she answered vaguely.

"What's that supposed to mean?" he asked, sounding exasperated. "I'm not interested in the details. It's just so awkward—I wish you would do something about it."

It was a natural request. The storm brewing between their team members was so fierce it even made bystanders like Nagi and Saiga uncomfortable. As she ruminated on the problem, a brilliant plan occurred to her.

"I just had a great idea! Will you help me out, Saiga?"

"What…? Me?"

"I can't do it alone! I need you! Please!" she begged.

"…I should never have said anything," he muttered reluctantly.

◆

It was Friday night, and the bar was overflowing with office workers excited for the weekend. The place served creative food and drinks, and it was Nagi's go-to spot.

"What a cool place!" Saotome said as they entered, instantly perking up.

"Right? Let's stuff ourselves!" Nagi answered.

"Count me in! I'm so happy you invited me. Thank you!"

Saotome had immediately said yes that afternoon when Nagi asked her out to dinner. Feeling a pang of guilt at Saotome's smile, Nagi glanced around the bar. To her relief, she quickly located two familiar faces at the counter. Evidently, Saiga had succeeded at inviting Keigo to the same bar.

"Wow! What a coincidence to see you two here!" she cried.

They turned around in unison.

"Oh, hello. How funny," Saiga said, sounding like he'd planned the line in advance. Keigo, on the other hand, seemed surprised. His eyes went wide.

"Nagi? …And Saotome…"

When he noticed Saotome beside her, his expression darkened visibly. Saotome looked equally disappointed.

"Wh-what a perfect chance to all have a drink together," Nagi suggested, as if to clear up the sudden awkwardness.

"Isn't it strange that we're on the same team but we've never had dinner together?" Nagi said.

Even after they'd moved to a private room and their drinks and food had been served, the conversation between the four of them was lagging horribly. Sensing that she was nearing the limits of her ability to carry the conversation alone, Nagi shot Saiga a silent plea for help. He shrugged and gave her a look that said "Good luck." *Figures.*

"B-by the way," she said to Saotome, who was silently eating sashimi next to her. "You know that Korean TV show you said you like? I watched it! I'd never seen a K-drama before, but it was really good!"

"You watched it?!" Saotome replied, her glum expression replaced by a happy smile. Gaining confidence from this positive response, Nagi went on.

"In fact, I enjoyed it so much, I told Keigo about it, and he said he liked it, too."

Nagi was so wrapped up in her plan, she didn't notice the emotion vanish from Saotome's face.

"There's a sequel, right? What's it about?" Nagi asked.

"Ah-ha-ha, I'm sorry. I just started hating that show, so I don't remember."

Just now? What does that mean?

"But I wanted to ask you about something else, Ms. Yoroizuka," Saotome continued, ignoring Nagi's confused expression. "I was thinking of buying a Christmas makeup set this year. Which of these do you like?"

She held out her phone to show Nagi.

"Oh, those are so cute! I'd buy both of them!" Nagi exclaimed.

"I know, right?!" Saotome said, nodding enthusiastically. Keigo watched the two women totally absorbed in conversation, his chin in his palm.

"...By the way, Nagi," he finally said.

"Huh?" she replied, looking up at him.

"My mom wants to have you over at our place for New Year's Eve this year. She said she's gonna get some crab from a friend."

"Wow, crab?! That sounds amazing! We can heat up sake in the shells afterward!"

"Of course. I'll buy a nice bottle and bring it over."

As Nagi nodded happily, Saotome interjected.

"Ms. Yoroizuka! Do you want to go to that new tart shop by the office sometime? I've heard their tarts are delicious, with a ton of fruit!"

"Ooh, I'd love to! We have to go—"

"Nagi! There's a new Japanese sake bar near my house. Wanna try it out with me?"

This time it was Keigo who interrupted. Just as Nagi started to nod, Saotome broke in again.

"She promised me first."

"No way. Nagi likes alcohol better than sweets, so I bet she'd rather go with me."

Caught in the middle of this escalating argument, Nagi was totally perplexed.

"Ms. Yoroizuka! You like sweets better, don't you?"

"Nagi! You're a drinker, right?!"

In the end, they both bore down on her at once. Driven against a wall, she curled up defensively in her seat.

"Um, I—I like them both…?"

"No fair!" they shouted in unison.

"Eek!" Nagi wailed. Maybe Saiga, who had been looking on dispassionately, would rescue her? But he merely shot her a glance and said, "…You'll have to sort this one out yourself." He then proceeded to bite down on a skewer of grilled meat. Her two other coworkers were now glaring at each other. Helpless to put a stop to it, Nagi hung her head.

◆

"Thank you, please come again!" the waitress called after them as they left the bar.

Nagi was exhausted. Keigo and Saotome had continued fighting the entire time, resulting in a less than amicable mood. In one sense, it had been a lively evening, but Nagi seemed to have failed in her plan to reconcile the two of them. It was depressing.

"Ms. Yoroizuka, I've got to get up early. Do you mind if I head home?" Saiga asked.

"Of course not… Thank you for spending the evening with us… Good night…"

"…Good luck," he said.

Her plight must have been dire enough to evoke pity even in him, because he glanced back sympathetically as he walked off. As she watched him go, she felt something soft settle against her back. She looked over her shoulder to find Saotome's small face buried there.

"Are you okay, Saotome?"

"I'm sorry… I must be a little tipsy…"

She lifted her head unsteadily and looked up apologetically at Nagi.

"No worries at all! You can lean on me until you feel better."

"Ha-ha… Thank you…"

Nagi squirmed internally at the full-on feminine charm she sensed in Saotome's vulnerable smile. Unlike Nagi, Saotome must have very low alcohol tolerance if she was like this after only one drink.

"Be careful who you show that expression!" she said, smiling wryly as she stroked Saotome's soft hair. Saotome pouted.

"…I only show it to you."

"Ha-ha, you're very cute."

As she hugged Saotome's small head soothingly, an idea hit her. Was this her chance?

"Hey," she called to Keigo, who was standing nearby. "I'm going to buy some water. Would you mind staying here with Saotome?"

"…Me?"

Nagi unwrapped her arm from Saotome and nudged her toward Keigo's back.

"You can do this," she whispered as she passed him on her way to a nearby convenience store.

I hope this helps them make up! Nagi prayed as she trotted toward the store. She didn't have the faintest notion how much she would eventually come to regret that decision.

Eighth Try

"You can do this," Nagi whispered as she rushed off to the store, leaving Keigo alone with Saotome. He sighed deeply. *Do what?*

"...I can't stand this!"

Keigo stole a glance over his shoulder at the sound of Saotome's voice, which had suddenly turned malevolent. A few seconds ago, she had been sweetly clinging to Nagi. Now she was glowering fixedly at him.

"Glare at me all you want. I don't care," he said.

Instead of answering, she clicked her tongue.

"Dammit... This isn't what I meant to happen...," she said, tottering to the curb and squatting down. Keigo suddenly remembered how little she'd drunk at dinner. Maybe her tolerance was super low after all. He crouched down beside her, starting to wonder if she really *was* feeling sick.

"Hey, are you okay?"

Just as he was about to gently place his hand on her back, she slapped it away.

"Please do not touch me. I hate men. And you, in particular, I detest from the bottom of my heart. So would you please stay away?"

Under her biting stare, his concern vanished.

"Is that so?" he said, quickly standing up and moving away from her. Watching her out of the corner of his eye, he angrily waited for Nagi to return.

"...Huh?"

Suddenly, he noticed three men huddled around Saotome. When had they shown up? They were staring rudely into her face.

"Hey, miss, have a few too many drinks? How about you come with us and rest for a while?"

They really thought that stale pickup line was going to work? Keigo started to walk toward Saotome, then remembered she'd told him to stay away and stopped himself.

As he debated what to do, he heard Saotome say, "Hey, quit it…" He looked over in surprise. One of the men had grabbed her hand, clearly against her will. Screw it. She could yell at him later. He ran over to her.

"Is there some problem with my friend?" he said, standing above them. The three men looked up in unison. From this close, he could see how young they were. They must be university kids.

"Oh… No, nothing at all. Let's get out of here, guys."

They stood up and slipped past Keigo as he loomed forbiddingly over them. He was glad it hadn't ended in a fight. Relieved, he took a step toward Saotome, who was staring up at him.

"…Didn't I tell you not to come near me?" she asked crossly. "What, you think you saved me or something?" He could handle this level of nastiness.

"Think of me as a utility pole," he replied.

She snorted but stayed obediently where she was. She acted completely different around him than she did around Nagi. It was amazing, actually. Stealing a glance at her prickly expression, he couldn't help but be impressed. He didn't know which version was the real her, but whatever the answer, it was clear how much she cared for Nagi.

"…So tell me—what do you like about Nagi?" he asked, genuinely curious. She glanced at him, then quickly looked away.

"She's cool," she muttered. "She's tall, and she's got a nice body and a pretty face, but more than that, she's got an amazing personality."

"How do you mean?" he prodded.

"...Once, I made a mistake at work, and it ended up causing some trouble for a client," she began haltingly. "It didn't have anything to do with Ms. Yoroizuka, but she said since she was my direct supervisor, she would go with me to apologize. On top of that, she stayed and worked half the night cleaning up my mess..."

Saotome blinked tenderly, as if she were replaying the memory in her mind.

"She didn't scold me at all. The only thing she said, once everything was over, was 'Good job today. You worked hard.'"

That was just like Nagi. Keigo couldn't help smiling as he remembered how she'd canceled her date with Mr. Cider Commercial to redo that proposal for him.

"I made up my mind to never make the same mistake again," Saotome went on. "Not for my sake—but for Ms. Yoroizuka's, because she was the one who went with me to apologize. No one had ever treated me that kindly before."

Being great at your job didn't guarantee you would be respected as a manager. Keigo felt like thoughtfulness was the extra piece you needed to gain the trust of your subordinates. But even managers were human. They came under pressure when they were busy, and sometimes they got angry. The amazing thing about Nagi was that she put all of that aside and prioritized consideration for other people.

"I see," he said in reply. He could probably spend his whole life trying and never catch up with her. He nodded, filled with a mixture of envy and pride.

"...And that's why you're so intolerable," Saotome said in a low voice.

"Huh?" Keigo blurted out. Suddenly, she was standing, looking at him sharply.

"You've got enough of an advantage just being a man, but on top of that, you're her childhood friend? What the hell?!"

Several people looked over in surprise at her loud declaration.

"It disgusts me to think you know sides of her I don't… Why you?! Why Ms. Yoroizuka?! It's so unfair!" she wailed.

"Huh? Please try to calm down…"

He reached out to restrain her, but she flung his hand away.

"You have everything!" she shouted. She glared hatefully at him, eyes full of tears. "Why can't you let someone else have Ms. Yoroizuka?! Aren't you happy enough already?!"

Happy enough? Him?

"…You're full of shit," he spat out.

She flinched in surprise. For an instant, he glimpsed fear in her eyes, but his anger was far from quelled.

"If I was happy enough, would I want her this much?! The one thing I want most in life has been out of reach for over twenty years! How could I be happy?!"

Always. Since he was a kid, for so long it boggled his mind. Always, always, always. In fifth grade, when a classmate had called her ugly, he'd wrestled them. Nagi had apologized in tears when she saw him covered in scratches and bruises, but he couldn't bring himself to tell her she was cute. In their third year of junior high, she told him she was dating someone for the first time. When he happened to see them together, the shock was so bad he developed a fever that night and couldn't go to school for three days. In their third year of university, they went to the beach with some friends, and he saw her kissing the guy she was dating in the shade of a rock wall. Wanting desperately to forget it all, he started dating the next woman who told him she liked him.

His love for Nagi had been shaken many times, but he'd never been able to give it up. He was still desperately hanging on to it. None of the women he'd dated had ever satisfied him—there was always a gaping hole in his heart. He felt like Nagi was the only one who could fill it. If he couldn't have Nagi, he was sure he would remain incomplete forever.

"You can say what you want, but I have no intention of leaving her alone. At least not until she personally asks me to," he announced decisively. Saotome's eyes went wide. Then she grimaced and looked down.

"…I hate you…," she said as if she were cursing him, her voice shaking. "I really, truly *hate* you…" Her eyes brimmed with tears. "I'm begging you—don't take Ms. Yoroizuka away from me…"

Her voice sounded like it was about to break. Tears fell between the fingers covering her face. As Keigo watched her, the anger swirling inside him subsided. He didn't like Saotome, but she was suffering for love, just as he was.

"Come on, Saotome, don't cry…," he said, reaching out to her.

"Saotome!"

A form stepped between them.

"What's the matter?! Are you all right?!"

Seeing Saotome's tears, Nagi pulled out a handkerchief and gently began wiping them away.

"…Keigo. What did you do to her?" she asked in a low voice, her eyes still on Saotome.

"I didn't do anything…"

"Then why is she crying?"

When he failed to answer, she stopped asking questions.

"Saotome, can you walk?"

Nagi wrapped her arm gently around Saotome's shoulders and helped her into a nearby taxi, then watched as it pulled into traffic. Keigo came up behind her and timidly said her name.

"Hey, Nagi…"

"I'm sorry. I should have thought twice before leaving you two alone."

Her voice sent a chill down his back. She still hadn't looked at him.

"…I'm going home now," she said. Without a single glance his way, she started off. Panicking, Keigo tried to stop her.

"Nagi!" he cried, grabbing her shoulder and half forcing her to turn toward him. Then he froze.

"Tell me what you said to Saotome… Did you really have to make her cry…?"

He hadn't wanted to see Nagi make that expression. Her sad face weighed on his heart a hundred times more than Saotome's tears had. He bit his lip and resigned himself to his fate.

"…All I did was tell her about the person I like. I can't tell you anything else."

He knew it was cowardly, but the truth was the truth. If Nagi let it go at that—

"Why would you say something like that to her?! You're insufferably dense!"

But her reaction was the opposite of what he'd expected. At her fierce accusation, he lost his temper.

"You of all people have no right to say that to me!"

She frowned. They glared blisteringly at each other until Nagi finally looked away with a sigh.

"…I've heard enough. I didn't know you were such an awful person."

He felt like she'd punched him. An awful person? Him? What the heck?

An inexpressible irritation welled up inside him. He realized he was furious. Furious at Nagi for having the nerve to insult him despite not knowing anything. And furious at himself for being able to dislike her even a little.

"Later," she said coolly, before starting off again.

Out of his mind with anger, he caught up and grabbed her.

"Which one of us is really awful?! I'm sick and tired of you not having a clue! Figure it out already!"

Her defenses were down, and it was easy to enclose her in his arms. He hadn't held her for ages. Her body was far softer and slighter than he remembered, more dear and more hateful.

"Hey…Keigo! Stop! Let me go!"

She struggled fiercely, but he only tightened his grip.

"I'll let you go if you promise not to run away."

"I promise! Just let me go! This is embarrassing!" she shouted. He finally released her. But to prevent her from leaving, he kept a tight hold on both of her wrists.

"I can't believe this! Out here in public!" she whispered with a shaky voice. Even in the dark, he could tell her cheeks were flushed.

"Nagi."

He wanted her to look at him, but she just stared more intently at the sidewalk. He could see her eyes darting around behind her eyelashes.

"If you don't look at me, I'll make you look at me."

Seeming to give in to his threat, she looked up at him. He caught her gaze and peered into her confused eyes. He wanted his dense old friend to know everything he was feeling, so he willed all his love for her into his stare.

He heard her gasp softly. Her eyes widened as if she had realized something. A second later, she turned away. For a moment, she said nothing, and all he heard was her nervous breathing.

"...Keigo?" she said after a while. "Is the person you like... someone I know...?"

"Saying you know them would be putting it mildly."

"Is that person...near you right now?"

"She's right in front of me."

This time Nagi was really and truly speechless. Keigo didn't know if the pounding blood he felt at her wrists was hers or his own. He'd come this far. Why not tell her the rest? The love he'd felt all through his life, the impatience, and the pain—everything. Would she accept it all with kindness?

"This isn't a prank...is it?" she asked in a feeble voice, looking down.

"I'm getting mad."

Her shoulders twitched at his low voice.

"O-okay, I get it. I believe you...but..."

"But what?" he urged, a little violently. She shuddered like she was frightened.

"I'm still in shock… I never dreamed that you thought of me like that…"

Keigo knew right away what she was going to say. It was ironic. After all, the reason he knew was because he had always been by her side, gazing longingly at her.

"It's just that…"

A sense of foreboding spread through him, chilling his heart. Her voice was boundlessly cruel, but even now, it was kind, too, because it was hers.

"…I'm sorry, Keigo."

The words were like a death sentence. He listened in a daze.

"Please let me go home."

Her wrists slipped out of his limp hands. None of this felt real. He watched her walk away without a backward glance like he was in a bad dream. How many times had he had this nightmare?

"Ha-ha… What the hell?"

The energy drained from every corner of his body, and he slowly crouched down. Everything was exploding into pieces, but for some reason, it felt terrifyingly unreal. He should have prepared himself better for this possibility. Then maybe he could have avoided feeling this way. Overwhelmed by crushing regret, he covered his face with shaking hands. Loss always came without warning. How could he have forgotten that? Just like when Nagi's father died…

It happened in the fall of his thirteenth year. He would never forget it. The funeral was held quietly, with only relatives and very close friends. It was an intimate ceremony. He remembered that only two or three people came from Teitou Bank to light incense. Her father had been made to take responsibility for the personal data breach, but the end of his life was so lonely it was hard to believe he'd been the head of system development at such a huge bank.

After the cremation, Keigo found Nagi hiding in a corner of the crematorium hallway as the sun set, crying.

"…Keigo?" she said quietly after he'd stood next to her for a while. "Can you tell me something, if you know the answer?"

Her tear-filled eyes turned desperately toward him.

"My father worked so hard for everyone. Why did they kill him?"

What a simple, painful contradiction. He couldn't find an answer. Maybe it was because he was young, or because he himself was so upset by the death of her father, who had always doted on him.

"I'm sorry… I don't know."

In place of answering, he wiped away her tears, and finally, unable to hold himself back, he wrapped her in his arms. He wanted to hide her sobbing body away from all the bad things in the world, but his arms weren't strong enough for that. It tore him up inside. Still, he hugged her tight, if only to protect her for that moment. Desperately, he cradled her in his weak arms.

He lifted his face, returning from the past, and looked at the arms that had once held her. Aside from a few moments ago, he had never held her before or after that day. He had thought she was strong, but back then, she had shown him her weakness. There was more than enough of it to make him want to protect her. But she would probably never accept such feelings from him again.

Nagi. Nagi. Nagi. He loved her name more than any other word in the world. And right now, it hurt like hell.

Ninth Try

Even if Keigo felt like the world was ending, time kept marching on indifferently. The old line about "time fixing everything" was definitely a lie. After all, a block of ice shattered to tiny pieces could never be put back together again.

"That should take care of it. If any other issues come up, please don't hesitate to contact us."

Keigo and Saotome left the factory, the clients bowing and saying their good-byes as huge machines started up behind them. The pair had come to fix a bug in the system at this textile mill. Saotome had originally been in charge of the account, but Nagi had asked Keigo to go with her, saying that if the bug was in the network rather than the system itself, his more extensive knowledge in that field would be needed.

"…Thanks," Saotome said curtly. As Nagi had predicted, the problem originated in the router, so Saotome would probably have had a hard time fixing it herself.

"…You're welcome," he answered brusquely, without looking at her.

Two weeks had passed since the worst day of his life. Saotome had been consistently frosty, and as for Nagi, they hadn't exchanged a word outside work. While Nagi and Saotome weren't on bad terms, Nagi was under the mistaken impression that Saotome liked Keigo and seemed vaguely reticent around her, as if she thought she'd wronged her somehow. And because Saotome thought Keigo was to blame for Nagi's distance, she was extremely cold toward him. It was like one big, vicious cycle.

Without another word, Keigo and Saotome continued onto the train. As Keigo sat glumly staring out the window, he remembered something.

"Ms. Saotome?" he said. She turned toward him crossly. "I'd like to drop off some papers with a client. Would you mind if we got off at the next stop? It'll only take a minute."

He happened to have some documents he'd promised to deliver the next time he was in the neighborhood.

"It's fine with me," she said, nodding grudgingly.

They got off together and walked the five minutes to the office building. He asked her to wait in the entry hall while he took the elevator upstairs and delivered the documents. The client offered him a cup of tea, but he told them a coworker was waiting downstairs and hurried back to the first floor. When he got out of the elevator, he spotted Saotome sitting on a sofa facing away from him. He was about to offer to buy her a can of hot tea from the vending machine to thank her for coming along.

But just then, he heard someone say, "…Saotome, is that you?"

He froze. The woman, a total stranger to him, must work in the building.

"Oh, it *is* you! It's me, Hirasawa! We were in the same class in junior high. Do you remember me?"

"…Oh, yeah," Saotome said, nodding like she'd just remembered.

"It's been ages! You're as cute as ever! Or maybe even cuter!"

"That's not true…," Saotome said, smiling a bit distantly. As Keigo tried to decide if he should interrupt, the two women kept talking.

"What are you up to these days?" Hirasawa asked.

"I'm working at an IT company."

"Wow! So you've got a regular job. That's a surprise!"

"Why?" Saotome asked, tilting her head quizzically.

"I mean…," Hirasawa said, smiling. "Knowing you, I thought

you'd be married to some rich guy and living a life of leisure by now."

There didn't seem to be any malice in the comment, but Saotome's voice when she answered was stiff.

"…I don't plan to marry anyone."

"Really? Why not?" Hirasawa asked innocently.

"Being single is more fun."

"Oh, that's right—you were famous for hating guys. And they were falling over themselves to ask you out anyway! You were incredible."

"Ah-ha-ha…"

Saotome laughed dryly, but Hirasawa seemed to have no intention of stopping her nostalgia session.

"That reminds me! Didn't you have a stalker? Your slippers and gym clothes always used to go missing, right? I still remember how everyone used to feel sorry for you. And that one time some creepy old man cut your skirt. Remember, on the way home from school?"

Saotome flinched visibly.

"It turned into such a big fuss," Hirasawa went on. "I mean, I can see how that would make you hate men. But it really is too bad, someone as pretty as you making up your mind not to date anyone…"

"Saotome," Keigo said, almost without realizing what he was doing. She whipped her head around to look at him, her face totally pale. "I'm sorry to have kept you waiting."

He walked over to her and looked at Hirasawa, who seemed surprised.

"Is this a friend of yours?"

"…We were in the same class in junior high," Saotome said quietly.

"Ah," he said, then turned back to Hirasawa and smiled. "Nice to meet you. Thanks for helping my coworker pass the time."

"Oh, not at all…," she said, shaking her head. For some reason, he felt like she was examining him closely. He squatted down in front of Saotome.

"Are you okay to walk?" he asked.

"Yes."

She stood up right away and turned bravely toward Hirasawa.

"See you," she said with a smile, then headed for the door. Keigo nodded at Hirasawa and followed Saotome.

"…"

As they walked back to the train station, Keigo glanced at her. The color had returned to her face, but her expression remained dark. He remembered her saying the other day that she hated men. He wanted to punch himself for never giving the slightest thought to the kind of life she had lived. Simply by virtue of living, every person goes through transformative events, just like Nagi had. The weight of the resulting sorrow could never be measured. It was possible that Saotome had experienced things in her life that were many times harder than Keigo could even imagine.

"…Sorry about the other day," he mumbled. She glanced suspiciously at him.

"Sorry about what?"

"About yelling at you and saying some harsh stuff."

There was an interval of silence before she finally replied.

"Are you apologizing because you feel sorry for me?"

"Huh?" he said, stopping in his tracks. She stopped, too. She turned slowly toward him—her gaze was icy.

"If you're feeling sympathy because you think I'm weaker than you as a woman, don't. Please don't try to help me or rescue me. If you genuinely feel bad, then don't give me any special treatment." She spoke quickly, then grimaced. "I'm begging you… Please treat me like you would any other person. *Just treat me normally.*"

She looked on the verge of tears, but Keigo couldn't think of anything else to say to her.

◆

They returned to the office without exchanging another word. Completely exhausted, Keigo dropped into his chair. First Saotome, then Nagi... Had he ever struggled this desperately to get along with people before? Across from him, Nagi was focused on her work with a serious expression. He couldn't remember her smiling at him even once in the past two weeks. They had often fought as kids, but they would always make up after a day or so. And look at them now. He could probably fix everything by apologizing and asking her to forget he ever mentioned it, but he couldn't bring himself to do it. How pathetic! He was supposed to be a grown man.

"What?!"

Keigo jerked his head up at the sudden shout from a nearby desk. It had apparently come from Saotome. She was staring in disbelief at her own monitor.

"No, this can't be..."

"What's the matter, Saotome?" Nagi asked, worry in her voice.

"Ms. Yoroizuka...is this...?"

She swiveled her monitor toward Nagi. Nagi looked intently at the words on the screen.

"All your files have been encrypted...?" she muttered.

Keigo jumped up.

"Nagi! Let me see that!"

Nagi hurriedly traded places with him, and he stared at the monitor. An unfamiliar browser had started up on Saotome's desktop, and English words filled the screen. Keigo stared in astonishment at the large letters at the top.

All your files have been encrypted.

"Everyone, disconnect your devices from the network and make sure no suspicious tasks are running!" he shouted.

Everyone in the office looked up in surprise.

"It's ransomware," he said as he hurriedly checked Saotome's computer.

Ransomware was a type of computer virus that took its name from the words *ransom* and *software*. Once it infected a device, all the data was automatically encrypted and became totally unusable. If you wanted to decrypt it, you had to pay a ransom to the virus's creators.

"Saotome. Have you gotten any suspicious e-mails lately?" Keigo asked. There were lots of ways for ransomware to infect a device, but e-mail attachments were the most common.

"E-mail…," she mumbled, fishing through her memory in a panic. Suddenly, she seemed to remember something. "Now that you mention it, last week I got an e-mail from a company I'd never heard of. There was an attachment titled 'Invoice,' and…"

"You opened it?"

"…I did…," she said, her voice barely audible as she nodded. That was most likely the culprit. Although most people knew about viruses, the criminals were typically a step ahead of their victims. They competed night and day to find new ways of spreading malware. Avoiding them completely was near-impossible. It was no wonder Saotome had fallen for it.

"But ransomware…," he muttered, a bad feeling welling up in the pit of his stomach as he accessed the shared server from Saotome's computer.

Ransomware didn't just encrypt the files of the device it had infected. In some cases, it also encrypted connected storage locations.

"…You're kidding me," Keigo whispered.

"What…?" said Nagi, sounding terrified.

"This is bad. It's not just Saotome's local file. The shared server has been affected, too."

"The shared server? …Wait, that's…"

Panic crept over her face as she realized what was happening.

"Yeah. The source code has been encrypted, too."

Nagi was dumbfounded. The development team that Keigo and the others belonged to kept their source code on the server so everyone could access it. A quick check revealed that the majority had been encrypted and was now unusable.

"No…that can't be…"

Saotome was so pale Keigo worried she might actually faint.

"Mr. Yuuki! Can we try one of the decryption tools available online?" Saiga suggested. He must have been looking into it while they were talking. He was right that free decryption tools could be found on the internet. But not all ransomware used the same encryption algorithm. New algorithms were being developed, decoded, and redeveloped every day. It was a real cat-and-mouse game. Of course, it would be nice if a decryption tool conveniently existed for the virus they'd been infected with, but…

"…No luck," Keigo said with a sigh after a quick search. Unfortunately, the right tool didn't appear to exist yet. Everything was going against them, and no one had anything to say.

"…I'm sorry!"

Saotome's voice broke the silence.

"This is my fault. I'm so sorry! I apologize!"

"Saotome, it's all right…!" Nagi said, trying to soothe her, but the other woman kept on apologizing desperately.

"Listen, the first thing we need to do is get the work that's due tomorrow completed. If we extract whatever source code is still okay and work together to rewrite the rest, I'm sure we'll make our deadline…!"

"That's impossible! It took us a month to write that code… How can we redo it all in a day?!" Saotome wailed tearfully. Nagi tried to calm her, but it seemed she could no longer hear Nagi's words.

"How can I ever make this up to you…?! I'm so sorry for causing all this trouble…!"

"Stop crying and pull yourself together!" Keigo shouted.

The whole office fell silent. Nagi, Saiga, and the teary-eyed Sao-tome all stared at him in shock.

"Just calm down. We don't know yet if all the data is perma-nently lost. I've heard that encrypted files can be restored from the registry. I don't remember the details, though, and I'd say our chances are only fifty-fifty," he continued.

He'd read an online article about it once. They might not be able to fully restore the data, but even if they could only save the source code, they'd be in decent shape.

"You're the lead on this project, right?" he said sternly to Sao-tome, who was standing next to him in a daze. "I want you to direct Nagi and Saiga on how to prepare to rewrite the source code. I'll try to do something about the data on the shared server."

He couldn't just "try"; he needed to make this work. Otherwise, he didn't think Saotome would ever be able to recover. They were still on bad terms, and he knew she hated him. But this was a special situation. He didn't fully understand her, but he did know she'd worked extremely hard to learn her job.

"It's going to be tough, but keep at it," he said.

"Mr. Yuuki…," Saotome mumbled in a daze.

"Saotome! Tell us what to do!" Nagi said eagerly.

"Yeah, I'll do whatever you say," Saiga added.

"…*Sniff.*"

For a second, Saotome seemed about to cry again, but she didn't. She violently wiped her eyes, and when she lifted her face, it was calm.

"All right! Let's do this!"

Nagi and Saiga responded to her firm declaration with stiff nods.

◆

"I can't believe it…"

"You recovered the data…"

Nagi and Saotome stared at the monitor in astonishment.

"I knew you could do it, Mr. Yuuki. Nice one," Saiga said as he delivered a cup of coffee to Keigo, who was sprawled, exhausted, on his desk.

"Hey... Thanks," Keigo said, drinking it down in a single gulp.

It was already eleven at night. More than six hours had passed since they detected the ransomware. Keigo had fumbled his way toward decrypting the shared server, then used the same strategy to recover Saotome's local files. Fortunately, there was no sign of other damage, and it seemed they had escaped with just those two locations being infected.

"Do you think we can make our deadline?" he asked. Saotome nodded.

"Yes, definitely!"

"That's a relief."

He stood sluggishly and left the office, saying he wanted to wash his face. He sighed in relief as he headed to the bathroom. He was mentally and physically exhausted, but he was also truly grateful they'd averted disaster. He rolled his shoulders, trying to undo the knots that had formed from concentrating so hard on his work.

"—Mr. Yuuki!"

Saotome was running after him down the hall.

"Thank you so much for today!" she said loudly, bowing her head.

"Don't worry about it. I learned a lot myself," he said, waving dismissively. But she stayed where she was, looking troubled.

"That's not all I wanted to thank you for... I'm also grateful you snapped me back to reality when I was panicking."

"Oh, that..."

She might be grateful, but he wondered how the others would view his yelling at a female coworker in the office.

"I'm sorry I yelled at you," he said. "I feel like I apologized for the same thing earlier today... Geez, I haven't learned anything... I really am sorry."

He scratched his head guiltily, but she quietly shook her head.

"No, thanks to you I was able to calm down. If anyone gets on your case about it, I'll give them a piece of my mind!"

She sounded so determined, he couldn't help smiling.

"Seriously, though, you did good work today," he said. "It was amazing how you got back on track so quickly."

While he was recovering the data, Saotome had directed Nagi and Saiga, efficiently and without complaint. He was truly impressed by her about-face.

"You were surprisingly manly. It was pretty cool," he said, then blinked in surprise. Saotome was bowing deeply to him.

"...I'm sorry for all the trouble I've caused you," she said to his complete shock. "I'll tell Ms. Yoroizuka that you're not the one I'm interested in. And I'll explain to the president that the episode with the love hotel was all a misunderstanding on my part."

"Really, are you sure?"

Keigo was bewildered. Admitting that it had all been a misunderstanding was equivalent to throwing away her trump card. There was clearly no gain in it for her. As he tried to figure out her motivation, she frowned slightly.

"...You're kind of odd, aren't you, Mr. Yuuki?"

Now she was insulting him? He was speechless. Then Saotome stretched as if to collect herself.

"Let the best man win. And no grudges!" she said defiantly. He offered her a wry smile.

"I won't hold it against you, but I might take a week or so off work," he replied.

"Nope, not allowed. Ms. Yoroizuka and I would have to pull your weight."

"You're merciless."

He smiled again, and she couldn't help smiling back.

Tenth Try

"Cheers!"

Five glasses clinked. It was New Year's Eve, the coldest night of the year, and the Yuukis and Yoroizukas were gathered at the Yuuki family home for their annual celebration.

"Wow, the crab is amazing!" Keigo's father said, holding up a crab leg and sounding very impressed.

"Nagi, Nae, please have as much as you like!" added his mother.

"Thanks!" they answered, smiling.

"Mom, this is seriously delicious!" Nagi said excitedly.

"Oh my, the meat is very plump and juicy," Nae answered mildly.

Nagi's and her mother's personalities were as different as their looks, but as Keigo knew well, they sounded nearly identical over the phone.

"Ahh, that was so good...," Nagi said with a sigh when the crab was finally picked clean, a satisfied smile on her face.

In contrast to the way she dressed at work, that night she was wearing a casual hooded dress with her hair half up. Keigo hadn't had many opportunities to see her in loungewear since they'd grown up, so there was something intriguingly fresh about her outfit.

"Hey, Nagi, didn't you want to try heating sake in the crab shell?" he asked, fully in relaxation mode, holding out a bottle of sake to her. Her smile instantly vanished.

"...I'll use my own, thanks," she said.

Their parents fell silent at her cold tone. In the midst of that strange quiet, she picked up the bottle in front of her.

"K-Keigo, I'll have some of yours," his father said, rescuing the orphaned bottle from his hands. *Sorry, Dad*, Keigo thought as he felt his mood plunge into depression. The truth was, he hadn't yet mended his relationship with Nagi. After the ransomware episode, Saotome had fulfilled her promise and told the truth to Nagi and the company president. Keigo had hoped that would fix everything, but reality wasn't so kind. Maybe that was to be expected. Clearing up the misunderstandings with Saotome didn't undo the fact that Keigo had confessed his love to Nagi and been totally shot down.

"Hey, Mom!" Nagi said as the group was starting to feel buzzed and the party was finally livening up. "The beer we brought is all gone."

She turned from the refrigerator to face Nae as she spoke.

"It is? I thought I bought plenty. Would you mind going to get some more?" her mother asked apologetically.

"Sure!" Nagi said with a pleasant nod as she wrapped a scarf around her neck.

"Keigo, you go along with Nagi and keep her safe," his father said. Needless to say, Keigo had been planning to do that anyway.

"Gotcha," he answered, standing up.

"I'll be fine by myself," Nagi said firmly. Keigo froze, half standing from his chair. "Be back in a minute."

She walked out the door without a glance in his direction. Only when he heard the entryway door shut did time start to move forward again.

"Did something happen with you and Nagi?" his mother asked suspiciously as he slowly sat back down. His father and Nae were also peering worriedly at him.

"No, nothing in particular…"

"Hmph. I thought you must have told her you liked her and gotten rejected."

Why were mothers so bizarrely perceptive?

Keigo silently sipped his drink.

"Oh dear, did I guess right?" she asked, wide-eyed.

Please, Mom, don't pour salt in my wounds!

"Well, if she turned you down, that's that. Anyway, go catch up with her."

"Mom, she just told me she didn't want me to come."

"Not my problem. What are you going to do if something happens to her?"

Prodded on by her words, despite not completely understanding them, Keigo stood up reluctantly, stuffed his phone and wallet in his pocket, and opened the entryway door.

"…Whoa!"

His exclamation came out in a puff of white air and vanished. Not only was it freezing, but it was snowing, too. A white film had already accumulated on the sidewalk, and he could see what looked like Nagi's sneaker footprints leading toward the road. He began following them cautiously forward.

"Nagi!"

Turning the first corner, he caught sight of her. She looked back in surprise, then immediately turned away again.

"I told you I'm going alone," she said curtly, before hurriedly walking off. He followed, irritated.

"Come on, it's not safe."

"I'm fine. Just go back."

He stubbornly kept pace with her as she accelerated, but her patience must have finally run out, because she abruptly whipped around to face him.

"I'm asking you politely. Please do not follow me— Ack!"

Suddenly, she slipped on the snow. As Keigo saw her begin to fall backward, a chill ran down his spine.

"Nagi!"

There was a wet slapping noise, a feeling of heaviness, and then silence.

"Damn...!" he gasped.

He let out a breath of mixed relief and surprise, his arms still clasping Nagi against his stomach. With a quick slide, he had succeeded in inserting himself between her and the ground when she fell.

"Are you hurt?"

He peered at her as she lay unmoving in his arms. Slowly, she turned toward him and nodded, a stunned look on her face. She seemed to be unharmed.

"Good. Don't scare me like that. I thought my heart was gonna stop."

He smiled wryly and stroked her hair. Just then, a large tear spilled from her eye.

"...Huh?"

For a second, he thought it was a snowflake falling from the sky. But as he watched, another clear drop of water, and then another, ran down her cheek.

"...U-ungh..."

Before he could figure out what was happening, Nagi started sobbing convulsively. As he listened in a daze, he felt like his body was sinking into the earth.

He could only think of one reason she would be crying like this. She must feel horrible that he had to rescue her after she'd rejected him.

He wished he had never told her in the first place.

He felt pathetic. What the hell was he doing, making her sob when she was the last person in the world he wanted to cry?

"...Keigo...?"

She made a strange gulping sound. He had pulled her silently back into a standing position, and now she was staring up at him with teary eyes.

"You go home. I'll do the shopping myself," he said, pushing her lightly toward his parents' house and stepping into the fresh snow in front of him. The two of them had walked the same path their whole lives. They had seen the same things, had the same experiences, and grown up together. But this was the last time they would do that.

"I'm sorry, Nagi."

Somehow, somehow, he prayed that she would forget the childhood friend who couldn't even bring himself to wish her happiness in years to come.

"W-wait!" she cried sharply.

He stopped. He heard damp footsteps approaching, and then she circled around to face him.

"Why are you apologizing?"

He couldn't help looking away from her persistent upward gaze.

"…Because I dumped my feelings on you and made you reject me… That's why."

He felt even more miserable after saying it. He stared down at the snow, afraid of what she would say back.

"…I don't remember rejecting you…"

Her words reached his ears.

"…Huh?"

Slowly, he looked up. Her confused face was right in front of him. She didn't remember rejecting him? What was she talking about?

"No, you… But you apologized to me!"

There was no way he could be wrong about something he recalled so clearly. She had definitely turned to him and said, *I'm sorry.*

"No…you're wrong! That's not what I meant by *I'm sorry*!" she protested.

"Then what did you mean?" he asked, at his wit's end. For a moment, she looked astonished; then she grabbed her head in frustration.

"Keigo, I swear… Why are you like this…?" she muttered.

Finally, she looked up at him with a frown. "I meant I was sorry for putting you through so much pain."

It took a long time for him to digest her words.

"Then why were you treating me so coldly...?"

"I was ashamed to look you in the face!"

She buried her mouth in her scarf and lowered her brows apologetically.

"I don't know how long you've felt like that about me, but that whole time, I've probably been hurting you, and I felt horrible about it...so...I'm sorry."

She said the exact same words she'd said the other day, but this time he had an overwhelming urge to hug her. Damn, he loved her so much. He loved her, he loved her, he loved her. His feelings for her looped around endlessly, overflowing the bounds of reason. They were constantly on the verge of surging upward and drowning him mercilessly. He knew he was at an impossible disadvantage, but even so, he couldn't free himself from the endless refrain of his feelings.

"Hello? Keigo...? Are you okay...?" she asked, peering into his face.

"Nagi!"

"Wah!"

She leaped back, startled by his shout. But he didn't care.

"A minute ago, you said you didn't remember rejecting me, right?" he asked, bearing down on her.

She took a step backward.

"Does that mean I still have a chance?"

"...A chance at what?"

"A chance to be your boyfriend," he said with zero hesitation.

"Uh...," she said idiotically, looking utterly confused. Her face turned bright red. "I...can't imagine that, so I don't know what to say..."

"I can imagine it very easily, because I've wished I was your boyfriend hundreds of times," he said decisively. She opened and closed her mouth without saying anything.

"Uhhh…?" she finally managed. "Wait, wait, wait…"

Succumbing to a rare level of panic, she gripped her head with both hands.

"But, but…if I dated you, things couldn't stay the way they are, could they…?"

"I suppose that's true. I'd kiss you and do everything else you're probably imagining right now."

"E…everything…?"

Her gaze darted around like she was envisioning what he meant by *everything*.

"Yes, everything," he shot back right away. "You'd probably be embarrassed, but there's no way I could stop myself."

This appeared to be the fatal blow, because Nagi turned beet red and covered her face with both hands.

"Stop! This is so embarrassing I think I'm going to faint!"

Her muffled voice escaped through the gaps between her fingers.

"Nagi."

He grabbed both her arms and gently pulled them down. When she looked up at him, her eyes were full of tears, and it seemed like she'd lost her nerve. He was hopelessly in love with each of her quivering eyelashes.

"If you'd rather die than have me as a boyfriend, tell me. But if not—"

He'd been wishing for it for so long. When he woke up in the morning, he wanted her to be the first person he said "Good morning" to. When he ate his meals, he wanted her to eat the same food from the same dishes and say "How delicious!" with him. When he said, "I love you," he wanted her to be the one who smiled happily and said, "Thank you." He didn't want anything grand. He just wanted the little, everyday things.

"I want you to let me keep trying. I want to become the special person you take for granted."

He was sure that would be enough to fulfill all his needs.

"All...all right..."

It was New Year's Eve, and the first winter snow was falling. Keigo had taken the chance of a lifetime, and Nagi had nodded and answered so softly he could barely hear her.

Eleventh Try

Keigo was kind. That kindness hadn't changed at all since they were kids. And that was exactly why Nagi had never made a point of deciding if she loved him or hated him. If she decided she loved him, he would become her boyfriend. If she decided she hated him, they would grow apart. There weren't any other options. That was why both choices utterly terrified her.

"...Nagi... Hey, Nagi!"

She looked up with a start. Keigo was looking at her suspiciously from the other side of the open door.

"We've reached our floor."

"Oh, s-sorry... Ack!"

As she hurriedly moved to step out of the elevator, the doors began to mercilessly slide shut, and without thinking, she stepped back. *Clank!* An arm reached out and stopped the doors just before they banged into her.

"Close call!" Keigo muttered in surprise, shielding her from the doors with his body. His massive shoulders and muscular neck were right in front of her eyes. He was so close she could feel his heat. She was aware of her own heart practically leaping out of her chest.

"Why are you so spacey?" he asked, looking at her with a wry smile.

"No reason! I'm sorry—thank you!" she said in an unnaturally loud voice before slipping quickly past him. There was no way she could scream, "Why?! Because of you!"

"I've never been inside a veterinary hospital before. Hope none of the dogs bark at me. What if I'm so tall I scare them?"

Two weeks had passed since the New Year, and both the office and the city were back in the swing of things. That day, Nagi was doing some routine server maintenance for Karasuma Veterinary Hospital, an account she'd had for a while, and Keigo was with her. She'd been there many times, so she was used to it, but Keigo seemed unusually anxious about the situation. It was totally like him to be worried about animals even though he was fearless with humans.

I want to be the special person you take for granted.

Nothing unusual had happened between them since he'd said those words to her. Nagi was hyperaware of him, such as in the elevator a moment ago, but he was acting exactly like he always did. She actually felt a little let down, though it was good that things weren't terribly awkward between them, since they still had to be together at work.

"Happy New Year, Dr. Karasuma!"

Although the head vet was still in his early thirties, she'd heard the locals thought highly of him. She had a good impression of him herself, since he always took the time to graciously interact with service providers like herself even though she was sure he must be busy.

"Nice to meet you. My name is Yuuki, with Sync.System."

"The pleasure's mine. I'm Karasuma, the head vet here."

Sliding Keigo's business card into his chest pocket, Dr. Karasuma led them to the room where the server was kept, then returned to his work with a polite nod.

"Let's get started," Nagi said. Normally, she performed the server maintenance herself, but that day she had asked Keigo to come along and was supervising as he did the work. As she expected, he checked each item efficiently, and they finished in half the time she'd planned for.

They went to look for Dr. Karasuma to tell him they were done and found him with a nurse in a room filled with dozens of cages, most likely for animals admitted to the hospital.

"Pardon us, Dr. Karasuma. We're finished looking over the system," Nagi said, and he glanced up at them. The nurse was apparently done speaking with him, and she nodded and left the room.

"Thanks for your work today. By the way, Ms. Yoroizuka, I have a question for you."

"Yes?" she asked, standing up a little straighter.

"I was wondering… Are you leaving the company to get married?"

"What?!" she blurted out loudly, completely caught off guard. "N-no, why do you ask?!"

"I thought that might be the reason Mr. Yuuki came along with you today…"

Since she usually did this work by herself, he must have thought she was training Keigo in preparation for quitting her job.

"Oh, no, not at all! I don't even have anyone to marry!" she said, shaking her head emphatically. "From now on, Yuuki and I will be performing the maintenance together, and I'll continue to handle your account just as I have in the past."

"Ah, I see," Dr. Karasuma said, looking relieved.

He saw them all the way to the back door when they left. Only once the hospital was out of sight did Keigo speak up.

"…You don't have anyone to marry, huh?" he said suggestively. She pouted and glared at him.

"I didn't lie, did I?"

"No," he said, smiling slightly. "By the way, are you free this Sunday? Want to go see a movie together?"

He held out two tickets. The second Nagi saw the movie title printed on them, she let out a surprised yelp.

"No way!"

Incredibly, they were tickets to an advance screening of a yakuza film she was dying to see.

"I won the ticket lottery," he said.

"That's amazing! I entered, too, but I lost!"

"Thought so. You were clearly upset the day they announced the results."

He flashed her a wry smile, and she could feel her face heating up. She'd found out she lost while at work and had momentarily escaped to the women's bathroom to get over the shock. It was embarrassing enough that Saotome, who happened to come in at the same time, had gotten all worried over her, but even Keigo had noticed?

"So? Wanna go?" he asked. She nodded right away.

"I'd love to! Thanks! I really, *really* wanted to see this movie."

"Glad to hear it. Should we meet there?"

"Sure! I can't wait. I heard the director was really picky about the action scenes. I wonder how they came out. I bet they're amazing!" she said breathlessly, before suddenly falling silent. Keigo was gazing at her with impossibly kind eyes. For some reason, she felt mortified. How could she have missed how he felt about her when he looked at her so sweetly like that?

"Um, so…," she mumbled.

"Yeah?" he prompted, tilting his head.

"Maybe this is a dumb question, but…um, what made you want to date me…?"

Not to brag, but she had somehow captured the love of a single man for twenty-some years despite having no outstanding features to speak of. The only thing she had to boast about was that she'd always been a fast runner.

"Well…"

Nagi waited nervously for a few seconds while Keigo appeared to think about it. Finally, he turned toward her.

"I can tell you if you want, but I have so many reasons, you'd probably be put off."

What? That many?

".........Okay, then never mind."

Part of her wanted to know and part of her didn't, but she figured his answer would make her faint with embarrassment, so she ultimately decided to pass.

"Should I e-mail them to you, then?"

"Like I said, never mind!" she snapped back, which made him laugh out loud.

◆

"Hey!"

It was 12:40 PM on Sunday when Nagi arrived at the train station near the movie theater where they'd agreed to meet. She found Keigo already there, waving excitedly at her. She stared at him in disbelief.

"What?" he asked with a half smile as she walked toward him. He was wearing a caramel-colored sweater and a navy-blue Chesterfield coat. She glanced at her watch. Yep, no doubt about it. They'd agreed to meet at one, which meant she was twenty minutes early. Normally, she aimed to arrive about five minutes ahead of time. But that day, she had finished getting ready more quickly than expected, and since she couldn't stand to sit around waiting, she'd decided to head out.

"...When did you get here?" she asked, a little grumpily. Somehow he'd managed to beat her there.

"Ten minutes before I figured you'd get here, considering you probably ran out of other things to do and left early."

The way he saw through everything she did was maddening.

"It won't be starting for a while, but should we go?" Keigo asked.

That's right. That day, they were going to see a movie she'd been looking forward to for ages. It would be no exaggeration to say the thought of this day had gotten her through the whole work week.

"Sure!" she said with an enthusiastic nod before following after Keigo.

"Looks like we're in the back row."

"Nice."

They set down their bags, feeling like they'd won the grand prize in the lottery.

"Would you mind watching my stuff?" Keigo asked, grabbing his wallet from his bag.

"Wait, I'll buy the drinks and snacks," Nagi insisted, easily guessing what he was up to. "At least let me treat you to that."

"Don't worry about it."

"No way. You bought the tickets."

She'd tried to pay for hers, but Keigo had stubbornly refused to accept the money.

"If you pay for everything, I'll feel so awkward I won't be able to enjoy the movie," she pointed out.

"What are you talking about?" he said with a wry smile, but she must have gotten through to him, because he obediently sat back down. "Okay, okay, I'll let you treat me. Thanks."

Nagi headed to the concession stand in high spirits and bought some popcorn and soda. She got two kinds of popcorn— one salt and one caramel flavored. Keigo liked to switch between sweet and savory, like she did, so she figured they would probably trade halfway through the movie.

She walked jauntily to the theater's back entrance, tray in hand, but stopped when she spotted the back of Keigo's head. He appeared to be talking to the person sitting to his right. Did he know them? She squinted, then stiffened. Bizarrely, it was

Dr. Karasuma. The hospital must be closed on Sunday. He'd probably won a ticket in the lottery, like Keigo. And by some inscrutable miracle, his seat was directly next to theirs.

It was awkward enough to run into a client outside of work. She could only imagine how uncomfortable things would get once she showed up. Dr. Karasuma thought they were no more than coworkers. Still, she couldn't very well watch the movie from where she was standing, so she steeled her will and started heading toward them. No sooner had she taken a few steps than—

"Oh, Ms. Yoroizuka is here, too?" she overheard the doctor saying.

She stopped in her tracks.

"Um…how are you two related?" he asked, sounding puzzled. A natural question.

"Actually, we're childhood friends. We grew up across the street from each other."

"Really? So you're just friends, then."

For a moment, Keigo clammed up. It only lasted a second, but a bead of cold sweat trickled down Nagi's back.

"…Yes, just friends."

He nodded. He was smiling, like one would expect in such a situation, but he sounded slightly stiff—although that could have been her imagination.

"Ah. Glad to hear it," Dr. Karasuma said.

What was that supposed to mean?

"Oh? And why's that?" Keigo asked.

"Nothing. It's just that she's such a wonderful lady, and the other day when she said she didn't have anyone to marry, it stuck with me. I thought I might ask her out to dinner next time I saw her…but coming out of the blue, I didn't know how she'd take it… What do you think, Mr. Yuuki?" he asked without a trace of malice. Nagi's mind was internally battling between the urge to immediately interrupt their conversation and the urge to flee as fast as she could.

"Why would you ask me?" Keigo said as Nagi waffled over what to do. His terrifyingly calm voice made her realize there was no way in hell she could interrupt them now.

"Because as her childhood friend, you seem likely to know how she would react if I asked her out to dinner."

As Nagi stood still as a statue holding her tray, she saw Dr. Karasuma grin at Keigo and was tormented by the possibility he would say something rude back.

"You have nothing to worry about. I'm sure she would take you seriously."

Keigo smiled placidly. He was perfect. Anyone watching would think he couldn't have cared less if the vet asked her out.

"Why not give it a shot?"

Keigo's words seemed to crawl down her back like a clammy snake. For a moment, she doubted her ears, but no—he had really said that. The second she realized this, she felt incredibly ashamed. What in the world had she been hoping he would say?

"...Oh, Ms. Yoroizuka, is that you?"

She looked up. Dr. Karasuma and Keigo were both craning their necks around to look at her.

"Uh.........oh, yes! Dr. Karasuma? Fancy seeing you here!"

She quickly pasted on a professional smile and sat down next to Keigo, with the vet on his other side.

"It really is a coincidence!" he replied. "I was quite surprised to find Mr. Yuuki next to me when I sat down. Imagine the chances we'd end up with seats right next to each other."

"I guess truth really is stranger than fiction. Do you like this kind of movie, Doctor?" she asked.

They chatted aimlessly for a few minutes until the bell signaling the start of the show cut off their conversation. The movie began playing, and Nagi turned her attention to the screen. She had been so excited, but as the title appeared, she felt nothing.

Whenever she caught a glimpse of Keigo out of the corner of her eye, she got so distracted she didn't even register the dialogue. She didn't get to trade popcorn flavors with him even once.

◆

"Ms. Yoroizuka, are you all right?"

The sound of Saotome's voice brought Nagi back from her daydream.

"Oh, yes, sorry! I'm completely fine!" she quickly answered, taking a gulp of her beer. She had been neglecting it, and it was now lukewarm. That day, they were holding a belated New Year's party for System Development Division One. Her colleagues, many of whom liked to drink, were letting loose and getting a little wild. Normally, she would have been right there with them, but...

"..."

Right now she just didn't feel like partying. The reason was no mystery. She stole a glance to the side.

"...Come on, Yuuki, hurry up and show me!"

"I told you, I don't want to! Hey, get your hand out of my pocket! Are you some kind of pervert?"

Yuuki was sitting with his broad back to her, joking around with a senior staff member in the sales division. She was glad he was fitting into the department so well, but when she saw him, her emotions were mixed. Lately, she couldn't stop thinking about his conversation with Dr. Karasuma at the theater.

She hadn't forgotten a single word he had said to her on New Year's Eve. She had gone over them so many times in her mind that if someone had asked her to reenact the conversation, she could have done it on the spot. He'd declared he wouldn't be able to stop himself once they were dating, and he'd told her he wanted to be "the special person you take for granted." But if so, then why had he said that to Dr. Karasuma? Had he been lying on New Year's Eve?

"—No way, you're kidding!"

The loud voice of the sales staff member echoed behind her and snapped her out of the mental spiral she'd fallen back into. She looked up. He was running toward her.

"Yoroizuka, you went to the same university as Yuuki, right?"

Overwhelmed by his odd excitement, she nodded, a little confused, and said, "Yes, and…?"

"Do you know this woman? Yuuki says she's his ex!"

Before she had time to think, he thrust Keigo's phone in front of her face. There was a picture of a man and a woman pulled up on the screen. The man was Keigo, looking slightly uncomfortable. She knew right away from his hairstyle that it was taken in university. Next to him, looking as relaxed as he was awkward, was a very pretty woman. She had expertly curled long black hair and large downward-sloping eyes. In direct contrast to Nagi, she had a sweet face. Judging by her arm stretched toward the edge of the frame, Nagi assumed the picture was a selfie she'd taken.

"…Yes, I know her…"

That was an understatement. Everyone in their class probably knew this woman.

"…She was our year's Miss Campus."

Although she'd never heard about Keigo dating her.

"Give me that!" Keigo yelled, wrestling his phone from the salesman's hand and bearing down on him with steely eyes. "Would you please give it a rest? I'm about to get very mad."

"Ah-ha-ha, sorry. She's so pretty I thought maybe you'd edited in a celebrity's face or something."

"You think I'd waste my time on something like that? Enough. We're going back to our seats."

He grabbed the older man by the collar and dragged him away.

"M…Ms. Yoroizuka…?" Saotome timidly addressed Nagi, who was in a daze.

"…Huh? What's wrong?"

"Um…you look scary."

Only then did Nagi realize that her face was completely blank.

◆

She was done. She didn't care. She didn't want to think about anything anymore.

"What?! You're not going to the after-party? …Are you sick?! I'd be happy to take you home!"

Nagi could usually be counted on to attend after-parties, but that night, she'd begged off, pretending she didn't feel well. She shook her head vehemently, not wanting to worry Saotome.

"Oh, it's nothing serious! Thank you, though. You go enjoy the after-party."

She said good night and waved to Saotome, then speed-walked toward the station. She wanted desperately to dispel the typhoon of unease swirling in her chest. She dove into the first karaoke place she saw, immediately ordered a beer, and started singing the most intense songs she could think of. For the first half hour, she sang whatever popped into her mind, but eventually, the mood of the songs calmed a bit, and for whatever reason, around the one-hour mark, she started singing sorrowful romantic ballads and feeling inexplicably depressed.

"Ugh…my throat…"

At last, having finished a song about unrequited love, Nagi set down her mike. The next song started playing right away, but her throat was at its limit, and she didn't think she could sing anymore. As she stared absently at the monitor and sipped her beer, a lyric scrolled across reading If only I knew how you felt, things wouldn't be so hard. The song had been popular when she was in high school.

"…If only I knew how you felt, eh?"

She laughed dryly. When it first came out, she hadn't thought twice about the lyrics. Who would have guessed that more than a decade later, it would be stabbing her straight through the heart?

"*Sigh...* Time to go home..."

Coughing, she left the karaoke place with heavy steps and started back to her apartment. She'd stopped in to sing karaoke because she wanted to release some tension, but now she felt even more depressed than when she'd started. As she walked through the ticket gate at her home station, she caught sight of her favorite *oden* restaurant. It was the same place where Keigo had listened as she talked about Kousaka and Saiga. He'd not only stayed up listening until two in the morning but walked her home afterward. The simple explanation was because he was in love with her, but what if that wasn't the case? What if he'd only done it out of kindness toward his old friend? But who would go that far for someone they didn't have feelings for?

"...Ugh."

She hated herself for obsessing like this. It was pathetic that she was using his kindness toward her as a measure of how much he cared for her.

Filled with self-loathing, she stopped in front of her building and dug around in her purse for her key. Just then, she caught sight of the faint glow of her phone screen.

"Huh?"

The display read 8 missed calls. Flustered, she unlocked her phone. They were all from Keigo. As she tried to grasp what was going on, her phone buzzed again. The name on the screen was that of her childhood friend.

"Hello?" she said after reflexively answering the call.

"Where in the world have you been? You didn't go straight home, did you?!"

She pulled the phone away from her ear at the sound of Keigo's shouting.

"Why are you yelling at me out of the blue? ...And anyway, how do you know I didn't go home...?"

"Because I went to your house! There was no answer when I rang the bell, and your room was dark… What were you doing out until this time of night?!"

"You came to my house? Why?"

"Because Saotome told me you weren't feeling well, obviously! You shouldn't be wandering around when you're ill!"

As she listened to him lecture her, her brain started to fog over again.

"Anyway, where are you now? Tell me so I can go there right away! Are you at home?"

She could hear traffic in the background of the call. Judging by how fast he was breathing, she guessed he had been zooming around outside in search of her. Instantly, it became hard for her to breathe. She didn't want to see him. She understood that very clearly.

"…It's fine."

"What? Why?"

"I feel better now, so you don't need to come over! Bye!"

Ignoring Keigo's *"Hey, wait…,"* she hung up. Stuffing her phone into the bottom of her purse as it started vibrating again, she ran through the entryway and pounded on the elevator button. There was no way in hell she could see him. Just talking on the phone was torture! If she met him in person, she might literally suffocate.

Once inside the elevator, she pretended the sounds of the machinery were drowning out the buzzing of her phone. She knew how incredibly awkward she would feel the next time she saw him, but that night, she just didn't have the mental space to think about the future. The elevator stopped on the fourth floor—her floor—but as she stepped out…

"…Huh?"

When she saw the figure blocking her way, she was speechless.

"What the hell…? Don't ignore my calls like that…," Keigo said between raspy breaths. His hands were planted on his knees, his phone still gripped in one of them. He looked about ready to collapse.

"Wh...why are you here?!"

"I finally spotted you outside your building...but then you ran into the elevator, so I followed you on the stairs...!" he said between pants, sinking into a crouch. "Shit...I'm beat..."

He squatted there limply until his breathing quieted, then slowly stood back up.

"We'll bother the neighbors out here, so let's go somewhere else," he said.

They walked over to the door of Nagi's apartment. As she turned her key in the lock, panic overcame her. She had wanted to avoid meeting him no matter what, and now here he was right next to her. She had no clue what to do or how to interact with him.

"Thanks," he said with a quick bob of his head as he stepped into the entryway. When Nagi started to take out a pair of slippers for him, he shook his head and said, "No, it's fine. I'll stay here."

Nagi turned toward him apprehensively, her eyes on the floor. Because of the step down to the entryway, his head was closer to her own than usual. That made her even less willing to look at him.

"...Do you feel okay?" Keigo asked, breaking the silence.

"Oh, yeah... Sorry for worrying you."

"That's good," he said. There was another silence.

She figured he could leave now that he knew she was fine, but he showed no sign of budging.

"Nagi," he finally said, his voice kind. "I was hoping you might tell me why you've been so cold toward me lately."

"..."

"To be honest, that kinda treatment really makes a guy depressed."

She could tell he was keeping his tone playful for her sake.

Nevertheless, her lips remained stiffly pressed together. As she stood there, fists clenched, she heard him sigh quietly.

"I bet it's my fault…right? I'm sorry," he said sadly, peering into her face. He looked so genuinely apologetic it made her chest tighten. How could she put him through any more suffering after seeing those eyes?

"…I heard you talking. The day we went to the theater, when I went to get popcorn. I heard you tell Dr. Karasuma that he should give it a shot and ask me out to dinner…," she said very quietly.

"Aha…," he said, nodding. "I'm sorry. Everything makes sense now."

He coughed softly.

"Will you let me explain?" he asked. "The first reason I said that is because I wanted to avoid messing up your relationship with the vet by blatantly opposing the idea."

She had figured as much, but she hadn't wanted to accept it, because she hadn't wanted to hear him say those words.

"I know…," she mumbled.

"Also," Keigo went on, "he's got something going on with that nurse from the hospital."

Going on? What was going on?

"I mean, I think they're seeing each other," he said.

Nagi stood there blinking for a long time, then finally blurted out, "What?!"

She thought back to the face of the nurse she'd seen with Dr. Karasuma when she and Keigo visited the veterinary hospital.

"There was a woman's purse and phone on the seat next to him at the theater," Keigo said. "A few minutes after the movie started, a woman came and sat down by him. Didn't you see? I glanced over at her, and it was that nurse. They had on matching rings at the hospital, too. I can't imagine any other explanation. You don't remember?"

Obviously, she'd had no idea. She was shocked by how poor her memory was.

"Um...so..."

A lot of things were starting to make sense, but now something else was bothering her.

"If he has a girlfriend, then why was he going on about dinner with me...?"

If she accepted Keigo's view of the situation, Dr. Karasuma was talking about asking a woman out to dinner in the middle of a date with his own girlfriend. Keigo frowned.

"He's probably a player."

What the heck? She stood there gaping.

"Anyway," Keigo continued, "I thought it was weird he was asking about you if he was there with another woman, but since you've known him a lot longer than me, I figured you must have realized what kind of person he was. You're not into womanizers, right? Since I knew you'd turn him down, I told him to go ahead and try. Anyway, with that type of guy, it's usually better to tell them outright that you're not interested."

"..."

"Oh, I see. You hadn't noticed, had you...?"

Keigo must have figured out why she wasn't saying anything, because he smiled and rolled his eyes.

"If he asks you to dinner, just turn him down. His whole situation sounds like a mess."

"...I'll do that," she nodded stiffly.

She resolved to maintain a positive relationship with Dr. Karasuma—as a client, that is.

"...I understand the situation with the doctor. I'm sorry for taking it the wrong way. But there's something else I want to ask you about."

The wry smile vanished from Keigo's face.

"Oh...about that picture?"

She nodded silently, and he frowned.

"Honestly, I just forgot to delete it, and that guy happened to see it…"

"That's not what I'm asking about!" she snapped before she could stop herself.

The image of Keigo with another woman popped back into her head.

"I had no idea the two of you were dating!"

"Yeah, I never told you about it… I mean, she asked me out, and then she dumped me right away, so I didn't even have time to mention it…," he said evasively. "The point is, we only dated for a really short time."

He shrugged. Nagi scowled, sensing he was trying to end the conversation as quickly as possible.

"I see. You 'only' dated her?"

He hesitated, his gaze darting away from her face and eventually landing on the floor.

"I mean…we did kiss a few times."

"You just kissed?"

"…And some other things," he said, sounding resigned to his fate. Her stomach churned.

"Is that so. How nice you were able to enjoy your time with Miss Campus."

She turned away. Now he was the one who looked sullen.

"Why are you mad about that?"

"What?!" she shouted back. She was about to say she wasn't mad, then thought better of it.

He was right. She was mad at him. And not just right now. She'd been mad at him for weeks. But why?

It only took her a few seconds to realize the answer. What an idiot she was. A twenty-eight-year-old woman who couldn't even put a name to her own emotions.

I'm jealous.

The second it hit her, she felt her cheeks rapidly grow hot and knew she must be blushing. Keigo, who had probably seen everything, tilted his head in confusion.

"I—I…"

"What?"

"…I think…I might be jealous…," she mumbled.

He instantly turned as red as she was. They stared at each other's flushed faces.

"…Nagi…are you serious…?"

Unable to hold out any longer, he covered his face with both hands.

"I said I *might* be! I'm not sure…but I feel like maybe that's what's going on…"

She took a deep breath and tried to calm herself, then reviewed the facts. There was Keigo's comment to Dr. Karasuma. Then there was the fact that he'd dated Miss Campus. Clearly, those things had put her in a crappy mood. With that much evidence, she couldn't very well deny it. She could remember feeling this way several times before, but never toward Keigo. And yet now, though it was slight—

"…Can I assume we're thinking the same thing?" Keigo asked. The excitement in his voice was unmistakable.

"I won't know unless we say it…"

It was all so mortifying, she couldn't bring herself to be any clearer.

"Then go ahead."

"You go first."

"Fine. I'll say it again," he said stoically.

He let out a long breath, then gazed solemnly at her.

"Nagi."

His commanding voice made her heart flip. She had heard him say her name hundreds, probably thousands, of times, but this time he sounded completely different—much more manly.

"Ever since we were children, I've been in love with you."

Ah, that's what it was. This was the voice he used to speak to the person he loved. She hadn't noticed it before, but he'd probably been speaking to her in that voice all along.

"Now it's your turn," he said immediately, as if to cover up his embarrassment. She took a deep breath, gathered her courage, and spoke.

"…I haven't loved you since we were children, but recently…I think I might…be falling for you…maybe."

"Hey! …That was the wimpiest confession I've ever heard!"

"I—I can't help it! It's the truth! I'll just have to fall more and more in love with you as time goes by!" she shouted frantically. Keigo took a deep breath.

"…I guess that's good enough," he said, reluctantly accepting her words. "By the way, Nagi. Can I go ahead and assume we're dating now?"

Nagi's heart flip-flopped again.

"Um…maybe?"

She nodded, and he nodded back. For a moment, they stared at each other in silence. Weird. If she wasn't mistaken, they were now officially a couple. So what was going on with this peculiar atmosphere?

It would probably be normal to kiss in this situation, but unfortunately, the mood felt completely wrong for that, and she had no idea how to move things in that direction. As she hesitated, a hand suddenly appeared before her.

"Here."

She looked up questioningly at Keigo. He glanced away uncomfortably, then mumbled, "…It's okay to shake hands, right?"

He looked exactly like a sulking child, and she couldn't help smiling.

"Yeah."

She placed her hand on top of his larger one. It was warm and just a little sweaty. A man's rough, angular hand—Keigo's hand, which she knew so well.

From this day forward, the man attached to that hand was her boyfriend. The thought was unbearably strange and made her very embarrassed. She looked shyly up at him and met his equally shy gaze. Then he broke into such a happy smile she couldn't help giggling, too.

"Okay."

"Okay."

That was how, in the winter of her twenty-eighth year, Nagi's friend of over two decades became her boyfriend.

Chapter 2.

My First Love
Was Successful?

Twelfth Try

Ai Saotome was sitting on the sofa in her room, drying her hair with a towel. She stared at the wall clock and thought about Nagi, who had looked gloomy all through the New Year's party earlier. Nagi had only drunk three glasses of beer the entire night, and on top of that, even though she always went to the after-party, that night she'd gone home alone instead. She'd told Saotome she didn't feel well, but Saotome knew right away that was a lie. It worried her.

Saotome waffled over what to do for a while, but she finally made up her mind to send Nagi a message and picked up her phone. Just then, a notification dinged. Who could it be? When she looked at the screen, she gasped in surprise.

"Mr. Yuuki!"

Fifteen minutes later, she was running to the nearby convenience store, only to find Keigo already standing in the doorway.

"I'm so sorry to bother you this late at night. Here, take this."

Puzzled, she took the bottle of iced tea he held out to her. The message he had sent read Would you be able to meet me somewhere? When she'd called him, he'd said he was at her local train station and so she'd given him directions to a convenience store close to where she lived.

"Did something happen?" she asked. He'd left the party that night right after Nagi had. What on earth could he want with her now?

"Actually, I came to tell you that Nagi and I are officially dating."

The plastic bottle dropped from her hand.

"As of…when?"

She didn't even care that the bottle was rolling away.

"Just now," he said, picking it up for her. As she listened in a daze, he explained what had happened.

"So…you're telling me you left the woman you just started dating to come tell me?" she asked, struggling to grasp the situation. If what he was saying was true, Nagi was alone in her apartment right now.

"Yeah, that's about right," he acknowledged.

She wondered how a woman would react to her new boyfriend rushing off right after they started dating. Wasn't that a special, once-in-a-lifetime kind of moment? Not that she wanted a boyfriend, but if she had one, she would definitely want him to stay with her.

"Nagi doesn't get mad over stuff like that," Keigo said with a laugh. "Anyway, it was more important for me to apologize to you."

He turned abruptly serious and bowed his head low.

"It's probably going to be tough for you to see us together. I'm genuinely sorry about that."

The whorl of his hair, which she didn't usually have the opportunity to see, was right before her eyes. A man had never bowed so deeply to her before. Ever since she was young, the men who approached her had always tried to win her over by showing off.

"Oh, no, that's…"

As she floundered, a man came out of the convenience store and gaped at them. She hurriedly grabbed Keigo's shoulder.

"M-Mr. Yuuki! Please stop bowing! I understand! It's fine!"

Finally, he straightened up. She knew right away when she saw his face so close in front of her that she was going to have to forgive him.

"…That's what's so irritating about you," she muttered.

"What?" he asked, puzzled.

"Nothing. Congratulations, that's great," she said quickly.

As she turned away, she noticed the expression on his face.

"What?" she asked.

"Nothing, I was just wondering if you were okay…"

"You what? Where do you get off being so condescending?" she snapped irritably. "You'd better watch out. If you let down your guard, someone else might take your place."

"That would be a problem," he said, smiling awkwardly.

"Was there anything else you wanted?" she asked.

"No, just that. I really am sorry."

She wasn't sure if he was apologizing for making her leave her house so late at night or for dating Nagi. Probably both. He really was infuriating.

"Good night, then," he said. "See you at work. Sleep well."

He retreated, that concerned expression never leaving his face. After watching him disappear down the street, Saotome slipped into the convenience store. She grabbed a shopping basket from the stack next to the door and charged straight to the corner with the candy and pastries. She grabbed items randomly from the shelf and stuffed them in her basket, and once it was full, she heaved it onto the counter. The attendant stared rudely at the overflowing contents.

"I'd like these, please," she said.

"Uh, yes, ma'am…"

After paying the astronomical total, Saotome walked along the darkened streets, bulging bag in her hand. *So it's come to this*, she thought. *I knew something bad was going to happen. After all, it was only after they started talking about Keigo's ex-girlfriend that Nagi's mood plummeted. Anyone would have noticed the shocked look on her face, even if they didn't have a vested interest like me.*

"Sigh…"

She looked up at the night sky. Why was it only on days like this that the heavens were clear and cloudless? The sight of those beautiful twinkling stars made her heart hurt. She thought back to Keigo's words and his expression as he bowed to her.

"…How could I complain when he was making a face like that?" she grumbled, beginning to cry. The wails she had been holding back spilled out all at once.

No fair! No fair, no fair, no fair! That man didn't play fair at all. Why did he have to be Nagi's childhood friend? Why couldn't he be worse at his job? Why was he kind even to his rival? She wouldn't feel so awful if he was the type she could look down on and resent with her whole soul, but—

"Ungh…"

She violently wiped away her tears. Taking a deep breath, she looked up again at the night sky and gradually calmed down. It was all right. She would limit her depression to the weekend, and on Monday she would go to work looking like she always did and give him a good shock.

Having made up her mind, she pulled an éclair out of her shopping bag and took a big bite.

"…Ahhh, so delicious."

She kept eating. The saltiness of her tears was blotted out by the sweetness of the custard cream, vanishing softly into oblivion.

Thirteenth Try

When Nagi thought back to her time in university, she remembered that for the first few months after she started dating someone, she always felt high. That feeling changed everything. The whole world looked more colorful, and if something bad happened, she would laugh it off right away. Recently, her love life hadn't been going well, and she'd been sure that if only she had a boyfriend again, every day would be a joy. Now she did, for the first time in ages, and he was her childhood best friend. She had expected that to transform her life, but—reality turned out to be a little more realistic.

"Hey, Nagi?"
She glanced up from her computer at Keigo.
"Aren't you going home soon?"
Looking at the clock, she saw it was after eleven at night. Then, glancing around, she realized they were the only two people left in the office. She had been so intensely focused on her work that she hadn't even noticed.
"Oh, yeah. I'm having a problem with some coding," she said wearily.
"What's wrong?" Keigo asked, walking over to her. The truth was, she had been wrestling with a bug for the past few hours and still couldn't figure out where it had come from or how to fix it. She was utterly drained and wanted to go home, but the deadline for this system was approaching, and if possible, she wanted to fix the bug that night.

"Hmm… Can I see?"

After she'd described the symptoms, he took the mouse and scanned the source code.

"…Ah, I see the problem. In this version of the framework, bugs pop up under certain conditions. This one is fairly minor, though, so it isn't widely known. I think we should be able to avoid it if we do this…"

He typed something into the keyboard and told her to test it out. She tried it again and found that the bug that had been tormenting her had completely vanished.

"Wow, you fixed it! Thanks! That's amazing! I was working on that for three hours!"

"I'm glad it's fixed. Next time, I wish you'd talk to me before struggling over it for so long."

He smiled wryly. She had to admit he had a point.

"What a relief… Now I can go home… Let me get you a coffee to thank you!"

She stood up energetically, but Keigo stopped her.

"Wait just a minute now. I didn't do anything to deserve a free coffee."

"But you saved my butt, and I want to thank you for it…"

If Keigo hadn't been there, she probably would have kept working past midnight. The coffee was nonnegotiable.

"Hmm," he said, pretending to think it over. "In that case, there *is* something I'd like from you."

"Okay, what? Your wish is my command!"

It was unusual for him to ask something of her. She nodded, a little elated, but for some reason he seemed reluctant to say any more. *I wonder if he's going to request something outrageous. What if he asks me for money? I mean, it's Keigo, so I wouldn't mind trusting him even if he needed a lot…*

"Um… Will you come over to my apartment this weekend?"

"Huh?"

All that buildup for such an ordinary request? She felt let down.

She'd hung out at his place plenty of times before. On New Year's Eve three years ago, when his parents were remodeling their house, everyone had a hot-pot party at his apartment. And last year one time when the two of them went drinking, Keigo had gotten smashed, and she'd had to drag him home. She'd been so exhausted she'd ended up spending the night on his sofa.

"You're inviting me over? That sounds great. That's all you wanted to ask me? You were having such a hard time getting the words out, I thought it was going to be something bigger." As she elbowed him cheerfully, she noticed he had a weird expression on his face.

"You don't get it, do you?"

"Get what?"

"This Sunday is our one-month anniversary."

One-month what?

She turned slowly to glance at the calendar on her desk, paused for a few seconds, and felt like she'd been struck by lightning.

"Oh…ooohhhh! That's right! We're dating, aren't we?! And it's been a month! I can't believe it's been that long! Time sure flies. Ha-ha-ha!"

"…Come on, you forgot?"

"Ah-ha-ha… No way, I wouldn't forget something like that…"

She laughed to cover it up, but a chill ran down her spine. Not only had she forgotten about their anniversary, she'd almost forgotten they were even dating. After all, they saw each other at work every day just like before, they didn't call or text each other unless they had some reason to, and since they both preferred to stay home, they didn't go anywhere together on their days off. With her everyday life virtually unchanged and the usual busyness of work taken into account, the fact that she was dating Keigo had been pushed far away into a remote corner of her mind.

"Okay then, great, I'd love to come over!" she said, flustered. Just then, she realized something. It was their one-month anniversary, and she was going to her boyfriend's house. Was it possible he was envisioning something a little different from what she was when he used the words *come over*?

"Um, did you by chance mean you wanted me to stay the night…?" she asked timidly.

"You don't have to if you don't want to," he said grumpily. So she was right.

"Don't be ridiculous!" she shouted. "Or, well, I mean, I'd love to stay over, but…"

"But?"

"B-b-but that…means…"

"What?"

"……Nothing."

She couldn't bring herself to ask him if he meant *that* kind of staying over.

◆

It was three o'clock on Saturday. Holding her traveling bag packed with her overnight kit in one hand, Nagi texted Keigo I'm almost at your place. After sending the message, she tucked her phone back into her bag with a sigh. The day in question had finally arrived. Just in case, she had preened every centimeter of her body the night before and packed a new pair of underwear. Of course, that was all just in case. She didn't actually think anything would happen, and she certainly wasn't expecting it to.

I'd kiss you and do everything else you're probably imagining right now.

She recalled what he'd said on New Year's Eve. As her imagination ran out of control, her whole body grew restless. She wanted to shout "Ahhh!" at the top of her lungs. They'd been dating for a month, but they hadn't even kissed. Maybe that was natural, since they hadn't really been on a proper date. She couldn't even imagine kissing him, it was so embarrassing. Plus, she felt like once they did, their relationship as lifelong friends would fall apart. And now Saturday had arrived, before she could figure anything out.

She walked along, deep in thought, then abruptly stopped. Someone was standing in front of Keigo's apartment.

"Hey."

It was him, phone in hand. He gave her a half wave. He must have come down when he got her message. The second she saw him standing there in blue chinos and a casual off-white knit shirt, her heart started pounding.

"H-hello…I'm pleased to see you on this very special day…," she said, bowing stiffly.

"What are you talking about?" he said with a laugh.

He took her bag, and they got in the elevator. She anxiously watched the numbers go up on the display.

"!"

She flinched. Keigo had silently taken her hand. She glanced at him in surprise. He was staring intently at the display panel. He looked vaguely nervous, and she could tell he was thinking about what might happen later, just like she was. Even though it was the middle of winter, his skin against hers felt damp with sweat. She was terrified he might be able to sense her pounding heart through their interlocked fingers. Unable to bear the relentless hum of the elevator machinery any longer, Nagi finally broke the silence.

"H-hey, it just occurred to me that we live really close to each other. That makes things easy! We don't even have to take a train to hang out."

It was only a fifteen-minute walk from her apartment to his.

"Oh…yeah," he said.

She was too nervous to notice the evasiveness of his answer.

"Did you choose this place because it was near my apartment? Kidding, ha-ha…"

"…Sorry I'm a stalker."

The smile vanished from her face. He was looking stubbornly away from her. She flushed as she realized the thing she'd been joking about was actually true.

"No, I-I'm sorry…"

This was awkward. She hadn't wasted any time sticking her foot in her mouth. Of course, he should have made up some excuse instead of being so idiotically honest!

As they stood there uncomfortably, the elevator finally reached his floor.

"We're here! Come on!" she said, practically leaping out of the elevator. Keigo showed her into his apartment.

There was a sofa, a low table, and a TV in the sunny living room. That was all normal, but Keigo's place featured something a little more unusual as well—a huge server rack as tall as she was and packed with wired-up devices. There weren't just computer parts, either. There were servers, too, which ordinary people didn't exactly keep lying around.

"This stuff always blows me away… Did you get more or something?"

"There's a new computer I built recently. A new kind of CPU went on sale, and I wanted to see how it performed."

"You're a true techie…"

Personally, she felt like one computer per household was plenty, but according to Keigo, different jobs called for different devices. She was looking over the rack with a mixture of shock and awe, suppressing the urge to ask him if this was his office or his home, when she heard him call her name. She turned around to find him sitting on the sofa, gesturing to her.

"Nagi, come sit with me."

"Oh, okay," she said, sitting down a safe distance from him.

"Want to watch something?" he asked, picking up the remote control. A long list of movies and shows appeared on the screen.

"I didn't know you subscribed to a streaming service!"

"I signed up recently."

"Cool! I was thinking of signing up, too... Wow, there's so much to choose from."

She'd never watched streaming TV before.

"Yeah," he agreed. "Oh, cool, they even have some super old-school stuff."

Nagi watched Keigo suspiciously as he kept saying "Wow" and "Cool" over and over again.

"Haven't you ever used it before?" she teased. He flinched. He'd said he subscribed recently, but he was acting like he'd just turned it on for the first time.

"Uh...um, well...," he mumbled. Suddenly, it dawned on her.

"Did you by chance get this subscription just so we could watch something today?"

He must have been embarrassed, because his mouth stayed set in a straight line. Finding this hilarious, she leaned forward and kept up her attack.

"I'm asking you a question, Keigo!"

"..."

"Speak up!"

"Fine! What's wrong with that? I thought watching a movie would help you relax!" he finally confessed. She burst out giggling.

"I knew it!"

As she shook with laughter, he muttered, "Why'd you have to ask if you already knew?" Watching him pout, she felt the tension melt inside her. So she wasn't the only one who'd been nervous about her visit.

"Thank you, Keigo," she said, laying her head softly on his shoulder just because she felt like it.

"...No biggie," he said brusquely, and sheepishly placed his hand over hers. The warmth of his slightly sweaty fingers felt just right.

◆

"That was so good!" Nagi said, stretching in her spot on the sofa as the credits started to roll.

"I'm getting hungry," Keigo said, glancing at the wall clock. It was already almost six. Nagi was starting to feel peckish herself.

"How about I cook something for us?" she suggested. She wasn't a great cook, but she could manage an edible meal. She figured it would be a way of thanking Keigo for letting her stay over, but for some reason, he just shook his head and headed toward the kitchen.

"That's a very tempting offer, but…" He opened the refrigerator and took out a white bag. "I've got some chicken in here."

He opened one of the produce drawers.

"And some vegetables."

He pulled out Chinese cabbage, mushrooms, and leeks before opening the cabinet over the sink.

"And I have this nice clay pot I got as a present at a wedding."

"You don't mean to say…"

Keigo glanced back at her with a grin.

"We're having *nabe* tonight!"

"Yes! I haven't had a hot pot in ages!"

"We can make it together."

She liked the way he wasn't offering to make it himself or telling her to make it. After they got everything ready, they toasted with cold beers and chatted about the movie they'd just watched. The pork-and-soy-sauce base Keigo had bought for the hot pot was fantastic, and after all the vegetables and meat were gone, Nagi finished off her meal with two helpings of rice simmered in the leftover broth. When they were done, she forced him to let her wash the empty pot and dishes. She meticulously dried everything and put it away before heading back to the living room, rubbing her overstuffed stomach.

"I'm done cleaning up," she told Keigo.

"Oh, thanks! I shouldn't have let you do that."

He stopped what he'd been doing at the computer and turned toward her.

"No way, you did the shopping. The least I could do was clean up."

She walked over and noticed he was programming something.

"Hey, you're not working, are you?"

"Nah, just analyzing that ransomware we got hit with the other day."

He must mean the virus that had infected Saotome's device. He'd managed to restore the encrypted files and reinstall the operating systems on her desktop and the shared server, which had also been infected. That should have been the end. So why was he using his time off to analyze it? Noticing her puzzled look, he explained.

"This encryption pattern hasn't been decoded yet. I thought I could analyze it and create a decryption tool."

His casual tone caught Nagi by surprise. The viruses currently circulating around the world had each been created by someone at least several times as smart as her. She might be a systems engineer, but she had no clue how to decode viruses. Keigo was probably the only engineer at Sync.System who could do it. She knew he'd always been incredible at programming, but after working on the same team with him, she was even more aware of what a genius he was. To be honest, his skills would probably be better used by a bigger IT company. In fact, the company he'd worked at straight out of university was so famous, just about everybody had heard of it. Nevertheless, he'd switched to Sync.System, a much smaller company, and he was still there. It was probably stupidly conceited of her to think she might be the reason—

"…Man, it's getting late. You take your bath first. I'll go after," he said, glancing at the clock on the monitor.

"Sure. Thanks," she said.

"Help yourself to the shampoo and towels and stuff."

She grabbed her toiletry bag and headed for the bathroom.

After undressing in the changing area, she covered herself with a towel and entered the room with the bath. Even though she'd been to his house multiple times, she'd never taken a bath there. As she timidly turned on the shower, she suddenly noticed something.

"Whoa, he's still using that? What a blast from the past."

A familiar light-blue bottle of body soap was sitting on the shower rack. It was the same brand his family used when they were kids. She remembered they used to take baths together all the time up through second or third grade. She remembered liking the slightly sweet-smelling soap. She used to make heaps of bubbles and pile them on top of Keigo's head. He hadn't hit his growth spurt yet, so he'd been about the same height as Nagi and as fine-boned as a girl. And look at him now! He must have grown in all sorts of—

"…No, no, no!"

She hurriedly chased away the racy image that had started to form in her mind.

"Gotta stop… I'm getting dizzy…"

She had a feeling her cheeks reflected in the shower mirror weren't flushed just because of the steam. She looked anxious. Thanks to the movie and hot pot, she'd completely let down her guard, but were they really going to fall asleep without anything happening?

That might have been the whole reason he invited her over on their one-month anniversary. Objectively, it was completely natural. Actually, it was unnatural that two grown-ups had spent the past month dating without so much as kissing.

"It's fine. Whatever will be, will be. No problem. Let it happen…," she muttered as she got out of the shower and put on her brand-new underwear and favorite pajamas. She took twice as long as usual to blow-dry her hair and apply moisturizer before returning to the living room with as natural an expression as possible.

"Sorry for taking so long," she said. Keigo was still sitting at the computer.

"Oh, you're out. Guess I'll go in now." He stood up, yawning. "Make yourself comfortable. If you're tired, you don't have to wait for me to go to bed."

Seeming not to notice her murmur of surprise, he stretched and headed off to the bathroom.

She couldn't very well fall asleep, even if he'd said it was okay. Feeling out of sorts, she went to the bedroom and warily opened the door. This room might well become the setting for that night's decisive battle. There was his semidouble bed. It looked like he'd bought new pillows for her—the ones on the bed appeared unused. She turned on the side-table lamp and sat down in the dim room, posed like *The Thinker*. Should she stay up or go to bed? After grappling with this question for a long time, she decided to get in bed and wait for him. If she got scared, she could just pretend she was sleeping. She curled up anxiously under the comforter. After a while, she heard Keigo open the bathroom door and walk toward the bedroom. Then the bedroom door opened. Lying with her face to the wall, she panicked and tried hard to even out her breathing.

"...Nagi?" he said softly.

The bed creaked. She desperately kept up her charade.

"Did you fall asleep?" he whispered. She felt him lie down next to her. Maybe because he'd just taken a bath, his back felt slightly warm. She couldn't see him, but he had to be really close. She could feel sweat on her clenched fists, and her heart was pounding. She could hardly breathe. What should she do? Sit up? Or keep pretending to sleep?

"...Good night."

She heard his voice just as her tension reached its peak. *Huh?* Then, after a few seconds, she heard him switch off the lamp. She huddled perfectly still on her side of the bed and focused all feeling into her back, but she couldn't sense any movement from him.

Was he really going to sleep?

Devastated, she silently turned her head toward him. In the shadows, she could see him lying on his back with his eyes closed. Apparently, he really *was* preparing to sleep.

"Ke…Keigo?" she said softly. Slowly, his eyelids opened.

"…Oh, sorry, did I wake you up?" he asked.

"Oh, um…no, but…"

He reached up a hand and placed it on the head she was hurriedly shaking.

"Go to sleep. Good night."

His hand stroked her hair gently a few times, then vanished with surprising swiftness. He must have sensed her disappointment, because he asked, "What's wrong?"

"Nothing, it's just…are you…n-not going to do anything…?" she mumbled, covering her mouth with the comforter.

"Do you want me to do something?"

She wasn't expecting that.

"…No, that's all right."

"Then don't ask."

He laughed, then rolled onto his back again and closed his eyes.

"I'm not going to do anything," he said. "If I wanted to do something, I would have done it a long time ago."

"Oh, really…?"

She wondered what that was supposed to mean, but at the same time, she wasn't exactly raring to go herself, so it was a relief to hear him say it.

"Okay…good night."

She nestled under the comforter and was closing her eyes when she heard Keigo say, "Um…" Her eyes snapped back open.

"In exchange for not doing anything, is it okay if I watch you sleep?"

"What…? No way!" she exclaimed.

"Damn," he muttered.

Of course she didn't want him to do that! Did he think any

woman could sleep peacefully while her boyfriend scrutinized her face?

"Then can we hold hands?" he asked, as if unwilling to give up.

"I suppose," she said, holding out her left hand. Keigo softly placed his right hand on top of it. This wasn't like the innocent hand-holding they'd done in the daytime. His fingers were laced deeply between hers. Her heart pounded, but his fingers stopped moving, and he simply held her hand. Her tension quickly unraveled.

Still, his hand was very big. As she gazed at it, it seemed like it might swallow up her own. She remembered how they'd shaken hands the day they started dating. She'd always been envious of his hands. He had beautiful nails and long, graceful fingers, and when they touched her, she felt completely at ease.

"You know, I really love your hands...," she whispered, pulling him closer and rubbing her cheek against his fingers. His warmth seeped into her, filling her whole body with relief. She felt as comfortable as if she were soaking in a hot bath. She sensed her eyelids slowly closing.

"Nagi..."

She heard his voice hazily through her fading consciousness.

"Hmm...?"

"Can I kiss you?"

Kiss? Huh? Did he just say 'kiss'?

"Huh?"

Her eyes popped open, and all traces of sleepiness instantly vanished. His face was right in front of hers, and he was gazing at her intently.

"Um...?"

Her feelings were in a jumble, but she instinctively tried to pull her hand away from his. He wouldn't let go. He squeezed her hand so that her fingers couldn't escape.

"If you're not sure, I can start with your fingers."

Start with? What did that mean? She was extremely curious,

but there was no way she could ask him. His unblinking eyes ardently sought her reply.

"I…suppose my fingers would be…okay…"

She couldn't turn him down. She didn't have the guts to cruelly reject those eyes filled with longing. As soon as she granted her permission, she felt something soft touch her left hand. His lips brushed her nails, then traveled up her fingers and onto her palm and wrist, leaving a trail of heat as they moved little by little up her body. They crept along the inside of her forearm and grazed her upper arm. Suddenly, the hand that had been holding hers was pushing down the collar of her pajama top to expose the base of her neck.

She jumped a little as his tongue ran along her clavicle. There was the tickle of his hair against her cheek and the smell of his shampoo. All her senses overflowed with him. She muffled a cry. On top of her now, he took his lips from her neck and lifted his head.

"Nagi?" he whispered. He was so close she could feel his breath. "Can I kiss your lips?"

It was the kind of question a kid in junior high would ask, but his voice was sexy enough to make her gasp.

"…Y-yes…"

She gave a tiny nod. Her heart felt like it was about to explode. She reflexively closed her eyes, and in the darkness, a soft sensation descended on her lips. It moved away for a moment, then returned from a different angle. It was a terribly deliberate kiss, as if he were testing the tenderness of her mouth. It felt innocent, like they were kids in junior high. So innocent, in fact, that it left her feeling slightly impatient.

"Nagi?" he whispered against her parted lips. She timidly opened her eyes. He was staring down at her with a look she'd never seen before. She guessed from the heat in his gaze that he wanted something more from her. What would he ask this time? The thought left her speechless.

" . . . "

As she stiffened, he stroked her cheek. He might have been trying to ease her tension, but her heart only beat faster.

"Is it okay if I do some other things?" he whispered gently, still adoringly caressing her cheek.

"What do you mean by...other things...?"

"How much are you okay with?"

There was no way she could answer a question like that with no advance warning.

"Ten, nine, eight..."

As she hesitated, he wickedly began counting down.

"Wait, wait, wait!" she screamed. "How do you expect me to answer that on the spot?"

"Well," he said, obviously not interested in her desperate protest. "How about you tell me to stop if you don't like it?"

"Huh?"

He kissed her lightly again, and she felt something tickle her stomach. His hand was under her top, swooping around to her back and unhooking her bra with unsettling ease. As his big hands covered her bare breasts, she instinctively pulled her mouth away from his.

"Um, um, um...," she said in a panic, weakly pushing at his shoulders. His body didn't move from on top of her.

"Yes?" he said with infuriating composure before calmly lifting her top. She flushed from embarrassment as her torso was exposed.

"I th-th-thought you said you weren't going to do anything...?!"

"I wasn't planning to, but there's kind of like this switch that gets turned on."

"What's that supposed to— Ah!"

She couldn't help moaning as he licked her breast. This was the worst. She hated it. She wanted to cry from embarrassment. He lifted his face unsteadily from her chest.

"Oh shit...," he mumbled, ripping off his sweatshirt. Nagi

thought she was going to stop breathing. She knew he'd grown up, but the body in front of her was so powerful it seemed to belong to a different person.

We're not kids anymore.

They were both adults now, and they could do things they couldn't back then. A shiver ran down Nagi's spine as that simple truth hit her with overwhelming force.

"Nagi…"

He pulled her close, and the heat from his skin made her dizzy. As his palms ran over every centimeter of her body, she felt herself sinking into the center of a sweet whirlpool. Scared of where she was going, she pressed her legs together just as Keigo's hand was about to touch her there. He looked down at her like he wanted to say something. She knew exactly what it was. She also knew from previous experience that if she let him, they wouldn't be able to stop themselves. But it was no good. She couldn't hold back her desire to see what happened if they went beyond being childhood friends—and she knew he knew she wanted it. His gentle but unrelenting fingers softly pushed her legs apart, and a sweet sensation flooded her body.

She couldn't help responding to each of his movements, and she knew he saw every one of her responses. She turned her face away in embarrassment, but he refused to let her, cupping her cheek in his hand and pulling her back to meet his gaze. Unending waves of passion swallowed her up, melting her into a puddle. She screamed his name until she was hoarse, and every time she did, he murmured, in a way so unlike him, how adorable she was, so that embarrassment and happiness jumbled together in a big mess she couldn't make any sense of.

As the last of the uncountable waves receded, she felt herself slipping into a bottomless ocean.

"…Nagi?"

She could distantly hear him calling her name as she sank

into the sheets. But she didn't have the strength to answer him or to fight the wall of white bearing down on her, so she closed her eyes.

"But we were still on fingers… Think you'll be okay next time?"

She heard him laugh wryly in the distance as she plunged into sleep.

Fourteenth Try

Monday morning was bright and sunny. As Keigo exited a convenience store near the office, a bag of drinks in one hand, he stopped short in surprise.

Nagi was standing in front of him, staring at him wide-eyed. They had bumped into each other on the way to work.

"Morning. Fancy seeing you here," he said, walking over to her. She mumbled "Hi" but didn't look at him. He guessed right away what was behind her brusque attitude.

On Saturday, they'd spent their one-month anniversary together at his apartment. They watched a movie, made a hotpot dinner together, and had some beer, and then he'd made a move—just a little one. He hadn't planned on it at all, and he'd been confident he could spend the night with her without doing anything. But once she was there in front of him, looking all vulnerable in her pajamas, he realized just how impossible it was for restraint to win out over desire. They didn't end up going all the way due to Nagi passing out, but on Sunday morning, she still seemed pretty upset with herself. Keigo had found the whole thing endearing, but it seemed she was so mortified she wanted to crawl into a hole.

"...Thanks for Saturday," she said in a low voice, her mouth buried in her scarf.

"The pleasure was all mine," he answered a little mischievously. She punched his shoulder.

"I swear..."

It was funny to see her this embarrassed, but he managed to

suppress his grin. She pouted, then finally mumbled, "I'm sorry…
I know I left you hanging…"

Apparently, she felt bad about falling asleep in the middle of
everything. True, he had to admit it had been a little tough on
him, but he was satisfied just to have seen a side of her he couldn't
normally see. And if he was being honest, he could probably go
six months just jacking off to the memory of that night if he
had to…but he knew if he said that, she would genuinely snap
on him.

"Don't worry about it. After twenty years of pining, you learn
how to go without," he said jokingly.

"…Oh, I see," she said, shrugging with irritation.

The conversation turned to chitchat, and as their office building came into sight, Nagi yawned.

"Didn't get enough sleep?" he asked

"Oh… No, not quite."

That was unusual. She had always loved to sleep and rarely
stayed up late.

"Did something happen?" he asked, slightly worried.

"Nothing big," she said, laughing a little reluctantly. "I was just
catching up on some work last night."

"You took work home? You're that busy?"

It was true she always seemed strapped for time, but as far as
he could tell, her schedule wasn't so tight she would need to work
on a Sunday. Could it be that she hadn't really had time to stay
at his place?

"Nah," she said, shaking her head. "I just had a couple of things
to finish."

She laughed it off, but it suddenly dawned on him that she
worked overtime almost every day. On late days, she stayed
almost until the trains stopped running, and on early days, she
still only left at nine. He'd almost never seen her go home at five.
He'd gotten used to staying late with her, but when he stopped
to think about it, wasn't she working a little too much?

"Hey, you stay late every day. Why not try going home early this week?" he said, concern in his voice. She smiled.

"Thanks for worrying about me. I'll do that."

He noticed his heart leaping at her easy smile. It was hopeless—he couldn't resist her. Would she get mad if he kissed her? They were out on the street, after all. She'd probably kick him into the road. Of course, if they were at his place, he could touch her as much as he wanted.

"Hey, Nagi, want to hang out again this—?"

"Good morning!"

Keigo jumped at the voice from behind him. He and Nagi turned around at the same time and saw Saotome, also on her way to work.

"May I join you two?" she asked.

"Of course!" replied Nagi, nodding.

"Yay!" Saotome grabbed her arm happily. "Ms. Yoroizuka, did you see yesterday's episode?"

"I haven't had a chance yet. But I recorded it and was hoping to get to it tonight."

He watched them out of the corner of his eye. As buddy-buddy as ever, it seemed. Saotome, still glued to Nagi's side, looked at him and grinned.

"Oh, I'm sorry, Mr. Yuuki. Am I getting in your way?"

Nagi probably hadn't caught the nastiness in her words. He'd been terrified of whatever vengeance she might wreak after he announced he was dating Nagi, but so far, she'd given no sign of doing anything. If she wasn't angry, then so much the better, but was it just his imagination, or was she flirting with Nagi in front of him a lot more often these days?

"Not at all. Your only opportunity to talk with Nagi is at the office, so go ahead and enjoy your little chat," he said as calmly as possible. Saotome giggled and returned the blow.

"Thank you for your thoughtfulness, but I sit right next to Ms. Yoroizuka at work. We have lunch together nearly every day. If you add it all up, I'm almost certain I spend more time with her than you do."

"Well, if you think about it, since I'm in the same office breathing the same air, I could say the same thing," he replied.

"I'm going to report what you just said to our boss as sexual harassment."

"Why?!"

"...Pfft, ha-ha-ha!"

For some reason, Nagi started chuckling as they continued to bicker.

"You two sure are good friends. I'm glad," she said.

Good friends? Us?

He threw a confused glance at Saotome. She was looking at him, equally baffled. After staring at each other for a few seconds, they both burst out laughing.

"Huh? Why are you two giggling all of a sudden?"

Nagi was peering at them suspiciously. She looked so funny, they both laughed even harder, unable to stop.

"No reason," Keigo said.

"It's nothing," Saotome added.

Their laughter melted away under the cool blue sky.

◆

"Hmmm... Thinking about the workers, I suggest we go with the plan that will be easier to implement instead of the cheaper one."

"Yeah, I agree."

"But if we go with that plan, the schedule will be pretty tight..."

Keigo and Nagi were sitting in a meeting space in one corner of the office, talking through a system they were going to propose to a client. Nagi was muttering away as she scrutinized the computer screen. Keigo liked to see her hard at work with a serious look on her face, especially since he knew how laid-back she was in her personal life. As he gazed at her, completely forgetting they were supposed to be having a meeting, her phone buzzed on the table.

"Go ahead," he said.

"Sorry," she replied, picking it up.

Since she handled multiple accounts, she got a lot of phone calls. Not just from clients, either. Saotome and various sales staff often came to her with questions. She always listened empathetically no matter how busy she was, which Keigo was sure everyone appreciated. On the other hand, he knew it must cut into her work time significantly. No wonder she had to work late so often.

He watched her as she talked, her expression serious. Once she'd finally hung up, she set her phone on the table and turned to him.

"Sorry to keep you waiting… Anyway, as I was saying…"

She stopped. Her phone was buzzing again.

"Sorry…," she said apologetically before answering.

"Yes, this is Yoroizuka. What, the numbers are off? Yes, yes… You're saying the figures from the automatic e-mails don't match up? …Yes, yes…"

Her voice was starting to sound troubled. Keigo looked up from the computer.

"I understand. I'll look into it today and get back to you…! Yes, I'm very sorry!"

She hung up.

"Everything okay?" Keigo couldn't help asking.

"Yes, it's fine…I think."

"…Hey, didn't you say you had a meeting after this?"

"…Oh, that's right!" she shouted and quickly began packing up her things. "Sorry, Keigo! Can we talk later?! I'm really sorry!"

"Wonder if she's really okay…," he mumbled as he watched her rush off.

◆

That night, in the hushed office, he went up to her as she worked at her computer.

"Nagi, look at the clock. It's ten already."

"Huh? Oh, it is!" she said, sounding genuinely surprised. She had seemed extra busy that day, running around from morning till night. As usual, they were the only two people left in the office.

"Remember what I said about going home early this week?"

"Oh yeah…," she said, apparently having forgotten. Her eyes darted around. "Ha-ha. Sorry. I can't believe how inefficient I am."

"I don't think that's the problem," he said, a little exasperated as he sat down next to her. "If you're in trouble, let me help. Is it about the call you got this morning?"

Since he'd stayed late with her, he was ahead on his own work. But she just shook her head cheerfully.

"Oh, I took care of that already."

"Then why are you working late?"

"Well, it took a little while to look into it, so I wasn't able to finish the work I planned to do in the afternoon."

"Then let me do the work from this afternoon."

"I'm almost done with it. You should go home. I feel so bad that you always stay late with me."

The message just wasn't getting through to her. Keigo quietly sighed. She smiled like everything was fine, but considering she worked this late almost every day, she had to be overloaded. And since she tried to take care of it all on her own, most of her colleagues didn't even notice.

"Listen, Nagi. If there's work you can delegate to other people, you should do that. If you don't, you're going to physically break down."

She must have picked up on his serious tone, because she stopped smiling.

"If you want me to go home earlier, then you need to go home earlier, too," he said. "Otherwise, I'll be too worried about you to leave."

He had to be a little sly in his wording. Nagi was so serious about her work, she didn't even know how to ease up. If he'd put it any other way, she probably wouldn't have listened.

"Nagi?"

She was staring silently at the floor. He peered at her face.

"…I'm sorry," she whispered. Then she looked up. "You're right. Let's get going!"

She shut down her computer and began gathering her things. Keigo sighed in relief.

"This can't be a one-time thing," he said, switching off the air conditioner and the lights.

"I know." She nodded. "This week, let's both get out of here as soon as the clock strikes five!"

She gave him an emphatic thumbs-up, then seemed to remember something.

"Let's do this right! How about we go for drinks the day after tomorrow? I know a bar that serves cheap beer on Wednesdays."

"Wow, you sure are enthusiastic all of a sudden."

Still chatting, they left the pitch-black office behind.

◆

Keigo didn't usually care for Thursday mornings, since it was still midway through the week, but on this Thursday morning he had a spring in his step. His pleas on Monday must have had an impact, because for the next two days, Nagi left work at five. Thanks to that, they'd been able to go out for a drink the night before, just the two of them, for the first time in ages. They hadn't stayed late, since the next day was a workday, but it had been fun to spend time together outside the office. And best of all…

Thanks for walking me home. Good night.

After tipsily thanking him for taking her home, she'd given him a quick kiss. It all seemed too good to be true. As Keigo waited for the office elevator, a grin spread across his face, and he didn't even bother to hide it.

"Morning, Keigo," came a relaxed voice.

He turned around. It was Ryou Yoroizuka, the president.

"Good morning!" he answered.

For some reason, Ryou gestured for Keigo to follow him. Wondering what was up, he walked with him into an empty corner of the hallway.

"Nagi told me you two started dating recently."

Apparently, she had done the proper thing and informed her uncle of their relationship. That was very like her. It made him happy to hear she was telling people they were dating.

"Oh…uh, yeah," he said, nodding vaguely.

"You look like a teenage girl!" Ryou said, his shoulders shaking with laughter. "Anyway, congratulations. Are things going well?"

"Fairly well. We've been doing some date-like things lately."

"Good. I was worried you might not get much time to spend as a couple, since she's so busy she's even working weekends."

"What?" Keigo asked in surprise. "What do you mean she's working weekends?"

Ryou seemed equally surprised by his reaction.

"She submitted a request to work both Saturday and Sunday, so I just assumed…"

Technically, employees were supposed to submit a request to the president if they wanted to work on weekends. That must be what he was talking about.

"Both days? When does that woman intend to rest?" Keigo muttered.

True, employees sometimes had to come in on the weekend to install a new system if those were the only days a client company was closed, but he didn't think that was the case this week.

"I was a bit worried myself, so I asked her about it," Ryou said, "but she insisted everything was fine…"

At last, it dawned on Keigo. Nagi was planning to use the weekend to catch up on the work she couldn't finish during the week. This wasn't what he'd meant when he told her not to stay late on weekdays.

He stormed into the office and found Nagi already there, working.

"Morning. Can I talk to you?" he said. She gave him a puzzled look.

"What's up…?" she asked, following him out of the office. He led her into a document room that hardly anyone used and got right to the point.

"I hear you're working both days this weekend."

He could see the muscles in her face tense. So Ryou had been right.

"…How do you know that?"

"I heard from the president," he answered stiffly.

"Ah… My uncle…" She awkwardly looked away. He could practically hear her thinking, *Damn, I forgot to tell him not to say anything.*

"Listen, Nagi. I was trying to say that you ought to cut back your overall workload, not that you should make up for the weekdays on the weekend."

He knew he sounded angry. She seemed to pick up on it, too, because she stared silently down at the floor. From the disgruntled look on her face, he gathered she wasn't going to swallow his advice meekly.

"Just give me the extra work. What's the job?" he asked sternly.

"…No, it really is fine!" she answered with abnormal cheerfulness. "If I do that, you won't be able to leave on time. Plus, if it's something I can take care of by coming in myself on the weekend, that's much better—"

"I'm telling you, that's the kind of thinking you need to change!" he shouted.

She flinched. As soon as he saw her wide eyes, he realized he'd gone too far.

"…Sorry," he said.

He was surprised by how much self-loathing he suddenly felt. It was crystal clear she was planning to work on the weekend because he'd told her to go home early during the week. She was simply trying not to worry him. It was his own fault for not predicting how she would react. She was his girlfriend, not his possession. His wishes didn't dictate her actions, and he didn't have the right to push his ideas on her.

"Listen," he said, taking a deep breath to calm himself before continuing. "Like I said before, I'm worried you're going to push yourself so hard you end up getting sick. Please don't try to do everything yourself. Lean on me a little."

Keigo felt a unique sense of purpose in his work. Knowing that the systems he created supported the lives of countless strangers was the special privilege of being a creator. But a lot of people in the field worked until they physically broke down and then quit. Keigo was sick with worry that Nagi would eventually reach her limit, too. The same had been true during the incident with Kojima. Just before the deadline for the Yummy Foods account, Nagi's team had been sucked into a bad situation thanks to a mistake on Kojima's part, and she had tried to fix everything herself. In the end, Keigo had butted in and averted disaster, but the incident was symbolic of Nagi's best—and worst—personality traits.

"I love to see you enjoying your work, and I love that you put your all into it. But what I want most is to see you truly happy."

She mattered more than anything to him. He wouldn't trade her smile for the world. People could call him an idiot all they wanted, but she meant everything to him.

"Would you worry this much about someone else?"

Her chilly voice broke the silence.

"What...?"

For a second, he didn't understand what she was saying. Just as he was about to ask what she meant, she shook her head and smiled.

"…I'm sorry, never mind. Can I take you up on that offer of a little help?"

Her smile was perfect—it was like she'd flipped a switch. Had he gotten through to her, or…? An indescribable unease lingered in his chest, but in the end, he simply nodded.

"Of course," he said.

"Thank you," she replied, her eyes crinkling into a smile. It was an apologetic expression, but one he was used to. Relieved, Keigo glanced at his watch. It was almost time for work to start.

"You have a meeting with a client this afternoon, right?" he asked.

"Yeah." She nodded, then stiffened. "Um…I might be a little late getting back…"

She sounded hesitant, like she was trying to gauge his reaction.

"I'll wait for you. We can go home together," he said as kindly as possible. She grinned like she was relieved.

"Ha-ha, thanks. I'll hurry back as soon as it's over."

Moved by her earnestness, he patted her head. She smiled happily, and he did, too.

"Do you think you can get away without coming in on the weekend?"

"Yes, thanks to you. I'll withdraw my request."

As he watched her smile and stroked her hair, a selfish thought rose up inside him. He wanted to ask if she would come stay at his place again this weekend. But asking her to stay two weekends in a row sounded greedy even to him. They had all the time in the world ahead of them. But just as he convinced himself to give up, she tugged on his sleeve.

"Hey, Keigo. Would it be okay if I come hang out again?"

"Huh?"

"Oh… You're busy?"

"…No, I'd love for you to come."

He wondered how well he'd be able to hold back this time.

Imagining himself forced through another ascetic trial, he was filled with a complex mixture of happiness and self-pity.

◆

"Mr. Yuuki, I'm going home now."

"Good work today. Take care on your way home."

Keigo glanced at the clock as he watched Saotome leave the office. It was after eight. He was now the only one left.

"That meeting sure is taking forever…"

Just as the thought crossed his mind, a message from Nagi dinged on his phone. It read, I'm on the train back right now, followed by a picture of a rabbit with its paws pressed together apologetically. He laughed, then replied, No worries, take it easy.

As he stretched and took a deep breath, he suddenly remembered their conversation that morning.

Would you worry this much about someone else?

Sometimes she said things that really cut. She was right. In part, he was so worried because it was her. Now, thinking about it calmly, he felt like he understood what she was trying to say. He was pretty sure she hated when he treated her differently than everyone else at work. If that was true, then even though she'd agreed to delegate some of her work to him this time, if left alone, she would probably go on accepting more and more work herself.

So what to do? He wanted to keep interfering, but if he went too far, he would just end up pushing her away. He thought for a moment, then abruptly looked up. His computer screen was glowing dully before him.

"…"

He looked around to make sure no one else was in the office, then slowly reached for the keyboard.

Fifteenth Try

It was lunchtime, and Nagi and Saotome were walking down the busy hallway toward the elevator. Saotome, a few steps ahead of Nagi, turned the corner and stopped short.

"…Sorry!"

Keigo had almost slammed straight into her. He stepped aside and allowed the pair to pass.

"You two going out to lunch?" he asked. They were both wearing their coats.

"Yeah, we're headed to a café nearby. We heard they have a limited-time-only fruit sandwich special."

"Would you like to join us, Mr. Yuuki?" Saotome asked. Keigo smiled wryly and shook his head.

"Nah, I just picked up something at the convenience store. Have fun, though."

"I see. Maybe next time, then."

"Let's go," Nagi said, walking past Keigo.

"Oh, Nagi," he suddenly said. She stopped.

"It's still cold out there. Take this."

He wrapped his gray scarf around her neck. As the smell of fabric softener grazed her nose, the memory of him holding her came flooding back. She could almost feel his touch.

"Be careful," he said, lightly placing his hand on her head. Then he started back toward the office, completely ignoring her flaming cheeks. Ever since he scolded her for staying late, he had been acting overprotective like this. She had stayed at his place again last weekend, and he'd stubbornly insisted on cooking for her and cleaning up afterward all by himself, saying she must be tired. She'd spent the weekend like a princess, doing nothing for herself other than bathing and using the toilet, which she had to admit *was* relaxing.

Can I kiss you a little?

When she'd agreed, he'd ended up giving her the kind of kiss that takes quite a lot of time and energy—with a little teasing thrown in. She blushed as she remembered everything that had happened.

"Is something going on with you lately?" Saotome asked as they continued toward the café.

"What? Wh-why?" Nagi answered, floundering in response to the candid question.

"I don't know…just a feeling."

Saotome giggled, but whether she noticed Nagi was flustered or not, she didn't say anything more. Nagi still hadn't told Saotome that she and Keigo were dating. There were two reasons. First, she didn't want Saotome to feel uncomfortable working on a team with the two of them. Second, she had thought for a while that Saotome was interested in Keigo. After Saotome admitted that the love hotel incident was a misunderstanding, she had said straight-out, "I'm not interested in Mr. Yuuki romantically." Even though Nagi knew she had simply misread the situation, she couldn't entirely shake her awkwardness about it all and still hadn't managed to bring up the topic of her relationship.

That said, she felt it would be unfair to Saotome to keep her in the dark forever. She gathered her courage.

"…Actually, Keigo and I are dating," she blurted out before glancing at the other woman. Saotome's big eyes were even wider than usual. It must have hit her hard after all. Growing anxious, Nagi hurriedly apologized. "I'm sorry for not saying anything."

"So you *are* dating! I knew it!" she said, sounding surprisingly nonchalant.

"You knew?"

"Seeing the two of you together these days, it's hard not to notice. I was wondering when you'd tell me."

She stuck out her tongue adorably. Nagi couldn't believe Saotome had known all along. She felt deflated.

"Congratulations," Saotome said with an ear-to-ear grin.

"Heh-heh… Thanks," Nagi said back, smiling weakly. For some reason, she felt a wave of relief wash over her.

"Now, go ahead and boast about it."

"What?! Our relationship is so ordinary. There's nothing to boast about!"

The two of them continued in a joking tone until suddenly Nagi's phone started buzzing. She looked at the display. It was a call from Yummy Foods. Everything had been going smoothly with their site since it was handed over, and she hadn't heard from them in a long time. Wondering what was going on, she picked up the phone. A panicked voice answered.

"Ms. Yoroizuka! I just sent you an e-mail, but you didn't reply, so I went ahead and called…"

"I'm sorry, I'm away from my desk right now… What's the matter?"

"None of our online sales web pages are visible!"

Nagi's stomach dropped.

"No matter how many times we press Refresh, it's all white. Can you please look into it right away?!"

"Of course! I'll go back to the office right now and see what's happening!"

When she hung up, Saotome asked her worriedly, "Is everything okay?"

"Um…it sounds like the Yummy Foods site isn't visible."

"What? Really?!"

It made sense that they would panic. If customers couldn't access an e-commerce site and buy what they wanted, they would most likely go to another company's site. That meant Yummy Foods was losing money by the second. Nagi would have to look into what was happening, and on the off chance it was Sync.System's fault, the company might have to pay for those losses.

"Sorry, I've got to get back to the office! Do you mind getting lunch by yourself…?"

"Of course not! I'll bring back a sandwich for you!" Saotome said firmly.

"Thanks!" Nagi shouted as she reversed course at full speed. By the time she opened the office door, she was panting hard.

"Hey, Nagi," Keigo said as she came in looking exhausted. He must have been in the middle of lunch, because there was a bottle of tea and two rice balls on his desk. "The Yummy Foods site is back up."

"What?! No way, reall—*cough, cough!*"

She'd run so hard that the shock had sent her into a coughing fit.

"Calm down," Keigo said, patting her back. When her breathing returned to normal, he showed her his monitor. "See?"

The website that had supposedly vanished looked completely normal. She tested it out with a few simple commands, and everything was fine.

"I checked everything, and there doesn't appear to be a problem with the system itself. They're using a rental server, and another user probably did some processing that took up a lot of bandwidth. I went ahead and reviewed the tuning on the database and found a spot probably causing a bottleneck. I've already fixed it and sent you the details in a chat message. You can take a look later."

All Nagi could manage in response to this brisk explanation was an embarrassed "Thank you…" She should have expected as much from Keigo. He was so fast, it was actually a little scary.

"You don't need to tell the client?" he asked.

"Oh, right!" she said, quickly pulling out her phone. When she told them the system was already working again, instead of being mad, the Yummy Foods employee thanked her for her quick work.

"Nice job," Keigo said after she hung up.

"Seriously, thank you… You did everything."

Thanks to his quick response, the damage had been minimized. But how had he found out about the problem to begin with? As she was wondering this, her stomach grumbled loudly. She apologized, her voice barely audible.

"No time to eat?" Keigo asked, suppressing a laugh.

"No…I came back when I got that call."

"No wonder you're hungry. Here, have this. I haven't taken a bite yet," he said, chuckling as he held out a rice ball. Nagi wanted to turn down the offer, but she was so hungry she gave in to his kindness.

"I'm sorry to keep leaning on you for everything… Saotome is bringing me a sandwich later, so how about I trade you that for this?"

"Seriously?" he said, laughing.

As they munched on their rice balls together, Keigo's phone started buzzing.

"Oh, it's Yuuma," he muttered. Nagi looked up. Yuuma Saeki was a high school friend of Keigo's, and Nagi had been in the same class with them.

"Hello. What's up? …Ha-ha, I know… This month, right?"

Keigo's casual demeanor as he spoke to Yuuma over the phone was a little different from the way he was with her.

"So things are moving along, huh? Uh-huh… Really? …I guess, but… Nagi, too?"

Keigo had sounded like he was enjoying the conversation, when his eyebrows suddenly drew together in surprise. At the sudden mention of her name, Nagi stopped chewing her rice ball.

◆

"Look, cherry blossoms!"

"Are they blooming?"

"Yeah, but I don't think they're all the way open yet. I couldn't see very well in the dark," Nagi said, turning away from the evening landscape outside the train window. It was the end of March, and the biting cold of winter had started to ease. They were headed home on the train, Keigo dressed in a suit and Nagi in a matching tulle top and skirt.

"Wasn't Yuuma's wife pretty? Her dress looked perfect on her," Nagi said.

"He kept bragging about how good a cook she was, too."

Keigo's friend Yuuma had gotten married earlier that day. Keigo had attended the afternoon ceremony, and since Yuuma had heard he and Nagi were dating, he'd invited her to the after-party as well. Nagi smiled to herself, remembering the way all of Keigo's high school friends had teased him.

"It sure seems like a pain to figure all this stuff out, though," he said, gesturing to the wedding favor on his lap.

"I know. I heard you have to give different presents to suit each guest."

"I've heard that, too. Like, some people have separate presents for relatives and coworkers...even for friends of the bride versus the groom. That's so much work," Keigo muttered as he peered into his bag. All of a sudden, he seemed to remember something. "Hey, didn't Nae say on New Year's Eve she wanted a new toaster?"

"...Maybe, I can't really remember."

"Let's bring her this," he said, holding up the favor bag. Apparently, he intended to give it to Nagi's mom.

"Are you sure? You really don't need to."

"Thanks to all these weddings lately, I actually have three wedding favor catalogs lying around that I still need to order from."

"I feel you...," Nagi murmured.

"Let's stop at your mom's house, then, okay?" Keigo said, smiling. "I know she'll be happy to see you."

"Okay, thanks."

They got off at the station near Nae's house and walked side by side through the cool spring night. Probably because he knew Nagi was wearing higher heels than usual, Keigo was walking extra slowly.

"Keigo?" she suddenly said. "Thanks for always thinking of my mom."

She had been really touched when he'd said her mom would be happy to see her. After her father died, it was thanks in large part to the support of the Yuuki family that the two of them had managed to get by. His whole family had been simply amazing.

"...I was thinking," Keigo said quietly. "If we stay together..."

"Yeah?"

"I don't know if we'd want to live in an apartment or set up a house, but if it's okay with you and Nae, I was thinking it would be great if the three of us could live together."

Nagi stopped walking and turned to Keigo. He was smiling, a gentle look in his eyes.

"She must be lonely all by herself in that house, and wouldn't you worry less if she was with us?"

Nagi was dumbstruck, partly from happiness but mostly from shock. She'd had no idea Keigo was thinking that far into the future. Although she lived on her own right now, she'd planned to eventually either move back home or get a larger apartment that her mom could move into. But she'd always wondered whether, if she got married, her future husband would take well to the idea of living with her mother. That worry had loomed over every relationship she'd had since her father died.

"What? Really, you wouldn't mind?" she asked Keigo in disbelief.

"Of course not," he answered, still smiling. "I'm obviously going to care about the person the person I care about cares about."

"I'm starting to lose track of who cares about who!"

"Point taken," Keigo said, chuckling. "Come on, let's go."

He held out his right hand.

"…Thanks, Keigo. I mean it."

She twined her fingers in his—she was being totally honest. Happiness welled up inside her, and she almost started crying. Keigo didn't say anything, but he squeezed her hand. It seemed like he understood.

They held hands as they walked through the neighborhood. When they passed their elementary school, she saw that the cherry blossom tree on the grounds was starting to bloom, floating like a peach-colored cloud in the dark. Although it was still a little chilly at night, lately she could feel the distinctive, soft warmth of spring. Nagi felt like the New Year had just passed, but it was already almost April. Which reminded her…

"Hey, Keigo! Isn't your birthday this Saturday? Is there anything special you want to do?"

Last year on her birthday, Nagi had managed to turn in the Yummy Foods project, and Keigo and Nae had treated her to dinner on a different day. She'd been thinking about how to repay the favor over the past few weeks. Right now, her plan was to do whatever Keigo wanted in the afternoon, then have dinner at a good restaurant and give him his present. She was surprised by how excited she was about spending his birthday together as a couple for the first time.

"Hmm…," he said, thinking it over.

"What is it? Anything is fair game!"

"Well, actually…*cough*."

She followed his gaze ahead of them and saw his mother standing outside Nae's house, smiling knowingly. She must have come over for a visit as usual. Keigo and Nagi instantly dropped hands, but it was too late.

"Caught you," his mother said, grinning with genuine amusement. Ignoring their panic, she rang Nae's bell.

"Nae! You won't believe it! Keigo and Nagi are here, and they were holding hands!" she said loudly enough for the whole neighborhood to hear.

"Stop it, Mom!" Keigo shouted.

"And you stopped by to give it to me? Thank you so much," Nae said happily, setting cups of tea in front of Nagi and Keigo as they sat side by side at the dining table.

"So? How long have you been dating?" Keigo's mom asked with a grin. She was sitting across from them with her chin in her hand. Keigo scowled.

"A little more than two months."

"You should have told us! It's your duty to your parents, after all."

"I've never heard of that duty... You're the last person I wanted to find out!"

"My, how impertinent! I think I'm going to tell Nagi about all the embarrassing things you used to say in your sleep."

"I'm sorry, Mom. Please don't do that."

Nagi laughed at their usual back-and-forth. Nae was laughing, too, but then she suddenly glanced into a Japanese-style room a little ways away.

"I'm sure your father is happy about this," she said.

Nagi's father was smiling kindly from his photograph in the shrine there. Just as her mom had said, Nagi felt like her father must be happy she was dating the boy he'd doted on like a son. Warmth filled her, and she grinned.

"By the way," Keigo's mom said, apparently having grown bored of teasing her son. "When's the wedding?"

Nagi choked on her tea. She shook her head vigorously as she wiped her mouth.

"No one's talking about a wedding! We just started dating! We're not ready for that, are we, Keigo?"

She turned to him for confirmation, then froze. He was staring at her in surprise. As she wondered how to interpret his expression, it gradually shifted to suspicion.

"...I thought you said you wanted to get married by the time you were thirty!" he said.

Her jaw dropped.

"What?! When did I say that?!"

She racked her brain, but she couldn't remember ever saying such a thing to him.

"When we were in our second year of high school."

"Our second year of high school?! How am I supposed to remember that?!"

She was already twenty-eight. That might be possible for Keigo, who had an unusually good memory, but normal people did not remember conversations from ten years ago. Strangely, Keigo seemed even more shocked than she was. He fell silent, and the three others watched him in confusion. What was going on? In the midst of the abruptly chilly atmosphere, Keigo stood up from his chair.

"...If you don't remember, it's fine. Let's get going. Ms. Nae, thanks for the tea."

He began gathering his things without looking at Nagi, then headed for the front door.

"Hey, wait! —Sorry, Mom! I'll come over again soon!"

After shoving her feet into her high heels, she ran out the door. Keigo was waiting for her, but as soon as she appeared, he strode off.

"Um...Keigo?" she called, running after him. He seemed upset and didn't answer. "Hey, Keigo? I'm talking to you!"

"..."

"Slow down!"

Losing patience, she grabbed his arm and forced him to stop. He turned silently toward her. His eyes were cold. Growing slightly scared, she whispered, "Sorry."

Timidly, she continued.

"Um...could it be you were...thinking seriously about getting married?"

What if he'd remembered her saying she wanted to get married by the age of thirty all this time and had been planning to make it happen?

"...If you don't remember, it's fine."

He didn't say yes or no, but his answer was more than enough for Nagi. She said nothing. Maybe she should have apologized some more, but she didn't feel like *sorry* would cut it.

"Honestly, please forget about it," he said quietly as she looked at her feet. "I'm a weirdo for remembering something you said more than ten years ago. But..."

She waited, but he didn't finish. She raised her eyes meekly and gulped.

"Keigo..."

His expression was so heartbroken, she could barely stand to look at him. She felt like her own heart was being ripped in two, but she knew he was in even more pain than she was, so she didn't say anything.

"Is it okay if we just go home?" he asked.

".........Yes."

They started walking along silently and didn't say another word the whole way back.

Sixteenth Try

"So that means for bugs number ten and twenty-five, the real problem is in this common function, so we'll need to start by fixing that to get at the root issue."

"That makes sense... But I wonder if we can still make the deadline if we start on that now..."

Keigo and Nagi looked at the monitor on her desk as they talked. They were finally getting ready to hand over the system that Acsis—the apparel shop—had ordered that winter, and they were now in the last stage of testing.

Once they'd sorted out the issue at hand, they fell silent for a moment.

"...Um, Keigo, I wanted to say...," Nagi began, thinking this was her chance.

"Right, I'll get back to work," Keigo said at the same time, before striding over to his desk. Another failed attempt. She stole a glance at him as he started typing, then sighed.

Five days had passed since Saturday night when they'd stopped at her mom's house, and it was already Thursday. The work week was almost over. Surprisingly, Keigo had acted like nothing happened on Monday. She had faintly hoped he was over it, but outside of work, he hadn't said a word to her. When they met in the hall, he avoided her, and at five, he went straight home. When she tried to talk to him while they were working, he shrugged her off. His birthday was only two days away, on Saturday. He hadn't even told her where he wanted to go or what he wanted to do. On the other hand, that could be her chance. No matter how stubborn he was, he couldn't avoid talking to her in the middle of their date on Saturday.

Anyway, the first thing she needed to do was apologize and get him to forgive her. Then she would go all out celebrating his birthday. That way, she could pay him back at least a little for everything he'd done for her.

"Sorry, Nagi, I forgot to ask you something," he suddenly called out to her from behind. She jumped up.

"Y-yes! What is it?"

"I'm sorry for the short notice, but can I have a paid day off tomorrow?"

She couldn't believe her ears.

"If we're too busy, I understand," he added.

"Um…it's completely fine as far as the schedule goes, but…," she began, flustered. Since she was team leader, she managed his schedule. "…Did something come up?"

For Keigo, who was probably the worst in the company at using his paid days off, this was an unusual request.

"Yeah, kind of."

"Oh, I see…"

Her resolve abruptly withered. She had been hoping he would let her stay over at his apartment on Friday night so they could start celebrating his birthday at midnight.

"Um…you're still free on Saturday, right?"

She assumed she didn't even need to ask, but she did so just in case.

"Actually," he said, "I'm busy until late on Saturday. I have a commitment I just can't get out of."

She couldn't believe her ears.

"What?"

She stared at him, taken aback.

"Sorry" was all he said.

It occurred to her that the previous Saturday, when she'd asked what he wanted to do on his birthday, he'd hesitated. *Hmm.*

Maybe this explained his strange reaction back then. Still, what commitment could he possibly have on his birthday? She desperately wanted to ask him but couldn't work up the nerve. He was free to make whatever plans he wanted, and it was her own fault for not arranging an official date with him.

"Oh, okay! When will you be free? I'd love to meet up with you when you're done," she said, trying to sound casual but hoping at the very least they could have dinner together.

"Probably around nine."

She couldn't help tensing up. That meant he was busy for the entire day.

"If you want to meet, can we do it after that?"

It wasn't like she could change anything by saying no.

"...Sure," she said, nodding apathetically.

Nagi stared at her phone and held her breath as she rode the last train home on Friday night. It was 11:59 and fifty-six seconds... fifty-seven, fifty-eight, fifty-nine. When the time changed to midnight, she hit Send on a message she'd written to Keigo reading Happy birthday. Her heart was pounding as she watched the screen, but even after a few minutes, there was no "message read" notification. She finally gave up and put her phone back in her bag before sinking into a seat. It had been a crazy day. Her mind had been so full of various thoughts on Thursday that she hadn't slept at all, and when she got to the office and saw Keigo's empty seat, she felt even more depressed. She was too tired to get much work done, and with the usual phone calls about this or that thing going wrong, she'd ended up staying till the last train. Plus, since she still hadn't completed her work, she had to bring her company laptop home to finish it over the weekend.

"...*Sigh.*"

She looked around. Everyone else seemed to be on their way home from drinking, relieved that the work week was over. Even though a lot of the other passengers were by themselves, too, she felt keenly alone. It was probably because she'd been taking the train home with Keigo lately. When she remembered his face, it felt like her heart was being twisted.

She was supposed to be with him right now. At the very least, she'd wanted to say "Happy birthday" in person, instead of via text message.

The two women sitting next to her got off the train, and three young guys got on and collapsed into the seats the women had just left.

"…And so I told her, 'Don't you think it's pointless clawing up every last yen like that?'" one of them was saying.

"Man, that's harsh," said his friend, guffawing along with the third man.

Nagi could smell the alcohol and oily food on them. There were always a lot of drunks on the last train on Friday night, but since at the moment she was not only sober but sleep-deprived, the smell of alcohol turned her stomach more than usual.

She leaned back in her seat and closed her eyes. As she breathed in and out in the dark, the noise around her faded. The rhythmic rocking of the train was so soothing. Her body sank into the seat, her exhausted mind freed from all its worries.

"…So whadda we do now? I want a new watch."

"…You know, that tablet last time brought in a nice pile of cash… Hey, look at that."

"…Hold on, let's watch her for a little while longer…"

Nagi drifted into a sound sleep, the conversation next to her no more than white noise in her ears. Red, yellow, green…brilliant fall leaves splashed against a blue sky in her mind's eye, swaying in the wind. Keigo was next to her. Instead of a suit, he was wearing a navy blazer. His high school uniform—how nostalgic. They were walking home from school side by side. She'd forgotten about it for a long time, but she'd loved watching the seasons change on that tree-lined road.

I think it must be a special relationship, Keigo said. His voice sounded more youthful than it did now. What were they talking about? She tried to remember, but the memory was like an empty hole she couldn't fill up.

A special relationship? she repeated.

He nodded.

More special than being old friends or boyfriend and girlfriend. The kind of special you take for granted.

What was this memory?

"Miss, miss! This is the last stop."

Shaken awake, Nagi opened her eyes with a start. There were blue seats, an institutional-looking door, and the faint smell of alcohol. She blinked, unsure where she was.

The last stop? As soon as the meaning of those words hit her, Nagi whipped her head around. Outside the window was the name of an unfamiliar train station. She had slept far past her own stop.

Flustered, she stood up. A powerful feeling of unease overtook her. She looked fearfully down at her seat.

"My computer… It's gone."

She was in shock. There was nothing there but an empty seat.

◆

"…I see. Thank you."

She nodded listlessly and hung up the phone, tormented by hopelessness. The station had just called to inform her that no computers had been turned in to the lost and found. She glanced at the wall clock. It was two PM. Over twelve hours had passed since her laptop was taken. When it happened, she had called the department head immediately to tell him, filed an incident report with the police, and then spent the rest of the night searching for it. But it wasn't so easy to find a missing laptop in the big wide world, and she had finally given up and returned home a little while earlier. The police seemed suspicious of the men who had been sitting next to her, but since there was no evidence, they couldn't take immediate action. To make matters worse, they said it was extremely rare for possessions to be recovered in cases like this. All she could do was spiral further into despair.

She buried her head in her hands. It wouldn't have been so bad if they'd taken her purse or her wallet. The big problem was the fact that a computer containing confidential client information was missing. It was password protected, of course, but someone with decent computer skills could simply remove the hard disk and extract the data directly. If that happened, it would be an absolute nightmare. The company would lose client trust and could face harsh public criticism for failing to teach its employees proper safety precautions. It would be just like what happened to her father...

"Bleh!"

Overcome by nausea, Nagi ran to the bathroom and threw up everything in her stomach. She hadn't eaten anything since lunch the previous day, so only gastric juices came up, but before she realized it, she was crying from the merciless waves of nausea.

"...Gah..."

Nagi moaned and gripped her stomach, which seemed about to turn itself inside out. What would she do if the computer wasn't retrieved? What if someone figured out the password and used client information for criminal purposes? What if the media got wind of it and they had to pay monumental damages? What if Sync.System went bankrupt and her coworkers ended up homeless? If that happened, how in the world would she take responsibility?

A chill ran down her spine. Just then, her phone, which she had left in her pocket, started vibrating. Her heart pounded when she saw the name on the display. It was Ryou. He must have heard what happened from the department head.

Gripped with fear, she answered the call.

"Nagi! They found it!" he shouted.

"What?" was all she could manage in response.

"Uncle Ryou!"

Ryou stood to greet her as she came running into his office. After receiving his call, she'd rushed out of her apartment with nothing but the clothes on her back.

"D-did they really find it?!"

"This is it, isn't it?" he said, holding out a laptop to the panting Nagi. Suppressing her excitement, she logged in with her password. The familiar desktop appeared. It really was hers.

"I-I'm so glad…"

All the strength drained from her body, and she sank to the ground, profoundly relieved. Then she leaped to her feet again and bowed deeply to Ryou.

"I am extremely sorry for causing so much trouble with my careless behavior! I am ready to accept any punishment you feel is appropriate."

She knew exactly how serious a mistake this was. It wouldn't be unusual for an employee to be fired for something like this, and at the very least, they could expect to be demoted or have their salary cut.

"Nagi. Please look at me."

But strangely, when Ryou placed his hand on her shoulder, she sensed no anger in it.

"Everyone makes mistakes. This time we were fortunate that no confidential data was stolen. You don't need to beat yourself up over it, although I'll probably need you to prepare a written apology. Anyway, just don't do the same thing again."

Was that really enough? She hadn't done it on purpose, but there was no question her lack of vigilance was to blame for the incident.

"By the way," Ryou said, breaking into her uncertain thoughts.

"The police said the thieves were university students and probably repeat offenders. Apparently, one of them knew about computers, and when the police showed up, he was in the process of extracting the files. Of course, Keigo was one step ahead of them."

"Did you say Keigo?" Nagi asked, confused.

"Go ahead and open up any of those files," Ryou said, pointing to the monitor.

She had no idea what purpose that would serve, but she did as she was told.

"Huh?"

A message reading This file is encrypted and cannot be opened appeared, and indeed, the file would not open. She tried a few more with the same results.

Had her laptop been infected with some strange virus? As she descended into panic, Ryou picked up his phone and made a call.

"...Hello. Yes, it's fine. Can you decrypt them now? Thanks. Talk to you later."

As she stared at him, astonished, Ryou turned back to her.

"Now try opening them."

She clicked a file that a moment ago had been impossible to open. Now it opened as usual.

"What's...going on?"

"Keigo found this computer for us."

Nagi had started to suspect as much, but it was still a shock to hear. How in the world had he found it when he had nothing to do with the entire incident?

"I told him what happened. I thought he might know some way to help us. He suggested that rather than locking the device right off the bat, it would be better to give the criminals some rope to hang themselves with, so I had him leave it operable for a little while and only remotely encrypt the important files."

It was true that if he locked the computer so it became unusable, the thieves were likely to give up and sell it off. On the other hand, if they thought confidential information was there for the taking, anyone familiar with computers would do their best to open the files. Keigo must have predicted that.

"While they were desperately attempting to decrypt the files, Keigo figured out their general location from the IP address. It was impossible even for him to pinpoint where they were, of course, so he spent the night searching for them...and thanks to his hard work, he was able to determine their address and inform the police."

Nagi hadn't slept in two days, and her brain was working slower than usual. But even so, she was able to understand at least one thing from all this explanation.

"So...I have Keigo to thank for everything...?" she asked haltingly.

"You do indeed," Ryou replied, nodding enthusiastically. "Make sure you thank him properly. I think he was with the police until just now and hasn't slept a wink."

Nagi glanced reflexively at her watch. It was already after three in the afternoon.

"But...I thought he said he had a commitment until late tonight that he couldn't get out of..."

◆

When Nagi rang the bell, the door opened right away.

"Coming! ...Argh."

As soon as he saw her face, Keigo made a rude sound of surprise.

"Uh... Aren't you kind of early?"

It was four. No wonder he sounded confused—they had agreed she would arrive at nine.

"Sorry. I know it's not the time I said, but I headed over anyway. Mind if I come in?" she asked, tilting her head.

"Um...can you wait a minute while I clean up?"

Looking a little panicked, he apologized and shut the door. A few minutes later, he was back.

"Sorry to keep you waiting."

"…No worries."

Nagi sat down at the low table in the living room. Keigo sat across from her and glanced around awkwardly. She was looking directly at him.

"My uncle told me what happened with the computer. Thank you so much. Because of you, we avoided disaster."

She bowed her head deeply.

"It was no problem, really," he said, shaking his head. "It was just…bad luck."

"No, it was my own fault," she countered flatly.

They were both silent for a moment. She might be imagining it, but Keigo seemed nervous.

"What about that commitment of yours?" she asked quietly. "I thought you said you'd be busy until tonight."

Keigo flinched. After a pause, and still looking away from her, he said, "Uh…it was canceled abruptly."

She'd had enough.

"Don't lie to me!" she snapped.

He glanced up like he'd been hit. She felt like she was looking him in the eye for the first time in ages. He seemed surprised, confused. She hadn't been expecting that.

"Are you mad because I didn't remember our conversation about getting married? You're right that I shouldn't have forgotten, but that's no reason to avoid me like this!"

After all, this was supposed to be a special day. She had wanted to hear him say how good the food was at the restaurant she'd found, see him smile as he opened his present, and hear him tell her how much fun he'd had at the end of the night. That's all it would've taken to make this day truly happy. So why had it turned out like this?

"It's your first birthday since we started dating! There won't be another our whole lives! Why did you say you couldn't meet until night? You sh-should have just told me if you didn't want to celebrate together!"

She hadn't only wanted to say "Happy birthday." She'd wanted to tell him all kinds of things. To thank him for everything. To say she was happy they were dating. To say she wanted to stay together.

"All I wanted in the world was to celebrate my special person's special day…"

She'd wanted to tell him how much she cared about him, after all these years of him caring so much about her.

"Nagi…"

Through her tears, she could see Keigo staring at her in astonishment. Probably because she'd just thrown a childish fit.

"…*Sniff*. S-sorry. That's all I wanted to say…"

Using her sleeve to roughly wipe away her tears, she quickly stood up. Now that she'd hurled all her anger at him, she suddenly regained her composure and began to feel embarrassed over her outburst. She grabbed her purse and turned toward the door without looking at him.

"I-I'll go home and come back again later…," she said.

She felt large fingers close on her right wrist. When she glanced over her shoulder, she saw Keigo gazing at her with a serious expression.

"Don't go," he said, pulling her back to the sofa. Ignoring her confusion, he headed over to the closet. When he returned a few minutes later, he was wearing a black suit with a properly knotted tie around his neck. Why was he wearing a suit, of all things? As she gaped at him, he gestured for her to follow.

"Sorry, Nagi, but would you mind coming with me?"

He took her hand and led her outside, then started walking to some unknown destination. She realized he was heading toward the train station. Was he intending to go to the office? On a Saturday?

She couldn't bring herself to ask him what was going on as he strode silently forward. When they reached the station, he paused.

"Mind if I stop here?"

They were in front of a florist that rented out a shop on the first floor of the building. She nodded, and he carefully stepped around the densely packed displays, before disappearing into the store. After she had looked at the flowers for a few minutes, he reappeared holding a bouquet. It was a subdued arrangement of blue flowers.

"Sorry to make you wait," he said, then headed for the ticket gates. They got on a train and rode for about twenty minutes before getting off. Right outside their stop was a large park with an athletic field and tennis courts next to it. Nagi visited that park without fail every year. Keigo walked right in without hesitating. She finally knew where they were going but thought it strange he would take her there on his birthday. Still, she followed him. The western sky glowed a deep red as he led her through the park. Maybe she was imagining it, but as they moved farther in and saw fewer and fewer people, she sensed his mood growing solemn.

Finally, they reached an expanse of gravestones. They were in the graveyard next to the park.

"Here we are."

Keigo stopped walking. The marker in front of them was engraved with the words YOROIZUKA FAMILY GRAVE. This was where Nagi's father's spirit had been laid to rest. Keigo squatted in front of the stone and gently placed the bouquet he'd brought on the ground.

"It's been a while, Uncle," he said, joining his hands in prayer. Nagi knew that although the Yuuki family wasn't related to the Yoroizukas by blood, they visited her father's grave every year on Obon.

"I came today to tell you something," he continued. "I'm dating your daughter."

A soft evening breeze ruffled the petals of the flowers in the bouquet. She remembered how she often used to bring her father flowers when she visited him in the hospital.

"I'm sure you realized it, but I've been in love with Nagi since before I can remember."

Whenever Nagi visited the hospital, her father would smile quietly at her while she told him what she'd been doing in school. There was always a bouquet of blue flowers, her father's favorite color, on the windowsill.

"For a long time, she didn't return my feelings—so long, in fact, that I started to have some doubts. But now she's accepted my selfish feelings and agreed to give me a fighting chance."

Now, he was talking to her father just like she used to, so long ago. Nagi gazed at him from behind as he kneeled before the grave, his back tall and straight.

"Still, I think it's inevitable that there will be times when we can't understand each other. When that happens, we'll probably argue."

His voice darkened slightly. Nagi felt the same. Now and then, for reasons both silly and serious, they would probably butt heads. Sometimes she might be hurt, and other times she might hurt Keigo.

"But even if we can't see eye to eye at times, I can say with confidence that I will never betray her."

Nagi knew how sad it felt when your values differed from those of the person you loved. It brought home that you were completely different human beings.

"No matter what happens, I will always protect your beloved daughter."

But maybe that wasn't necessarily a bad thing. After all, the reason fighting with Keigo was so painful was because of how much she cared for him.

"May I have your daughter's hand?"

A strong wind shook the trees surrounding them. Nagi closed

her eyes instinctively, then slowly opened them again. A moment ago, Keigo had been kneeling and facing her father, but now he was standing and looking at her. She had the feeling he had just said something incredible, but maybe she'd imagined it. The instant her eyes met his earnest gaze, though, she realized it had all been real.

"...So will you marry me?" he asked, holding out the paper bag he had been carrying since they left his apartment. "Please look inside."

Before she realized what she was doing, she had taken the bag. It felt heavy. She expected it to contain a ring, but—were rings this heavy?

Flustered, she pulled open the bag. *Huh?* There was a scrapbook inside. It was sturdily made, its wooden cover inscribed with intricate designs. As she flipped it open, her eyes widened. There was a photograph of a gracefully curved ring. Next to it was a handwritten note reading, Would definitely look beautiful on Nagi. They say the V-shaped design makes your finger look longer.

"Is this...?"

She turned the pages in a daze. Each one had a photograph of a ring and a handwritten note on it.

Stone will come out if knocked hard, but great design.

Not many design options, but solid post-purchase repair service.

This line includes wedding rings, so she could wear them together.

The album was filled to the very last page with clipped-out pictures of engagement rings and detailed comments.

"Um, what is this...?" she asked, closing the book.

"Please choose the ring you like," he answered nervously. Seeing that she still looked confused, he went on. "I thought that instead of me choosing one for you, you might prefer to make the final decision yourself. On the other hand, if I just said to pick any ring, you might have a hard time, so I went ahead and chose some I'd love to see you wear."

"...Why didn't you just give me a premade catalog?"

"Because they include prices, of course."

How like him to think of that. Half surprised and half impressed, she flipped through the book again.

"I thought you didn't like making stuff like this..."

If she remembered correctly, he had always done well in math, science, and gym and miserably in art and music.

"I worked on it every day when I got home, but for some reason, it still took me a month..."

Now it made sense why he'd been leaving work early recently. He must have been chipping away at it every night.

"Also, I have to apologize to you about one thing. I was planning to finish it by tonight, but it's not quite done... I'm sorry I'm such a clumsy oaf..."

"Is that why you took yesterday off?" Nagi asked, clapping her hands together. So *this* was the commitment he couldn't get out of.

"Yeah... I wanted to give it to you by the end of the day on my birthday no matter what."

"...Why?"

"Because I'm such a coward, I could never propose to you if I didn't use my own birthday as a deadline."

As Nagi watched his large form hunch over, she felt something rising in her chest.

"Bwah-ha-ha-ha!"

Keigo stared at her wide-eyed as she burst out laughing. Apparently, she found it so hilarious her eyes teared up, and she had to apologize to him between gasps for breath.

"I'm sorry, really... This is all just so unexpected...!"

She'd never heard of anything like this. Who would expect to be proposed to at a graveyard with a scrapbook instead of a ring?

"...I'm sorry," he said guiltily. "I overthought it to the point where this was the only thing I could come up with."

"That's not what I meant," Nagi said, still grinning from ear to ear. He could have proposed romantically in a restaurant with a view of the city lights, using a ring he'd chosen himself. Instead, he'd decided to let her choose the ring she would treasure her whole life. And before he did it, he'd stood in front of her father's grave and announced his intentions.

"Thank you, Keigo," she said.

She knew he'd thought long and hard to come up with a once-in-a-lifetime proposal, even though he was horrible at surprises. She could never express in words how happy that made her.

"...*Sniff.* Thank you..."

There were so many reasons for the tears that suddenly overflowed from her eyes. Even she couldn't name them all.

No matter what happens, I will always protect your beloved daughter.

She repeated the promise he had made to her father over and over in her heart. It made her so happy. Ever since the day her father died, she had lost the sense of security that comes with knowing someone will protect you no matter what.

A shadow fell across her vision. She looked up and saw Keigo standing right in front of her.

"You don't have to give me an answer right now," he said, softly wiping away her tears as she sobbed. What a fool he was. Didn't he know she already had her answer? She opened both arms wide and clasped them around his tense body as tightly as she could. She loved him. That thought came to her very clearly as she embraced him.

"If you'll have me, then yes, with all my heart!"

She was certain this wasn't a momentary feeling. One day, her passion would probably cool down enough that standing next to each other would feel completely normal. But when she imagined the emotions that would remain with her even then, she knew her place was with Keigo.

There might be a long road ahead of us, but if we're together, we'll be able to stay true to ourselves.

"...Of course. Thank you," he replied at last.

Against a breathtaking sunset, Keigo smiled like he was going to cry.

◆

Will you marry me?

Nagi had never guessed that one little promise would make her so happy, even though it didn't change the rest of her life at all.

"You certainly seem in good spirits lately, Ms. Yoroizuka."

At the sound of a voice from beside her desk, Nagi stopped her cheerful typing and looked over questioningly. Saotome giggled and pointed to her own cheek. Only then did Nagi realize she had been grinning like an idiot.

"S-sorry..."

"You don't have anything to apologize for. This is the happiest time of your life. It's only natural to smile!"

Nagi apologized again and tried to press her lips together, sure they would curve back upward if she wasn't careful. Two weeks had passed since Keigo proposed to her. Although they hadn't yet decided the details of their wedding or marriage registration, they wanted to keep things moving and had gone last week to tell their parents. Nagi couldn't help grinning when she thought back on how happy they had been when they heard the news. Keigo's parents had immediately said they wanted to celebrate and started cracking open beers, ignoring their son's protests that it was still daytime. Nae and Nagi had smiled and watched the usual Yuuki family antics before sneaking off to the Japanese-style room to toast by themselves.

Congratulations, Nagi. I wish you all the happiness in the world.

Nagi felt an odd mixture of sadness and joy as she watched

Nae's eyes fill with tears, and she cried a little herself. Then, earlier that week, they'd told Ryou and their department chief, as well as Saotome and Saiga. At first, it had felt like a dream, but as they went through the requisite steps, the word *marriage* began to feel real.

The happiest time of your life.

Saotome's words might be the perfect way to express the present moment. The buzz of the intercom brought Nagi, who was grinning once again, back down to earth. She hurriedly picked up the phone.

"This is Yoroizuka," came Ryou's mellow voice. "Sorry to bother you during work, but would you mind coming to my office?"

"Um...just me?"

"Yes, just you," he said.

Nagi put down the phone, stood up, and left the office. Whatever could he want? She assumed it had to do with the wedding, but in that case, he probably would have asked for Keigo as well.

She stepped into the president's office still lost in thought. Immediately, she saw two unfamiliar men sitting on the sofa. When they saw her, they stood up and held out business cards.

"Nice to meet you. I'm Sedani, from Houkoku Bank."

"I'm Matsushiro."

Confused, she took the cards, then did a double take when she saw the company name. Houkoku Bank was one of Japan's most prominent megabanks. Nagi was aware that bank representatives often visited the president's office, since bank loans were indispensable for running the company. But why would they need to talk to her?

"Nagi, come sit down over here."

Following Ryou's direction, she took a seat on the sofa across from Sedani and Matsushiro. The air of mystery was making her increasingly nervous.

"An employee here, Keigo Yuuki, has declined a job offer from our bank," Sedani said quietly, putting down his teacup.

Nagi had no idea what he was talking about.

"...Excuse me?" she said hoarsely, breaking the momentary silence.

"I'm sorry, Mr. Sedani. I haven't filled her in on the details," Ryou said as Nagi sat frozen, completely bewildered. Sedani nodded.

"Please allow me to explain," he said. "Our bank is currently transitioning our core system to a new one. We've been told that the transition will take almost seven years, so it is quite a significant project."

Nagi had heard about Houkoku Bank's core system transition project in the news. She had also heard that transferring core systems in banks was extremely difficult. Most banking systems were designed in the 1980s and '90s and had been operating for over twenty years by now, and in some cases almost thirty. During that time, new functions had been patched in and code rewritten many times without a break in operation, meaning most of these systems were incredibly overgrown. On top of that, since the systems were old, the engineers who made them were starting to retire, and none of the younger employees had a handle on the whole picture. This so-called "black box" problem was severe. To transfer a system like this, you first had to analyze the complicated patchwork of source code and come up with a cautious, detailed plan—all of which required a very high skill level. These factors combined to make bank system transfers particularly difficult. They were infamous in the IT world.

"The project was first conceived about six years ago," Sedani continued.

Nagi and Keigo would have been in their fourth year of university then. Nagi had only heard about Houkoku Bank's system transfer in the news recently, but apparently, it had been in the works for quite a long time. The lengthy period of media silence was probably a reflection of the bank's own caution surrounding the project.

"Around that time, Mr. Yuuki won the grand prize in a programming contest sponsored by our bank. Were you aware that he made a name for himself in distinguished programming contests starting in university?"

She had known that, even though he was in the humanities program, he had studied programming on his own and entered some contests on the recommendation of an engineering professor. She'd also heard rumors that he received some sort of prize.

"As contest judges, we had the opportunity to view his entry, and…frankly speaking, I was amazed by his ability. Normally, when you say a university student is gifted, there's still a limit to the kind of code they can produce. But Mr. Yuuki's code was perfect. Not just perfect—it was so cutting-edge it went beyond what we had envisioned."

There was a certain zeal in Sedani's words. Finding it odd, Nagi looked again at the business card he had handed her, and gulped. His title was printed in small letters at the top: MANAGER, CORE SYSTEM DEVELOPMENT DIVISION, IT SYSTEM UNIFICATION GROUP.

"At the time, we knew that we would be transitioning the core system in the near future, and we were looking for outstanding developers. Needless to say, Mr. Yuuki was our top candidate."

Nagi was finally starting to understand the situation.

"We knew how talented he was, and in the future, we wanted him to play a central role in the project," said Matsushiro, picking up where his colleague left off. "We approached him repeatedly about taking a job with the bank."

Nagi stared silently down at Matsushiro's business card, which read LEADER, HUMAN RESOURCES MANAGEMENT DEPARTMENT, PERSONNEL GROUP. She had completely misinterpreted who these men were. These weren't ordinary bank representatives. One was from the department that handled core systems engineering, and the other was from human resources. Judging by their titles, they were both fairly high-ranking.

"You want Keigo to join Houkoku Bank…?" she asked, her voice very quiet. Her heart was starting to pound unpleasantly.

Matsushiro nodded.

"Yes, but as a condition of taking the job, he said he wanted to gain experience at other companies for several years. We accepted that request and decided to keep an eye on his development until the official start of the system transfer project."

"And you're saying that time has come…?"

"That's right," Sedani said decisively. "When Mr. Yuuki joins our staff, we intend for him to take on a central role in the project. It will of course depend on his performance, but if he does well, it's likely that in the future he will be appointed head of system development—the same position your father held."

A shiver ran down Nagi's spine. She realized why her heart had been pounding so hard. Houkoku Bank had taken over Teitou Bank, where her father had worked as head of system development.

"…You know about my father?" she asked shakily. Sedani glanced down and nodded.

"We were colleagues. I worked on the core system at Teitou Bank."

Nagi gasped. All the dismal memories hidden deep inside her heart came flooding back as if a dam had been broken. Her father bowing his head in front of the exploding flashbulbs. Her father shut up all day in the house with stubble covering his chin. Her father's bony body lying on a hospital bed, staring up at the clear blue sky. Her father smiling eternally in a photograph surrounded by piles of flowers and the sound of chanted prayers.

She stood up with a clatter. Everyone in the room stared at her, their eyes wide.

"Are you going to tell Keigo to die this time?"

She was proud of herself for not shouting the words. That's how powerful her rage was in that moment. This was no joke. Wasn't her father enough for these people? Now they wanted to condemn Keigo to the same fate?

"Not at all," Sedani said. In contrast to Nagi, who was struggling to control her temper, the man from the bank remained extremely calm. "You work in the same field, so you probably understand that banking systems do not allow for even the smallest error. It's necessary to manage client information with the utmost caution and attention to detail. It would be no exaggeration to say that information is equivalent to our customers' lives. That's exactly why we want someone as talented as Mr. Yuuki involved in this project in a pioneering role. Don't you agree that will help prevent anyone in the future having to make the same sacrifice as your father?"

"I...," Nagi said, about to contradict him, but Sedani continued.

"This is what Mr. Yuuki himself wanted."

Shock quelled Nagi's explosive anger.

"...What?"

That couldn't be. She had never heard him say anything about this.

"It's true, Nagi," Ryou said. "Keigo has always wanted to work on banking systems."

Nagi stood rooted in place.

"Why...?"

"I couldn't say. You'll have to ask him. But for now, please sit down. You're treating these two gentlemen rudely," he said sharply.

She did as he asked, feeling ashamed, and bowed to Sedani and Matsushiro.

"...I'm sorry for getting upset."

"No, it's a completely natural reaction. I'm sorry we didn't explain things better," Sedani said, bowing his head in return. Glancing considerately at Nagi's downturned face, he continued in a serious tone. "It's just that, as I mentioned earlier, Mr. Yuuki has rescinded his acceptance of the job offer from our bank...

And that's what we came to speak with President Yoroizuka about today."

"It came as a surprise to me, since I always expected Keigo to eventually take a job at Houkoku. Nagi, do you know anything?"

She slowly looked up, only to find all eyes on her. She knew they wanted an answer, but she didn't know anything. To the contrary, she, more than anyone, wanted to ask Keigo why he'd declined the offer.

No matter what happens, I will always protect your beloved daughter.

The ray of light she had thought was illuminating her darkness flickered out so easily. Just like the irreplaceable human life that would never come back to her.

Seventeenth Try

Would you mind if I came over to your place?

The message from Nagi arrived just after eleven at night, as Keigo was getting out of the bath after work.

"Sorry to come over on such short notice."

When Keigo opened the door, she was standing there as motionless as the night itself. As he gestured for her to come inside, he noticed she was still wearing the same clothes she'd had on at eight when they left the office together.

"You haven't taken a bath yet? Did you eat?" he asked.

"Um...," she said vaguely, then grew quiet again. Finding this strange, he went to pour a hot cup of tea and set it in front of her.

"Thanks," she said, smiling brightly and wrapping both hands around the mug.

"...Is something wrong?" he asked, resting his chin in his hand. If something came up, she usually gave him a quick call or sent a text. It was unusual for her to come to his apartment like this. She set the mug down on the table.

"Today I met with some people from Houkoku Bank," she said quietly.

Silence filled the room. They stared at each other, the only sound the ticking of the second hand on the clock.

"...What?" said Keigo finally. "You talked...? But why?"

"They wanted to know why you turned down the job at the bank. Uncle Ryou was there...with Mr. Sedani and Mr. Matsushiro."

It was a shock to hear those familiar names coming from Nagi's mouth. He knew the two men well. Not only had they praised his entry in the bank's programming contest, but they had offered him a job at Houkoku Bank in the midst of a massive hiring slump. They had even gone along with his selfish request to spend a few years gaining experience in other fields, and they sent him thoughtful messages at regular intervals asking how his work was going and offering a sympathetic ear if he ever needed advice.

A month ago, he had made the painful decision to turn down the job with Houkoku. He had talked with them about it many times. They had humbly asked him to reconsider, and he had apologized profusely but told them his mind was made up. He thought they'd backed off—but now it seemed they'd pulled Nagi into it. The truth was, although he still had some regrets, he had felt like it was resolved. That was why he hadn't brought it up with her. Obviously, that had been a mistake, and now she'd found out in the worst possible way.

"...I'm sorry I didn't tell you," he said in a small voice.

She didn't say "That's fine" or even "How could you?" Instead, she said, "There's one thing I want you to tell me. Why banking systems, of all things?"

Her voice was so quiet, it was hard for even Keigo to make out the emotions behind it.

"If something happens, don't think you'll get away with a written apology. They'll put you in the news and treat you like a criminal. That's how my dad—"

"I know."

Maybe because he'd interrupted her, she slowly closed her mouth instead of finishing her sentence. Keigo understood very well what she was trying to say.

"I know," he repeated. "That's why I turned down the job. It's over, so let's just forget about it."

He knew that was an absurd way to dismiss the topic, but he didn't want to talk about it with her any further. There was a reason he'd kept quiet about it, and there was a reason he'd turned down the job. He had thought it through at great length himself and come to a decision.

"…"

Another dismal silence descended between them. He felt extremely uncomfortable.

"…Am I the reason you turned it down?" she finally mumbled.

"No!" he said, unconsciously rising in his chair. She stared at him with a strange composure. Under her gaze, which seemed intent on exposing every last emotion inside him, he finally surrendered.

"…I'm sorry," he said. "You're right."

Even after he admitted this, he felt her gaze continuing its harsh interrogation. He let out a long breath and gave in.

"Once the project began at Houkoku Bank, I knew I'd be super busy. I wouldn't be able to see you much, and I knew you'd worry about me. Plus…"

"If you leave our company, you won't be able to protect me like you have until now?" Her voice had an obvious coldness to it. "You put surveillance software on my devices, didn't you?"

This question, even more than the last one, froze him to his core. He was at a loss for words.

"I knew it," she muttered. "I thought it was odd. When the problem with the Yummy Foods site came up, you responded before I told you about it, and when my laptop was stolen, you were able to operate it remotely. That would all be possible if you were monitoring it."

"…"

"I'd been wondering about it for a while, but when I heard about the Houkoku Bank situation, I knew for sure. If you were willing to give up a job like that for me, then surveillance didn't seem out of the question anymore. I still couldn't believe it, but I poked around and found a program I didn't recognize. It was a real shock."

Everything she'd said was true. He had grown worried when

she started staying late at work every day and had installed a homemade surveillance program on her laptop under cover of a business e-mail. The software allowed him to view, from his own computer, not only the messages she got in her in-box but also the websites she visited, the files she opened, and even the location of her laptop. It also enabled him to remotely operate her computer. Concerned that she was working too much, he carefully monitored the data from her laptop to stay a step ahead of her.

That said, being concerned was hardly a justification for monitoring someone else's computer. He sat there as silent as a rock.

"Just as I'd expect from you," Nagi said with a half smile, "the program was very well hidden, and I had quite a hard time finding it. But I did manage to uninstall it, and I'd appreciate if you would refrain from putting weird software on other people's computers in the future."

At this point, there was nothing he could say to excuse his actions.

"I'm...s-sorry," he said almost inaudibly, his back as straight as if he were delivering a formal speech. He glanced timidly at Nagi. She was sitting wordlessly with her arms folded. He knew she must be mad, but for some reason, he couldn't find a trace of it in her expression.

"My uncle told me you've always wanted to work in banking systems."

"...Yeah."

That had been his dream, although she was the only person he'd never been able to tell.

"But now you're going to give it up and blame it on me?"

"I'm not blaming you. I'm doing it *for* you," he retorted. It might sound like they were arguing semantics, but to Keigo, the distinction was of utmost importance. "I think you've misunderstood, so let me say this. I don't blame you for any of this—not one iota, and if anyone says otherwise, I'll deny it with everything I've got. Even if everyone tells me I'm making a mistake, and even if it makes my whole life pointless, that's fine. I'd much rather see you at ease, with a smile on your face…"

"When exactly did I ask you to protect me that way?"

Her voice wasn't loud or rough. Nevertheless, Keigo's own stuck in his throat, and he was unable to say anything else. He realized something then. He had been completely wrong to think she wasn't angry.

"…Na…gi…"

She was furious. She might be the angriest he'd ever seen her. That was how cold and sharp her gaze was. It made him feel like hundreds of needles were piercing his skin.

"Nagi, listen to me!" He was shouting despite himself. "The whole reason I did this was because I care about you—!"

"Yes, I know," she interrupted calmly. "I can see how much you care for me."

She smiled—a smile so sad, Keigo felt like he was going to break down in tears.

"I'm sure that to you, I'm a precious, precious burden."

"Stop!" he said, jumping up and grabbing her shoulder. "Nagi, I'm begging you—don't talk like that! I turned down the job because I wanted to! It's not your fault! So…"

He wanted to say, "So don't despise me," but he couldn't, because he saw the tears falling silently from her eyes.

"…I'm sorry," she said. "Though I know it's already too late."

He couldn't bear to hear any more, but his ears continued to mercilessly absorb every word she said.

"If I'd known you would give up your dream because of me, I would never have let myself fall in love with you, and I would never have become your girlfriend. And…I would have said no when you proposed."

She kept saying sorry over and over. He didn't want to hear it.

He wanted to run away from this. But his gaze was riveted to her sobbing form, and he couldn't move.

"If I could rewind time, I would go back to just being your friend."

The look in her eyes was chillingly distant, as if the two of them had always existed in separate universes.

Eighteenth Try

Heavy. Her head was heavy. Her body was heavy. Her heart was heavy. Everything was heavy. It was a Monday in late April— a week before the Golden Week holidays—and Nagi could barely lift her feet as she headed to work.

If I could rewind time, I would go back to just being your friend.

Ever since Friday night when she said those words to Keigo, they hadn't been in touch. That night, she had ignored his pleas to stay and had gone home, practically running away. She had thought about apologizing many times on Saturday and Sunday, but she didn't have the courage to call him, and he didn't contact her.

Was this the end of their relationship? How had he interpreted those words, recklessly said at the height of her emotion? It was possible when he saw her that day at work, he would say he wanted to break up. She had imagined it incessantly over the weekend. Each time the thought ran through her mind, she felt like her heart was being crushed. But another part of her thought it might be best to end things. If they kept dating, she would probably only be a burden on him. Precisely because she cared about him so much, she wasn't confident she could live with that.

"Good morning."

The moment she stepped hesitantly into the office, she glanced at Keigo's desk. Fortunately, he wasn't there. It seemed he hadn't arrived yet. Strange—he was normally at work by this time. Nagi had just sat down at her desk, feeling slightly relieved, when Saotome called out to her.

"Ms. Yoroizuka, I wanted to ask you about Mr. Yuuki…"

"What? What about him?" Nagi asked, flinching.

"Is he all right? He seemed quite sick…"

"Huh? What are you talking about?"

"Oh, you didn't hear?" Saotome asked in return, sounding surprised. "He called the office a minute ago. He said he was staying home because he had a high fever. I assumed he'd already spoken with you…"

"No, I hadn't heard…but I might have missed his call."

She checked her phone, but there were no notifications on her home screen. Her heart dropped. Why hadn't he told her? He didn't have to call her first, but he could have at least let her know. He must be so mad he didn't even want to talk to her.

"A-anyway, thank you for telling me."

Nagi forced herself to smile. Maybe he would send her a message later. She made up her mind to stop obsessing over it and focus on work. After checking her phone once more—still nothing—and stuffing it into her bag, she turned to her computer and tried to clear her mind.

To make a long story short, Keigo never got in touch. The next day he stayed home again, calling the office to say he was still sick but not contacting Nagi directly.

"…Hmm…"

It was nine o'clock at night, and Nagi was staring down at her computer screen in the empty office. Since Keigo had taken time off work, she was handling the planning portion she'd intended to assign him, but it was complicated and not going very well.

She pressed her temples and soldiered on, but she eventually hit a wall and leaned back in her seat, staring at the ceiling. It was hopeless. She'd gone over it so many times she didn't know up from down anymore. Instead of struggling along by herself, it made more sense to ask Keigo's advice. She started to talk to him through the gap between their monitors.

"Hey, Keigo, can I ask you something…?"

Slowly, she closed her mouth. *That's right. Keigo isn't here.* That was why she was handling the planning in the first place. What was wrong with her brain? Fed up with her own spaciness, she flopped down on the desk.

If Keigo took the job with Houkoku Bank, would work be like this all the time? As she stared at his empty desk, loneliness washed over her. Belatedly, she realized she couldn't take his presence for granted.

The sound of her phone buzzing jolted Nagi out of her thoughts. Maybe it was Keigo. She pounced on her phone, then did a double take at the name on the screen.

"Hello, Nagi? Sorry to call you so suddenly. Are you still at work?"

It was his mom.

"Yeah, I'm still here. What's wrong?" she answered.

"I'm so sorry to ask you this, but would you mind bringing Keigo something to eat on your way home from work?"

"Um…"

Ignoring Nagi's vague answer, his mother went on talking.

"I happened to call him about something just now, and he told me he's not feeling well. It sounds like he has a fever and can hardly even move. I'm sure he won't die if we leave him alone, but if he did happen to die, that would be a problem, so just in case…"

If he was that sick, why hadn't he asked for her help? Nagi quickly pushed down the dark emotions surging in her chest.

"Of course! Do you think some yogurt or one of those pouches of rice porridge would be okay?" she asked, pretending everything was fine.

"Oh yes, that would be plenty," his mother agreed. *"I think you can just leave it hanging on the front door. Don't go inside—we don't want you getting sick, too!"*

"I won't," Nagi said. She hesitated for a moment, then said timidly, "Did…Keigo seem all right? Is he really that sick?"

"Well, his usual pattern is to stay sick for a long time, but he

always recovers in the end, so I don't think you need to worry that much."

Like his mother said, Keigo had always been prone to fevers. It happened less now that he was an adult, but it seemed like he'd gotten really ill for the first time in ages, so she couldn't help being concerned.

"...He's always been kind of frail," she mumbled. His mother gave a short laugh.

"He's got a soft heart. Especially when it comes to you."

"What? Me?" Nagi asked, perplexed.

"Yes," his mother continued. *"He's always been like that. Whenever anything happened with you, he would get sick. I remember the same thing happened in junior high. He got a terrible fever, just like now."*

His mother giggled.

"Apparently, he bumped into you leaving school with your boyfriend. I couldn't stop laughing, but for him, I think it was quite a shock."

Nagi smiled wryly. As usual, his mother was merciless toward her son.

"And normally he has a heart of steel! You're his only weakness," she said, sounding resigned. *"Looking at it that way, you really are the only one for him."*

I'm the only one for him.

"Well, I'll stop at his apartment on my way home."

Nagi hung up, turned off her computer, and gathered her things. On her way to his apartment, she stopped at a twenty-four-hour supermarket and bought some frozen meals, jelly drinks, and a cooling gel patch. When she got to his building, she noted the lights were out in his windows, then took the elevator upstairs. She hung the heavy supermarket bag on the handle of the door she knew so well. But once her right hand was freed of the bag, it refused to return meekly to her side. Instead, it reached slowly for the doorbell.

You really are the only one for him.

She remembered his mother's words as she gently brushed the button.

"Me too."

He was the only one for her, too. But…

She bit her lip, lowered her hand from the doorbell without pressing it, and turned around. Just before she reached the corner, she looked back. Maybe she was expecting something. But the dark door remained closed with the white plastic bag hanging silently from its handle.

◆

She had a dream. It was hazy but full of brilliant color. She was back in her second year of high school.

…Ah!

She was trudging through a residential neighborhood when she heard a voice ahead of her and glanced up. Her childhood friend was standing in front of her, looking at her in surprise. He must have bought a snack to eat on the way home from school, because he had a convenience store bag in his right hand and a roll stuffed with yakisoba noodles in his mouth.

What's wrong? he asked. It was a natural question. Her eyes were red from crying.

…My boyfriend broke up with me, she mumbled. A fresh wave of tears flowed from her eyes. A few minutes ago, the college guy she'd been dating for around four months had called to end things.

Oh… You mean him—that older guy?

Yeah… He told me he'd rather date someone shorter.

Oh…I see.

He glanced away awkwardly.

Well, bye, Nagi said and started walking toward her house.

Hey, wait, he said, running to catch up with her. For some reason, she glared at him as he matched his pace to hers.

…What's with you? she asked.

What? Can't I walk home with you? Why are you so mad?

Why? she said, stopping. She couldn't forget what had happened two months earlier, that summer. She'd been on her way to a date with her boyfriend—crap, no, her ex. She had on makeup and more grown-up clothes than usual when she happened to run into Keigo on the street, and he'd insulted her.

Don't tell me you forgot what you said to me! "What are you dressed up like that for? That stuff looks bad on you!"

She'd been so furious, she remembered every word he'd said. They'd argued, and she hadn't spoken to him in the intervening two months.

I forgot, he said casually. She gaped at him, incensed. He started fidgeting with the convenience store bag.

Take this, he said, holding out a soda-flavored popsicle. *Eat it and cheer up. You like these, don't you?*

...I like them, but I don't want one right now. Anyway, it's cold out.

Are you kidding? he asked. Ignoring his shocked expression, she sighed and started walking again. Keigo caught up with her and took his place by her side like he belonged there.

Popsicles taste better when it's cold out, he muttered, opening the package.

Just as she was starting to get genuinely annoyed, he said, *Hey, Nagi?* and tugged on the bag over her shoulder from behind. She yelped, stopping.

...Come on, what now?

Look up.

She scowled but did as he said. Brilliant red, yellow, and green leaves were spread across a clear blue sky.

Wow, how beautiful! she cried as she spun around, mesmerized by the fall leaves. *Aren't they amazing, Keigo? They're so pretty...*

She glanced at him, then snapped her mouth shut. She had assumed he was looking up at the leaves, too, but for some reason, he was staring at her and smiling.

...You don't need to wear makeup or grown-up clothes. That carefree smile is more than enough.

His big palm reached out and ruffled her hair before quickly vanishing again. She patted her hair back in place, then mumbled without much confidence, *You think so?*

Definitely, he said, looking over his shoulder and grinning so his eyes crinkled up. When she saw that smile, filled with a confidence she didn't understand, she thought he was an idiot but also that maybe he was right.

...Okay, then, she said.

Yeah, he replied. This time she was the one who ran after him. *Hey, can I have that popsicle after all?*

He handed it over, and she licked it as they walked together down that tree-lined street under the beautiful autumn leaves.

Keigo, look! she said, yanking hard on the hem of his blazer.

Hey! he groaned, before looking in the direction she was pointing. A man and a woman were holding hands beneath a flurry of fall leaves. The woman was wearing a pure-white kimono set off by the man's indigo *hakama* trousers. At first, Keigo was so distracted by this striking pair that he didn't notice a man nearby with a large camera and a woman holding a white reflector.

How lovely! said Nagi. *They must be taking wedding pictures.*

The street was famous locally for its fall leaves, so it wouldn't be surprising if the couple had chosen it for their wedding portraits. The bride, all in white, surrounded by brilliant fall foliage looked positively magical, and Nagi couldn't help cooing, *She's so pretty!* over and over in excitement. Keigo, meanwhile, was scowling.

I'd be way too embarrassed to take pictures in a place like this... Ouch!

She was so mad at him for destroying the mood, she pinched his side hard.

I swear, this is why I hate guys!

Ignoring his pain, she turned back to the couple. Silver wedding rings glittered on their entwined hands. Though they seemed embarrassed, they were beaming from ear to ear, positively glowing. Nagi couldn't help staring at them.

…They really are beautiful. They're so lucky, she whispered dreamily. Keigo, who was still rubbing his side, followed her gaze to the happy couple.

After staring at them for a while, he suddenly asked, *Do you want to get married?*

Um…I'm not sure. I can't imagine it.

Yeah, you don't even have a boyfriend… Owww!

She pinched him even harder than last time.

How about you stop pouring salt in my wounds? she said.

You're so violent…, he moaned, his eyes tearing up. Ignoring him, Nagi started walking.

…But I wonder…, she said softly, shading her eyes as she looked down the endless row of trees. *What's marriage like? It must be different from dating someone.*

Keigo thought for a minute.

I think it must be a special relationship, he said.

A special relationship?

He nodded.

More special than being old friends or boyfriend and girlfriend. The kind of special you take for granted.

His smile as he said this was a little more grown-up than usual.

The kind of special you take for granted… Hmm.

She wondered if, when the two of them grew up, they would both meet someone like that. She tried to imagine it, but unfortunately, she couldn't envision a future in which two people they didn't know where standing by their sides.

Then I'd like to get married as soon as I can, she said cheerfully. She thought for a minute, then added, *…Okay, I've made up my mind. I'm getting married by the time I'm thirty!*

She pumped her fist for emphasis.

Where did that come from? Keigo said with a wry smile.

I mean, I want to enjoy that kind of special you take for granted for as long as possible, she said. After all, it sounded like a very happy way to live.

Well, good luck, Keigo said.

Why do you sound so apathetic?

That was her dream. Hazy but full of brilliant color. They were young and simple and still thought living your life by someone's side was a beautiful, sparkling thing.

◆

"Um...are you okay...?" Saotome asked as soon as Nagi arrived at the office on Wednesday morning.

"What? Why?" Nagi replied. She was feigning ignorance, but she knew why Saotome was asking. She was probably worried because Nagi's eyes were red and puffy from crying. But Nagi just kept smiling and tilting her head inquisitively, and eventually, Saotome seemed to get the hint.

"Nothing... Never mind," she said, shaking her head slightly.

Nagi turned on her computer, still smiling. She knew Saotome was watching her with concern, but Nagi pretended not to notice and started checking her e-mail.

"Um, Ms. Yoroizuka?" Saotome said hesitantly as Nagi typed a response to a client. "I noticed something yesterday when I was looking at the design specifications. It's this part here..."

Nagi rolled her chair over to Saotome's desk and looked at her monitor.

"I was thinking that for this design class, rather than forcing it all together, it might be better to separate it out."

"Interesting... I think you're right. That means we'll need to adjust it to fit with the part Keigo designed..."

She peered through the gap between their monitors.

"Keigo, can I ask you something...?"

Quickly realizing she was talking to an empty chair, she stopped short. She'd done it again.

"Ha-ha… Sorry. Keigo's out again today, isn't he?" she said, trying to brush it over with a smile.

"Ms. Yoroizuka, would you like to go outside for a minute?"

Saotome had already stood up and was holding Nagi's arm.

"But we just got here…"

"It's fine. We'll just take a little break. Come on."

Half dragged by Saotome, who was surprisingly strong, Nagi wound up on the terrace. This area, with its tables, chairs, and parasols, was crowded during lunch but deserted at this time of morning. Nagi sat down in a chair near Saotome and looked at her, puzzled.

"Um, Saotome, what's going on?"

The other woman held out a brown paper bag.

"Will you share this with me? I found a really good donut shop."

Nagi had been too shaken to notice Saotome grab a snack as she brought her outside. Ignoring Nagi's confusion, Saotome noisily pulled some donuts out of the bag.

"Here you go. This is my favorite."

She held out a churro dripping with chocolate. Nagi reflexively took it and bit into the tip as Saotome watched.

"This is delicious!" Nagi blurted out. The outside was crispy but it was chewy inside. The dough must have had cinnamon mixed in, further enhancing the flavor.

"I'm so glad. That place is really popular, and they sell out quickly, but today I happened to be there when they opened and got lucky," Saotome said, smiling happily.

"Really? Thank you for sharing such a rare treat with me…"

"Of course! Everything tastes better when you eat it with a friend."

Saotome took a big bite of her own donut.

"Ahh, this really is delicious," she said, still grinning.

"…Thanks, Saotome," Nagi said before taking another bite of donut. She hadn't felt like eating breakfast, and her empty stomach made the donut taste even better. She was savoring the gentle sweetness as it spread through her when Saotome shocked her out of her reverie.

"...Mr. Yuuki was planning on quitting, wasn't he?"

Nagi stared at her, the donut still in her mouth.

"H-how did you know that?"

"I overheard the department head talking about it with the president... Sorry for being rude and listening in."

Nagi shook her head. His transfer was still up in the air, and Nagi had no idea what the best outcome would be.

"Is that why you're not yourself?" Saotome asked. Nagi could tell from the look in her eyes that she was genuinely worried about her. Realizing she couldn't go on lying, she haltingly began telling the other woman what had happened the week before.

She told her how Keigo had been recruited by Houkoku Bank starting in university. How he'd put them off for several years, saying he wanted to get more experience. How he'd just turned down the job for good. And how she herself was probably the reason.

"...So that's what's going on," Saotome said quietly when Nagi was done. Having finished every last crumb of her donut, she folded her napkin pensively.

"Ms. Yoroizuka, I adore you."

Nagi, who had been staring down gloomily, looked up in surprise. Saotome's big eyes were gazing straight at her.

"Um...where did that come from?" she asked, confused. Saotome's serious expression dissolved into a smile.

"Heh-heh. I just wanted to say it."

Nagi smiled softly at Saotome, who was tilting her head sweetly.

"Thanks. I adore you, too."

"Yaaay! Thank you!" Saotome answered a little bashfully before growing solemn again and quietly casting her gaze downward. "...But I know I can never beat Mr. Yuuki."

"What?" Nagi blurted out. Saotome looked up at her.

"This is just my opinion," she said, smiling. "But when it comes to you, Mr. Yuuki…well, I hate to say this, but his feelings aren't at all shallow. I think he's thought about the situation thoroughly and made his decision."

Keigo had always been very efficient about his studies and work, but that didn't mean he wasn't deliberate or careful. The same went for his relationships with people—including friends, family, coworkers, Nagi, and even himself.

"No matter what anyone says or does, I don't think he's going to change his mind," Saotome said.

Nagi nodded. Precisely because he approached everything in life so sincerely, all the counterarguments in the world probably wouldn't convince him he was wrong.

Of course, if she was being honest, Nagi didn't want him to take the job with Houkoku Bank. She didn't want him to have anything to do with banking systems. She wanted him to stay by her side for the rest of her life and never do anything that might cause her anxiety.

But more than that, she wanted to see him achieve his dreams.

Her feelings were so complicated, she felt like she was only understanding them now. She didn't want her own selfish demands to be the reason he gave up his lifelong dream or squandered his abilities. She wanted to be the one standing by his side, quietly supporting him as he poured himself into doing what he loved. How could she make him understand that? She remembered how stubbornly he had stuck by his decision.

"But, Ms. Yoroizuka," Saotome continued. "I think you can change his mind."

Nagi looked up, stunned. "You do?" she asked.

"Not just because he loves you. I mean, of course he has a soft spot for you…but I know you well, and I'm certain I'm right about this," Saotome said confidently.

As Nagi looked at her in astonishment, Saotome reached out her hand.

"The Ms. Yoroizuka I love doesn't just sit back quietly and let other people protect her."

Saotome placed her hand over Nagi's where it rested on the table. The fingers that squeezed hers were delicate but somehow strong and unwavering at the same time.

"I think you already know what you need to do."

It was like Saotome's hand was leading her forward. Keigo was kind and strong and always put Nagi first. She cared about him deeply. But because Nagi had wavered for so long, he was about to choose the wrong path. Her current approach wasn't working. No matter how supportive she tried to be, her intentions would never get through.

Which meant the only option was for her to change.

She loved Keigo with all her heart. That was why she made up her mind to let go of the happiness of absolute security.

Nineteenth Try

It was the Thursday morning after his third sick day in a row that Keigo first sensed an impending crisis. For the past few days, his fever had been going up and down erratically with no sign of stabilizing. He definitely hadn't recovered, but he felt like he couldn't take any more time off, so he put on a mask and dragged his weary body into the office.

"Morning…"

Somehow he managed to make it through rush hour, and he arrived at his desk several times more exhausted than usual and collapsed into his seat. Gripping his spinning head, he read through the backlog of e-mail. There was a message from Nagi saying she'd finished his part of the system design, so he didn't need to worry about it. *Oh yeah.* He needed to apologize to her for missing three days of work. He stood unsteadily and was about to call her name when he stopped short.

"…Huh?"

She wasn't there.

"Oh, Ms. Yoroizuka won't be in for the rest of the week," Saotome said.

"What? She won't…? Why not?"

"Don't ask me. But how are you feeling? I appreciate your coming into work, but I hope you don't keel over. That would be a real hassle."

Unsure if she was worried or angry, he mumbled a listless "Sorry" and sat back down. For a few seconds, he stared vacantly at the ceiling.

What had he been trying to do? Oh, that's right. He was going to send Nagi a message. His brain still foggy, he fished his phone out of his bag. Even moving his fingers was a struggle. He opened the messaging app. What was this? He saw a two-day-old message from Nagi saying, I left some food outside your door.

The night before last, as he lay in bed, Keigo had heard a noise outside his apartment and gone to check on it. No one was there, but a bag full of food and cooling gel patches was hanging on the knob. He had assumed it was from his mom. The idea that Nagi had brought it never even entered his head. This was bad. He had been too delirious from the fever to even check his messages. At one point, he had started writing a text telling her he was sick, then gotten distracted sending a message to the office and ended up forgetting to finish the one to Nagi, even though it was more important.

"…Dammit…"

He slumped in his chair, gripping his head. Just when they'd parted in anger, he'd gone and poured oil on the flames. What the hell was he thinking?

The important thing now was to apologize. He forced his sluggish body back into a sitting position and composed a message to Nagi. He apologized for not telling her he was sick and for being too out of it to read her message, let alone respond to it. He also apologized for making her cry during their last conversation.

Miserable, he read over his message full of apologies, then gathered the courage to hit Send. But she didn't respond that day, or the next, or even the one after that, and then it was the Golden Week holiday.

◆

It was the third day of the long vacation and the weather was gorgeous. Keigo, who had finally started to feel better, went to Nagi's apartment building and stood outside. He had sent her several more messages in the meantime but hadn't heard a word in response. He was genuinely starting to get worried, which was why he'd come to her apartment. But now he wondered if she would think he was weird for showing up without telling her first. He had a feeling he could never redeem himself if that happened. But it was still better than not seeing her at all. He felt like if they didn't meet even once over the holiday, she might get tired of him for good.

Steeling his will, he took the elevator up to the fourth floor, where her apartment was. On the way up, he imagined the scene over and over. The first thing he would do was apologize. That was essential. If she was still mad, he would give her the tart he had brought along right away. If she wasn't mad but instead creeped out…he would cross that bridge when he came to it. *You got this, future me. Please just let her be angry.* Still praying internally, he stepped out of the elevator, then stopped short.

"…Huh?"

Something was odd.

As soon as that thought crossed his mind, he dashed toward her apartment. The door was wide-open, and loads of blue protective coverings were taped to the wall outside. He had a bad feeling about this. Peering in the door, he discovered a tall stack of folded cardboard boxes in the entryway. He was bewildered. He hurriedly double-checked the apartment number, but there was no mistake. This was her unit.

"What's going on…?" he mumbled in a panic.

Suddenly, a man emerged from the back of the apartment.

"Excuse me, are you an acquaintance of the resident?" the man asked him.

He was wearing a blue jumpsuit—obviously a worker for a moving company. He frowned suspiciously at Keigo, who was standing frozen in the entryway. Keigo knew he must look suspicious, but he nevertheless pushed the man for information.

"Uh…is the resident moving?"

He knew there was no way the man would say, "Oh, no, she's not moving." But he prayed he would all the same.

"Yes…," the man replied.

Shit, Keigo thought. *I can't handle this.*

There are countless things in the world that can't be fixed with love alone. No one can grow up without realizing that. But if it was humanly possible, Keigo wanted to keep loving Nagi like he always had.

When exactly did I ask you to protect me that way?

Keigo remembered the day Nagi's father was cremated. The day he first held her. The day he realized with disappointment that his arms were too young and weak to protect her like he wanted.

I'm sure that to you, I'm a precious, precious burden.

He had been dragging her down ever since that day. Nagi had always seen much further into the future than he had, and while he struggled to find his way, she had always turned back to offer a helping hand.

If I could rewind time, I would go back to just being your friend.

He hated that idea. He finally had what he'd always wished for. He didn't want to go back. He wanted to stay the way they were. But Nagi didn't feel the same. All because he couldn't control the scale of his desires.

It was always like that. Wishes didn't come true. If pursuing them was this painful, he should let go, but he couldn't even do that. He got hurt, hurt her, hated it, then fell in love with her all over again and got hurt again. When would he ever escape this endless cycle? How many more repetitions of the loop would it take for his love to be rewarded?

He awoke to the sound of rain. He stared up at the ceiling in his dim room, then looked over at the clock. It was four in the afternoon.

"Shit… I overslept…"

He got up slowly and pushed the curtains open a crack. Heavy rain clouds covered the sky, and tiny droplets streamed down the window. It was the middle of Golden Week, and yet it was raining. Keigo picked up the thermometer he had set next to his bed and took his temperature. It beeped twice, and he squinted at the display window. Thirty-seven point five degrees Celsius. He let out a long sigh. His temperature had been going down, but no doubt because of what had happened the day before, it was up again.

He was sick of his own weakness. Swearing at himself, he stood up unsteadily, got a bottle of mineral water from the refrigerator, and poured some down his dry throat. Suddenly, he noticed something was amiss. It was hard to think straight, but after a moment, he figured it out. The sound of falling water was too loud to be coming from the rain. Belatedly, he realized it was the sound of the shower. The fog vanished from his brain.

"You're kidding me…!"

Apparently, he'd been so out of it that he left the shower running. He ran to the bathroom and, not stopping to wonder why the light was on, pushed the door open.

"Eeek!"

"…Huh?"

Nagi was standing there stark naked. What was going on? He must be hallucinating from the fever. He was astonished by how ill he must be, yet he couldn't take his eyes from the apparition in front of him. Her hair was stuck to her flushed cheeks, and fine droplets of water were dripping down her slender neck and between her breasts as if drawn there. The night she slept over, it had been too dark to see well, but now he could tell that, while her breasts were small, they were exactly to his liking.

"…I've always been more of a shape guy than a size guy."

"Whatever, just close the door! You're so stupid sometimes!" she shouted.

This was followed by a vigorous spray from the shower directly in his face.

◆

Nagi was standing in front of him with her arms crossed imposingly. He was sitting cross-legged, and she, now fully dressed and with her hair dried, was looking down at him with an icy gaze.

"I told you, I thought I left the shower on, so I went in to turn it off... I was definitely not trying to sneak a peek."

"Even if that's true, you could have closed the door more quickly."

"Uh... Well, I have a fever, and I'm not thinking straight..."

"..."

"...Sorry, that was a lie. I thought I might as well take advantage of my good luck."

With a loud smack, her hand came down on the crown of his head.

"Owww...," he said, pressing his hand to it.

"I swear," she said with a sigh.

"Anyway, what were you doing in my bathroom at this time of day?"

"What do you mean, what was I doing? I couldn't get in touch with you since last night, and when I came to your apartment, the door was unlocked, and you were inside, passed out in the living room! So I carried you to your bed, and that got me all sweaty! And when I said I was going to take a shower, you said okay!"

"...Really?"

"Really!"

He searched his memory, but the last thing he remembered was leaving Nagi's apartment and coming home. Still, the sweatpants he didn't remember putting on and the cooling patch he didn't recall sticking to his forehead proved she was telling the truth.

"Sorry for causing you so much trouble...," he said, bowing his head as she pouted. He was disgusted with himself. Dammit, all he ever did anymore was apologize to her. No wonder she was fed up with him. He slumped over, feeling like the world was ending. She must have felt sorry for him, because her brows drew together slightly.

"No, I'm sorry for not returning your messages. How's your fever?"

Resigned, she stretched her hand out and touched the back of his neck. Even at a moment like this, she was kind. He glimpsed concern flickering in her eyes.

"Uh…it came down some…"

"Number?"

"I think it's a moderate fever."

"The truth."

"…Thirty-seven point five."

"So it didn't come down!" she snapped.

"Sorry," he said, apologizing yet again.

"Why do you lie to me?!"

"I thought you'd worry about me…"

"Don't you know I'll worry more if you lie?! You're so stupid sometimes!"

That was twice in the same day he'd been called stupid. The energy drained from his body, and he let out a very long sigh.

"…You're always telling me to rely on you, so why do you never rely on anyone yourself?" she muttered, before jumping up. "Anyway, you need to lie down right now. Come on…"

She froze. He had grabbed her right hand. In the sudden silence, he could hear the rain hitting the window. Her hand was limp, giving no sign of returning his squeeze. If he let go, he was half convinced she would float off somewhere.

Do you want to break up?

He couldn't bring himself to utter the one question he most wanted to ask. He heard something rustle.

"Keigo?"

That single word was enough to make him to look up at her. She was kneeling in front of him, peering into his face. Unless he was imagining things, her expression was apologetic.

"I remembered our conversation about getting married by the time I turned thirty. I'm sorry I'd forgotten."

She reached out her right hand and laid it softly on his cheek. Warmth radiated into his skin from her gentle caress.

"But that was just a childish dream of mine. You don't have to bend over backward for it."

She apologized again, and he realized he wasn't the only one saying sorry all the time lately.

"…No," he mumbled.

She looked at him quizzically.

"That's my own wish."

He took her hand and squeezed it. Because of the rain, the room was permeated with gray. Still, when he closed his eyes, he could see the scene from that day as brilliantly as ever.

"…You hate your birthday, don't you?" he asked. She looked at him in surprise.

"You knew that?"

Of course he did. He knew that every year, when the anniversary of her father's death approached, she got depressed. He also knew that she tried as hard as possible to prevent anyone from noticing.

"I thought that maybe if we got married on your birthday, you'd like that day a little more."

No matter what he did, September 17 would probably always be a sad day for her. In which case, the best approach was to overwrite it with happy memories. Those had been the thoughts in his mind on that fall day in high school, when he imagined her dressed in a pure-white kimono beneath a swirl of brilliant fall leaves.

"So if I took the job with Houkoku Bank and gave myself a year to get used to it…we'd still have six months until your birthday, right? I thought we could get everything ready in that time and get married on your thirtieth birthday."

He hadn't planned on telling her about his idea, but now the cat was out of the bag. She sat in front of him with her mouth hanging open. The question "You planned it out in that much detail?" was written all over her face. Yes, he had. Starting quite a long time ago. And quite earnestly.

"I have two big goals in life," he said, figuring at this point he may as well tell her everything. He scratched his head and went on haltingly. "One is...to marry you. And the other is to work in banking system development."

Her expression grew serious.

"When your father died," he continued, "I remember you said, 'My father worked so hard for everyone. Why did they kill him?'"

"...Yes."

She nodded sadly, her eyes downcast.

"I guess...I wanted to prove to you that hard work doesn't always go unrewarded."

On the day she asked him that question, his younger self had only managed to say "I don't know." Even now, as an adult, he probably wouldn't be able to give her the right answer using words alone.

"I thought that if I successfully completed the Houkoku Bank project and was able to continue living happily by your side, eventually growing old together...then maybe your trauma would go away..."

If he couldn't answer with words, he would answer with his actions. Even if it took years and years and transformed his life in the process.

I want to enjoy that kind of special you take for granted for as long as possible.

Simply because he loved to see her smile.

"...But as it turns out, I can't have both things at the same time."

He laughed dryly. It really was true that if you chased two

dreams, you wouldn't achieve either one. He'd wished for too much, and now he was on the cusp of losing everything.

"I'm sorry, Nagi."

Sorry for being the way he was.

"...You really do think only of me," he heard her say from above. Keigo looked up unsteadily.

"Check this out."

She thrust a piece of paper in front of him. He took it, confused. The first thing that popped out to him were the words *Notice of Employment*.

Employment? Where? And more importantly, of who?

As he read over the paper more carefully, his face stiffened.

"But...this can't be..."

He glanced up in disbelief. Nagi nodded.

"That's right. I took a job at Houkoku Bank."

He was flabbergasted. There had to be some mistake. Unfortunately, no matter how many times he looked, Nagi's name and *Houkoku Bank* were still written on the paper.

"If the reason you're hesitating about the job is because I'm at Sync.System, then if I move to Houkoku Bank, the problem will be solved, right? So I went ahead and applied for a midcareer position. They required a university degree plus at least two years' experience, so I qualified," she said casually as he continued to burn a hole in the paper with his eyes.

"And...they hired you?"

"They did. For now, I'm an associate, but they have an employee registration system, so as long as I pass the test, it sounds like I'll be hired on a permanent, full-time basis. I'd better start studying!" she said energetically. For some reason, when she saw Keigo staring at her in a daze, she burst out laughing.

"I know this is sudden. I was surprised myself when I got the job. By the way, it's in operations. It has nothing to do with your department, but it's related to IT," she rattled on with a nonchalant smile as Keigo sat there, reeling. "Also, I'll tell you right now that I have no intention of letting you protect me like you've been doing. I'm going to work my butt off to get permanent status, then keep on going until I'm in a position to give my two cents about your work. You'd better be ready!" she concluded, grinning mischievously. Normally, that expression charmed the socks off him, but he was in no state to be charmed right now.

"Wait, wait, wait, you're talking about quitting Sync.System?" he said, lunging forward like he was going to grab hold of her.

"That's right," she said blithely. "The president and department head both agreed, and so did Saotome and Saiga. Of course, it will take some time to train someone for my position, so I won't leave for a month or so. Oh, by the way, this is my new address. They let me move into company housing early."

Nagi took a notebook out of her bag and held it out to Keigo. Her name and address were written on it.

"…So that's why you moved…?"

"You knew I moved? Sorry for not telling you sooner. I figured you'd try to talk me out of it, so I decided not to tell you until it was all finished."

So that was the story. Keigo felt like collapsing into a heap as she apologized again, but he quickly pulled himself together.

"But wait…!"

His mind was still in a fog, and he couldn't tell what Nagi was thinking behind her business-as-usual expression, but he did know one thing. This was all a huge mistake.

"You have to turn that job down immediately! You probably still have time!" he pleaded desperately, grabbing her shoulders. It was all his fault that she was acting so recklessly.

"I'm at Sync.System, and your uncle is, too, so you'll be safe there! Sure, some people might be jealous or prejudiced against you…but I'll protect you from them! Plus, it's hard to move to a new environment! Why would you go out of your way to put yourself in that situation—?"

"So what?!" she interrupted sharply. He fell silent. She jumped up and glared at him. "I know all that! I know Sync.System is a comfortable place to be! If I just stayed put, as long as you were there, I know you'd keep me safe!"

With each word she spoke, another thin veil descended over her eyes. And each time, as if in tandem, her voice quavered. By the time she said, "But none of that matters," she was nearly crying.

"I don't need the kind of safety that's like a chain dragging down the person I love! I'll take that stupid safety and crumple it into a ball and throw it away!"

But she didn't cry.

"Nagi…"

Keigo couldn't look away from her eyes, they were so close to overflowing with tears. But the tears stayed there, refusing to flow. They seemed to him like Nagi herself, about to step into an unfamiliar world despite her fear.

"…Listen, Keigo," she said quietly as she sniffled. "I want you to work like your life depends on it to make that project a success. I don't have that kind of ability, but you do."

She squatted down slowly so she was at eye level with him.

"Not just anyone can do what you're trying to do. It truly is amazing."

Her trembling hands embraced his cheeks. He felt the touch of her gentle fingers. Happiness overcame his heart and he could hardly breathe. Her fingertips were filled with things he loved.

"So please. Go out and build systems to support the lives of all sorts of people."

Her fingers slid down his cheeks and wrapped slowly around his back. A familiar scent tickled his nose. Nagi's scent. Her arms squeezed his tense body tight.

"And I will stand by you. No matter what."

There wasn't the slightest uncertainty in her words as she whispered into his ear. Suddenly, he felt like he understood. Why had he been so single-mindedly fixated on protecting her? It wasn't about one person protecting the other and the other person being protected all the time. Maybe *that* was the secret to the kind of special you took for granted.

"Nagi..."

He lifted his arms, which had been hanging limply at his sides, and wrapped them softly around her. Following her lead but still unsure of himself, he timidly hugged her slender form, so slight it might disappear beneath him. She squeezed him harder, and affection welled up inside him until it was beyond his control.

He loved her. He loved Nagi. No matter how many times he thought it, it wasn't enough. He knew how painful it was when his emotions overflowed until he was drowning in them, but he never learned his lesson and stopped loving her. After all, that love was the source of his happiness.

"...Shit," he mumbled, burying his face in her shoulder.

"What?" she asked.

He slowly leaned back from her and gazed straight into her puzzled eyes.

"I really want to take you to my bed. Is that okay?"

He knew full well he was saying something outrageous with a completely straight face. It made sense that she blinked two or three times and frowned suspiciously.

"Didn't you say last time that you'd learned how to go without?"

"Your power has surpassed my training, Nagi," he said decisively.

She laughed, a little taken aback.

"You're so stupid sometimes, Keigo."

She tapped his cheek, and the next instant, she was pulling him toward her. His breath stopped as her soft lips touched his. The kiss was finished in an instant, but before he could lament her absence, she pressed her body against his.

"...Yeah, let's go to the bedroom," she whispered, her cheeks flushed. He couldn't tell whether it was his heartbeat racing or hers.

"Okay...," he murmured.

That was the last time that day he acted with any semblance of rational calm.

He'd been wishing for it for so long. When he woke up, he wanted her to be the first person he said "Good morning" to.

"Good morning, Keigo."

When he opened his eyes, there she was in the translucent morning light. Wrapped up in white sheets, smiling at him as he slipped in and out of a dream.

"Are you still sleeping? Let's get up!" she said, reaching out a finger and stroking his hair adoringly. Unlike the previous night, when her hands entwined with his had been burning with passion, they were cool now. The morning was like a dream, but it wasn't a dream.

"...Okay. Good morning, Nagi."

The first person he said "Good morning" to that day was the person he loved.

When he ate his meals, he wanted her to eat the same food from the same dishes and say "How delicious!" with him.

"Wow, this donut is amazing."

Their matching plates each held a donut and a serving of Italian salad. The steam from their big mugs of café au lait brought the smell of coffee to his nose.

"Right? Saotome told me about the place that makes them."

Wearing his T-shirt, her hair slightly messy from sleep, she happily took a bite of her donut.

"Women always know the best places. Seriously, though, this is really good."

Keigo sat across from the person he loved, eating the same

food from the same plates and talking about how delicious it was.

When he said "I love you," he wanted her to be the one who smiled happily and said, "Thank you."

"...Nagi?"

It was the kind of easygoing afternoon particular to weekends. Nagi, who was sitting on the sofa reading a magazine, looked up when he said her name. The knowledge that her gaze was meant for him alone was enough to make him suddenly emotional.

"I love you."

The words spilled from his lips as naturally as blinking and as urgently as breathing. As usual, she giggled and asked, "Where did that come from?"

"I just felt like I had to say it, no matter what."

"What the heck?" she said, laughing.

Then she nodded, and for some reason, her smile looked a little resigned.

"Thank you," she said.

Keigo said "I love you" to the object of his affections, and she smiled happily and told him, "Thank you."

He'd always been the type to stick with things and keep his possessions for a long time. The same held true for his childhood friend Nagi Yoroizuka. He couldn't even remember how long he'd felt this way toward her. Now he was twenty-eight years old, and he still loved her from the bottom of his heart, unconditionally.

"I love you, too, Keigo."

Theirs was the special kind of love you took for granted, for the person dearest to you.

Last Try

She used to hate birthdays. You're supposed to have gained a year's worth of experience, but she always felt like she'd lost something in equal measure.

"Happy birfday to…Mommy! Happy birfday to you!"

A lisping voice was singing in a dim room lit only by the soft light of candles.

"Thank you, Itsuki! When did you learn the birthday song?"

Nagi stopped clapping along with her son's singing to stroke his head.

"Grammy taught me!" he said, pointing to Nae.

"Itsuki's a talented singer. He's such a good boy," Nae said, patting his head. Itsuki smiled proudly.

"Who wants a piece of cake?" Nagi asked, getting out the plates.

"I do, I do!" Itsuki said, shooting his hand up into the air.

"Would you like the chocolate decoration, too?"

"Yes!"

She set the piece of chocolate on his plate, and he stared at the letters on it.

"Congratulations, Mom and Dad…?" he spelled out, having recently learned his letters. He tilted his head quizzically. "Why is Daddy celebrating, too?"

"Because he's just finished the big project he's been working so hard on."

"Oh," he said, smiling at the person next to Nagi, although she wasn't sure if he understood what she meant. "Then happy birf-day, Daddy."

"Ha-ha, not quite, but thanks."

Keigo grinned and ruffled Itsuki's hair as the boy chomped into the piece of chocolate. He had a good appetite lately. So good that Nagi thought, before long, he'd be able to eat an entire cake. He was definitely his father's son. As Nagi smiled wryly at him, a glass appeared before her.

"Here, Nagi. Why not have a drink for once?"

"Oh, thank you!" she said, taking the glass. Keigo filled it with wine. She filled his in return, and they quietly toasted.

"Happy birthday."

"Congratulations on finishing your project."

Houkoku Bank's seven-year-long system transfer project had finally wrapped up that summer. It had been going on the whole time as she started her new job with the bank, got pregnant a few years later, took maternity leave, and returned to work. It had really been a long time. She didn't know the details, since she was in a different department, but she knew it had been an enormous undertaking. Keigo must have fought his way through a lot of obstacles. It wasn't unusual for him to stay at work until late at night for days in a row, and for a while, he'd even spent his time at home working. But he hadn't complained once, and she thought he was amazing for pushing through as a core member of the project.

"Thanks. Sorry to make you worry all these years. Also, I'd better apologize in advance for all the worry I'm sure I'll inflict on you in the future... Sorry."

She couldn't help laughing at the fact that despite everything, he still sounded so unsure of himself. She sighed. He'd probably still be like this in fifty years.

"No worries," she said reassuringly, softly placing her hand over his bigger one where it rested on the table. "I told you, didn't I?

I'll stand by you no matter what, so all you have to do is keep heading forward."

She was sure it would always be like this. Keigo would always be kind, and she would always feel this way toward him.

"...I know," he mumbled. His eyes creased with relief. Nagi loved that easy smile from the bottom of her heart.

She used to hate birthdays. You're supposed to have gained a year's worth of experience, but she always felt like she'd lost something in equal measure. She'd thought that once you became an adult, you only gained stupid things eons away from dreams and ideals. And yet...

"Here's to our future, Nagi."

As each difficult yet beautiful year passed by, it filled Nagi with more memories of the people she loved. That was why, these days, she could hardly wait for her birthday to come around.